# A Horse of a Different Color

by

## Halle Kenton

**A Horse of a Different Color**

Cover Art by *Tina Lynn Stout*

The Wild Rose Press, Inc.
PO Box 708
Adams Basin, NY 14410-0708
Visit us at www.thewildrosepress.com

Publishing History
First Edition, 2024
Trade Paperback ISBN 978-1-5092-5274-9
Digital ISBN 978-1-5092-5275-6


Published in the United States of America

He studied the muted flush on her cheeks and the slight increase in her breathing. His clasped hands tightened as he fought the urge to pull her against him, to kiss the stiffness out of her. His urge had nothing to do with her desire to help Mr. Tibbles, although that was commendable. It was the mix of pride and vulnerability and fire and guts, and the damn rag on her head. It was her pink, moist lips and the fact that she disliked his wealth and upbringing and…

"Are you an alcoholic?"

"What?" Her glance narrowed with disbelief.

"Do you have a problem with alcohol?" he repeated, unable to let it go, even though sparks darted from her eyes.

To hell with the sparks. He'd committed himself, and he wanted an answer.

She opened her mouth, her indignation front and center.

"Just tell me," he said.

Her mouth made quirky, little movements like she wanted to spit. He watched her struggle before she jerked to a stand and shouted, "No!"

He dropped his head and closed his eyes when she stomped off. She was halfway out the door when she flew back to grab her boots.

"Stop," he ordered, unsurprised when she didn't.

She smacked the door frame with her exit.

He followed her out. They weren't finished, not by a long shot.

## Dedication

This book is dedicated to my wonderful writer friends—Shelley Shepard Gray, Cathy Liggett, Heather Webber, and Julie Stone—who stuck with me on the long road to publication. You're the reason I never gave up and I love you all.

Chapter One

Cheyenne shook herself awake and found her pillow wet...again. Since her daddy's death and her recent move back to Lexington, her dreams always ended this way. Every episode of fitful sleep, made worse by a case of freaky summer flu, produced a scene from her Kentucky childhood and Daddy was in all of them.

She swiped at the tears to focus on the newly familiar walls of her bedroom. At least this time she didn't need to visit the barn. Her last check at ten had reassured her the horses were all bedded down for the night. She snuggled deeper under her grandma's quilt and tried to clear her mind.

"Think like a horse, Cheyenne, if you want to stay one step ahead."

Her eyes cracked open.

Either Daddy was hangin' with the Big Guy upstairs, or Mufasa had invaded her bedroom.

"Daddy?" she said to the darkened room. "Mufasa?" She waited a few seconds and gave it one last try. "God?"

Her heavy eyelids drifted shut. *Whatever.*

Right now, she wasn't moving for anyone. Well, maybe God, but he'd apparently relocated to greener pastures. She didn't blame him. The flu was, after all, contagious.

Then she noticed Daddy was back. When she heard her own four-year-old voice, she listened in.

"Daddy, why do you have that band-aid on your finger?"

Walker Modine put down the chipped coffee mug and glanced at his hand before his gaze turned to his daughter.

"Your daddy stopped thinkin' like a horse, darlin'."

She inspected the flesh-colored covering, now dirty at the edges like the rest of her daddy's big hand. Her nose wrinkled at the smell of the brown water he used to clean his barn cuts.

"Did the horse think your fingers were carrots?"

Daddy said horses thought little girl's fingers looked like carrots so she must always feed treats from a bucket, not her hands.

Her daddy shook his head.

"Did you forget to whistle?" she asked.

She didn't know how to whistle yet but he said to make a noise like whistling when she walked under a horse's belly so the horse knew she was there.

"No, honey," he answered with a slow smile. "I didn't forget to whistle. What I did forget was fly spray. I was tappin' a nail in the shoe of the big bay I just bought..."

"Oh, Daddy, you made a boo-boo!" she giggled and pointed out the obvious with great pleasure. "Did a horsefly bite his balls and make him kick?"

Her daddy's injured hand flew to his mouth, and his eyes got squinty with tears but she knew he tried not to laugh. His eyes always cried when he laughed, which confused her almost as much as thinking like a horse. She never cried but if she did, it wasn't because something was funny.

"Who told you about a horse's balls?"

*His voice sounded like he was trying to hocker up a piece of meat stuck in his throat.*

*"Billy."*

*She didn't think she was telling on her brother but the look on Daddy's face got strange. Maybe she wouldn't tell the rest of the story—how she stood underneath Old Blue's belly in the pasture one day and looked at his balls and his hangy down thing when Billy caught her and pulled her away. Billy said that wasn't the way to learn to whistle when she explained it to him.*

*Then he told her about balls, which made real good sense because that's what they looked like to her—balls in a bag.*

*She stretched out her arms to make the funny look on Daddy's face go away. Uncle Lyn said that was how she wrapped her daddy's little finger. That didn't make any sense either but Daddy nodded when Uncle Lyn said it so she did it anyway.*

*He lifted her into his lap.*

*"Let's forget about balls for a while, honey. Just remember what your Daddy tells you. Always think like a horse if you want to stay one step ahead of him."*

Her eyes shot open, and she bolted to an upright position.

"Dinah!"

She muttered to the shadows in the room and crawled from the bed.

"Thank you, Daddy, for reminding me that the devilish mare you bought me knows no limits when it comes to tricks."

For the last week, Dinah had shown daily signs of giving birth, exhausting Cheyenne with frequent trips to the pasture and barn to check for any progress. Much to her irritation, the foal had yet to appear. Knowing Dinah, the birth would be tonight since Cheyenne's strength was missing in action.

And, of course, there would be problems. Dinah was too old for this nonsense. Cheyenne swore she'd keep a strict eye on the mare from now on since she now had first-hand knowledge of a stallion's ability to jump *three* fences to copulate with a mare in heat.

Cheyenne lifted her jeans from the bedpost and prepared to leave. She found the flashlight on the kitchen sink and surveyed the night dark landscape as she made her way outside. Her unsteady steps echoed on the stone walk while the flashlight beam bounced ahead of her. Heat lightning illuminated the scattered clouds, followed by muted thunder. She tried to count the seconds between the two but gave up. Heaving sure made a girl tired.

A weatherman had predicted scattered showers, but she didn't remember which night. As vague as the last three days were, she didn't even recall when she'd heard the forecast. She shook her head and chided herself for worrying about something so uncontrollable. This was Lexington, it was July. Let there be rain, and steam, and heat.

When she reached the barn, she used her body weight to slide the heavy door open. She leaned against it for a moment to collect her strength, feeling like one of those rubber-legged Gumby characters.

Cheyenne directed the light toward Dinah's stall. Sadly, no gray Thoroughbred head stared back.

"Shit, Daddy."

A hugely pregnant mare didn't lie down just to catch a few Z's.

4

Cheyenne moved closer and angled the flashlight inside the stall. She knew what she'd find. Dinah's head came up then flopped back to the straw-covered floor. The horse's stomach rippled with contractions, and her big body filled the space, even though it was the largest stall on the property.

"What's going on, babycakes?"

Cheyenne eased aside the stall door and moved to the business end of the mare to check out the action. The straw at Dinah's rear was soaked. No doubt the wetness came from a ruptured water bag, which meant foaling would occur within the hour. Finally, Dinah was ready to pop. Thank you, Jesus—*not*.

Cheyenne crouched down to watch. Within a minute, she straightened and headed to the sink to disinfect her hands and arms. One hoof and a nose did not a normal birth make.

"Daddy, if you're anywhere close, I could use some help here."

Her voice sounded like a shout in the heavy silence. When there was no response, she turned on the tap as hot as possible and started to scrub.

A similar problem had occurred with Dinah's third foal ten years before. Cheyenne had fixed it then, and she was determined to fix it now. She wasn't about to let a little flu stand in the way. Besides, the mare had saved Cheyenne's butt on occasions too numerous to mention. It was only fair that Cheyenne now return the favor.

She came back to the stall to find Dinah's neck and flanks dark with sweat, which gave the already oppressive air a distinctively horsey odor. Cheyenne scooted into position on the floor and placed a hand on the mare's rear for stability. After the last contraction ended she carefully inserted her arm into the birth canal.

"Dinah, no turds. I've reached the end of my patience here."

Just as she located a hoof bent the wrong way, another contraction cut the circulation in her arm, and the hoof slipped from her grasp. She struggled on with increased frustration as what little energy she had disappeared.

She sat up and made an effort to stop her dizzy head from circling. All kinds of aches had reappeared. Her fever had broken earlier that day but she was still weak, and nauseous. She thought about calling Billy but as soon as the idea popped into her head, she rejected it. He was at least thirty minutes away. By the time he got here, it might be too late.

Then there was the matter of pride, the Modine curse as her daddy called it. Grandpa Modine had it in spades, but it skipped a generation and concentrated all its fury in Cheyenne. Her fierce independence and willful nature were legendary within the Modine clan. That meant she never called her family for help unless it was a matter of impending, painful, prolonged death—*her* impending, painful, prolonged death.

"Whiskey," she muttered. "I need something to make me numb."

She lurched to her feet and groped for any handy support to help her across the barn. When she leaned down into the tack box, the blood rushed to her head and lights exploded behind her half-closed eyelids. She fumbled around for the bottle and scraped her knuckles on a shedding blade before finally locating it under a saddle pad.

First, she poured a small amount of whiskey, the

brown water of her childhood, over the scrapes on her fingers.

"Holy crap!"

She blew quick puffs of air to ease her burned knuckles, before she brought the bottle to her lips, threw back her head, and swallowed at least two shots.

"Oh, God!" she whimpered and bent double to hold her stomach.

Fire streaked down her throat, and she barked to clear the sting while tears erupted from her tightly clenched eyelids. She'd eaten next to nothing in the last forty-eight hours. That meant the whiskey had already corroded her stomach lining.

When she stood a minute later, she noticed her lips were almost numb. That was good. Her stomach still felt like a ship on high seas but this was an improvement over the last two days.

She moved to the blackboard on the tack room door. Her farrier, Joe Dawson, had recommended a vet at the Bourbon County emergency clinic. *If* Dinah needed professional help Cheyenne wasn't about to let damaged pride and a precarious budget stand in the way. Calling a vet in the middle of the night was different from calling family. Any experienced vet knew horses almost always foaled in the still, wee hours. They expected the hassle and were well-paid for their trouble. Of course, that was one of the reasons why her daddy never called one.

Cheyenne found the phone number on the board and tried to memorize it. Maybe she didn't need a vet.

She stepped back into the stall and leaned over the neck of the laboring horse. When she bent down to whisper "wubby, wubby, nummy, oogie" into Dinah's ear, the unbalanced position, or maybe the booze, sent her face first into the horse's bony jaw. Cheyenne flailed in the straw for a good ten seconds before she managed to inch herself up into a sitting position.

Okay. A vet it was. He'd be on his way if she wasn't able to fix the problem or if she passed out, whichever came first.

Chapter Two

Jack Carter had his feet propped on a desk while he swapped llama stories with Gray Benson, Jack's best friend from their vet school days. Gray owned the clinic and had just mentioned "spit", which made Jack speculate on how much and how far. The conversation hadn't degenerated as much as it could considering the late hour.

Chris Crockett, the kid who answered the phone most evenings, entered the room and interrupted their laughter.

"Doc Carter," Chris said. "The owner of a farm out on Winchester Pike is on the phone—a problem with a foaling mare. Can you go?"

Jackson Beauregard Carter III threw his head back and mumbled an obscenity. Why hadn't this call come two hours ago while he still had some energy?

"What's the problem?" he asked.

"Says one of the foal's front legs is bent back," Chris said.

*Christ, that means someone had their hand where it wasn't supposed to be.*

He looked at Gray.

"Another client practicing medicine without a license," they said at the same time.

Either didn't want to pay a vet bill or thought he knew as much as the vet. Jack had seen both in his ten years of practice and his memories of the outcomes weren't good.

He uncrossed his long legs, stood, and reached for his bag on the chair next to him.

"Tell 'em I'll be there as soon as I can. Then tell them to keep their hands out of the horse until I get there. Also, tell them…"

He stopped and again looked at Gray.

"…hell, never mind. I forgot what I was going to say."

Jack turned to Chris. "Wanna come?"

Chris was pre-vet at the University of Kentucky. The kid would jump at the chance to assist with a difficult foaling. Tonight, though, Chris's throat flushed a curious red.

"Uh, well, Doc, it's like this," Chris stammered. "There's this girl, uh, after work…"

Jack grinned and held up his hand. "Say no more. I remember. Barely."

Chris mumbled thanks and disappeared. Gray smiled at Chris's retreating figure before his gaze shifted to Jack.

"Sure you don't want me to handle this one? You've already put in enough hours today by the sound of it."

"Nah, no problem," Jack replied. "I'm gonna give the poor horse a break."

They laughed again. In their vet school days, Gray had avoided horses at all costs while Jack tackled every equine ailment known to humankind. Even now, with a busy horse practice of his own, Jack volunteered his time at Gray's clinic.

"See ya later, bud. Don't wait up," Jack called as he strode down the hall. He stuck his head into the front office.

"Text the directions to my phone, will ya?"

Chris texted in record time like every other Gen Z Jack was familiar with. Jack looked at his phone to make sure he got the address.

"Didn't know there was a farm between Only Chance and Dixieland Stables," he said to himself, then caught the owner's name.

"Whoa. Great name. Brings to mind one of those classic movies about the old west, the ones that always ended in a gunfight," he joked.

The kid gave him a blank look which made Jack feel every bit of his thirty-six years.

"You know, Burt Lancaster, Kirk Douglas." He waited. "The Earps, Doc Holliday, the Clanton Gang." He held up his phone. "Cheyenne Modine."

Chris still looked confused. "Yeah, Doc."

Jack shook his head. These twenty-somethings had no idea what they were missing. Jack and his dad had watched all those movies at least ten times in Jack's younger years. It was one of the few things they'd done together, way back when.

"There are two barns beyond the house. The horse is in the barn on the right. Owner said the door to the barn will be unlocked and a light is on outside the stall."

Jack nodded and exited the side door to his truck. His jaw cracked with a wide yawn, and the tiredness from his long day seeped through his bones as he climbed into the cab.

He needed to talk to Gray about fewer hours at the clinic, especially when the Three-Day Event was in progress at the Horse Park. He had been there most of the day and the work, combined with the typical

Kentucky summer weather, was killing him. As Gray had reminded him earlier, days that stretched from six a.m. to midnight made Jack a very dull boy.

****

Cheyenne rummaged through the tack box for the bottle of whiskey. She'd placed it back in the box, with the hope that out of sight meant out of mind. Huh. Obviously not. She ignored the grit, brought the bottle to her lips and took a deep swig. Her cough echoed through the barn as another fireball singed her vocal cords and shredded what was left of her tonsils. Nausea lingered but she was too blitzed to care.

She trudged back to the stall and listened to the labored breaths of her mare.

"What's taking this yay-hoo so long?"

Dinah rolled her eyes in agreement.

"That's what I like about you, girlfriend." Cheyenne rubbed Dinah's ear. "We have a meeting of the minds on the really important stuff, don't we?"

Bolstered by the alcohol, Cheyenne headed back to the sink and tried to ignore the way her boots never lost contact with the floor. She was shuffling, for God's sake. She had a vision of herself, doubled over the edge of the sink while her head dangled near the drain, her legs seesawing back and forth on the other side. She might have laughed if not for another wave of queasiness. Instead, she scrubbed her arm pink and returned to the horse's rear, careful not to touch anything on the way.

For a moment Cheyenne lost focus and Dinah's broad butt swam before her eyes. Then she found the right insertion point and plunged in clear up to her armpit.

****

Jack leaned against the frame of the open stall door and watched the lower half of a human body writhe at the gray mare's rear. It was a toss-up on who grunted the loudest. He made out slender jean-clad legs and hiking boots in the low light before a string of curses erupted at the mare's tail.

"I'll be damned."

He was tired as hell but he knew a woman's voice when he heard it. Impressive, but not unusual. The horse industry in the Kentucky bluegrass had advanced in the last twenty years. The good ole boy network was still around but many women were now on the scene, which was a good thing.

His client's current position, however, wasn't good. His earlier irritation returned when he realized she had disobeyed rule number five on Jackson Carter's list of commands.

*Thou Shalt Not Put Arm in Horse's Birth Canal Even If You Are the Horse's Owner.*

"Ms. Modine, you did call for a vet?"

His sarcastic question was meant to warn and her legs stilled.

"Yes, dammit, what…took you…so long?"

Her head popped up but her speech was slow and slurred.

*Okay. So much for thinly veiled sarcasm.*

"Real sorry about that, Ms. Modine."

*Aww, shucks, ma'am, move your butt so I can do my job.*

"Why don't you stand so I can take a look? Unless, of course, you think there's room for two arms in that channel?"

*Uh, oh. I'm such a bad boy. It just slipped out. I*

13

*swear.*

He stepped over the legs of the horse and deliberately directed his flashlight into her face. He knew she'd appreciate he did it with a smile.

She threw up a hand to ward off the bright light but not before he noticed she was sweaty, flushed, and covered with dirt. Her lips tightened as she stood, her stance unsteady.

When she tottered out of the way, he caught a whiff of her perfume and jerked back. *Whoa.* That was a scent not easily forgotten, he thought, as his hold tightened on the flashlight. With his experience, he should be able to determine maker, price, and fermentation process.

"Perfect end to a perfect day," he grumbled and didn't care if she heard. As he counted in silence, he shoved the light in her direction.

His father was a reformed alcoholic. For the first ten years of Jack's life, their home environment was a living hell. Then, in a pathetic example of history repeating itself, he had married a woman whose Bible was *The Bartender's Guide.*

His knees snapped in the silence when he bent down for a cursory look. When he rose to search for a place to wash, he glanced again at Ms. Modine. Her tight brows told him she was anxious. Too bad he'd run out of comforting words.

"Sink?" he asked, his voice harsh even to his own ears.

She pointed and her arm waved like a flag in a slow breeze.

"To the right of the stall door, about ten feet." This time her enunciation was precise.

He gritted his teeth and walked away before she

finished.

At his return to the stall, she knelt by the mare's head and gave him a quick glance. He assumed the prone position to start his own examination. Hammered or not, he gave her credit for knowing enough to call a vet when needed. This little guy jerked his leg back like it was a game every time Jack touched him.

They were both quiet as the minutes ticked by. He looked at her a few times while he worked. Her glance had turned into a hawkish stare. Sort of like that scene his dad showed him from that old movie. Yeah, they were dueling except with eyeballs.

Despite her messed-up face and hair, she appeared young and pretty.

His body noticed and he looked away, so pissed with himself he wanted to spit. *Spit, right. Think about llamas. Maybe if I think long enough about all things gross and disgusting, I'll manage to lose the erection.*

He glanced back at her. A definite spasm in his groin told him llama spit wasn't quite up to the task.

Chapter Three

Cheyenne needed to have a talk with Joe Dawson the next time she saw him. "Old" Doc Carter was about ten years younger than Joe and had a personality only a mother could love. Of course, with his looks, who needed a personality? Hell, for that matter, who needed a soul?

His dark hair had a slight curl and his coveralls, those all-in-one uniforms popular with veterinarians in the horse business, fit as if tailored for his body alone. Cheyenne fought a grin when she noticed how much dirtier the blue fabric was now as he rolled around in filth. His arms were tan and muscled. She watched him grimace and detected dimples. How irksome. Dimples, and he wasn't even smiling.

Yes, if she'd been any other woman—and if she was being tortured on the rack—she'd admit he was attractive. *Really* attractive. The kind of attractive that made a woman giddy and prone to say stupid, gushy things because every nerve in her body pulsed with need.

But she was drunk, sick, and worried. Right now, pulsing was beyond her.

Not that he gave a shit about her impression of him. Drunk or not, she was alert enough to notice how he looked at her. He was a snob. She didn't come up to his standards, probably because her farm wasn't Shining Star or Windhaven.

She knew his kind like the back of her hand. Jack Carter was a member of the elite, from his patrician nose to the tips of his, probably, pedicured feet. Of all the rotten luck, she had to get one of the new breed of vets multiplying like rabbits in the Lexington Thoroughbred business. Because most of their four-legged clients were worth millions, these guys thought their excrement didn't disintegrate the ozone the way everyone else's did. Had her lips worked in a reasonably normal fashion, she'd tell him just what she thought of his patronizing attitude and lack of professional demeanor.

Professional demeanor, lol. What a joke. His could be summed up in one word. Surly.

"I need more light down here."

Yep, definitely surly. When he gritted his teeth at the next contraction the straight whiteness nearly blinded her.

"What in the hell for? Need to buff your nails?"

"Just do it!" he barked. She flinched and thought it was possible she'd gone a little too far with that remark.

He sat up and grabbed the flashlight away from her.

Only the appearance of the foal's nose and both front hooves kept her from adding to the insult. By now, Dinah had no push left. Carter lobbed the flashlight back to Cheyenne and waited for the next contraction, to help ease the foal's body out. Dinah lifted her head as the bulk of the foal slithered onto the stall floor. Cheyenne gasped with relief when she noticed the baby draw a breath.

"It's a colt," Carter announced.

*Don't smile, dimples, your face might crack.* It looked like the corners of his mouth fought for position. Then, like the sun appearing through gray clouds, the frown disappeared, replaced by a reluctant grin.

17

"He's beautiful," she whispered, awed once again by the miracle of birth. "I was a little worried. Dinah's not as young as she used to be."

"Yeah, well, happens to all of us." His eyes roamed her face, and when he continued to stare, she stood and stumbled backward. Because she watched him watch her, she backed into the wall and smacked her butt, hard.

"Ow."

His eyebrows shot up.

"I'll get my checkbook," she said and rushed out. At least, she thought she rushed. Speed had become a relative concept.

**\*\*\*\***

Jack's initial impression was right. Despite the drunkenness, dirt, and low light, there wasn't a man alive who wouldn't find her physically attractive. The rationale carried some comfort given the way his body continued to react.

His frustration increased when memories of his ex-wife intruded. She was beautiful in a completely different way—sophisticated, tall, blonde. When he couldn't live with her excuses any longer, their parting had been quick and bitter. After the divorce, she married a plastic surgeon and moved to Long Island, where Jack assumed she was drinking herself to an early grave. He had loved her once. Convinced she was never going to get help for her problem, that love had died a painful death.

He flexed his shoulders and turned to concentrate on the mare and foal. Dinah stood to nuzzle her offspring and within minutes, the foal was on its wobbly feet in search of his first meal. Jack stayed in the corner of the stall to watch the cycle of first recognition play out before him. It was always a reward, one of the best parts of a job that had no bad parts.

He pinched the bridge of his nose and closed his eyes with an amendment to his last thought. He loved his job but he preferred that drunk, gorgeous women not call for help at an hour so late he had no strength to keep his penis from adopting a mating posture. Even though she was out of sight, he had to fight the attraction with visions of every loathsome substance he'd ever removed from his refrigerator.

After a few minutes, when he was sure the mare and foal were okay, he left the barn, removed his coveralls, and packed his equipment in the truck. Impatient, he studied the farmhouse. More than enough time had passed and his body had begun to signal an immediate need for rest.

Finally, he gave up and stomped to the house. A dim light shone in the deserted kitchen. He stared through the screen door before he knocked.

"Ms. Modine, I need to be heading home," he called. He waited but there was no response.

He had his hand on the doorknob when he heard the far-off sound of a flushing toilet. A door squeaked in the house interior, boots scuffed through a hall, and she appeared, her clothes, hair, and face still a mess. Her spiritless stance poked a small, make that tiny, hole in the bubble of his anger.

Jack watched her cross the kitchen floor, grab the kitchen table for support, and sway as if she was about to fall.

"Shit."

He swung the door open and moved toward her, intent upon helping her to a chair. When he came up

19

behind her, he caught her elbows, and she rested back against him for a second. Then, with a moan, she clamped her hand across her mouth and leaned in the opposite direction. His hold on her arms broke too late. She bent over and spewed an unholy mess all over his recently cleaned work boots.

****

The distinctive sound of retching greeted his return to the kitchen. He looked at his watch, then his cell phone, and finally the clock above the sink. Sadly, they all seemed to work.

After losing dinner, lunch, breakfast, and maybe a few meals from last week, she had hurried back to the john and slammed the door behind her. Every swear word the U.S. Navy taught him had filtered through his brain but when he'd opened his mouth to rant, all that came out was an exhale of utter disgust. He went outside to wash off his boots, again, returned to the kitchen, found a disinfectant under the sink, and cleaned up the mess on the floor, which told him he might be in shock.

Horses didn't vomit. He'd been pissed on, crapped on, bled on, snorted on—horses were capable of producing copious amounts of snot—but vomit just didn't happen. Shock, that's what it was.

He sat down and listened to the muffled sound of dry heaves.

*Why in the hell am I still here?* He folded his arms and closed his eyes. He was here because he'd never heard someone be this sick for this long. And she was alone.

Jack leaned forward and ran his hands through his hair, not surprised to see straw drift to the floor. He argued with himself for a minute but lost. At the bathroom door, he listened to the sound of misery.

"You might want to remember this the next time you decide to get wasted," he said.

It was a half-hearted attempt to chastise and he knew it. Sometime between vomitus eruptus and now, he had acquired empathy. He wanted to shake some sense into her but not even her inebriation and his hyper reaction to the foul habit would allow him to kick her when she was down.

Besides, anger took too much energy.

"Ms. Modine, is there anything I can do for you? Anyone I can call?" He placed his hand on the doorknob and pressed his ear to the wood to hear her reply.

"No, Dr. Carter, it's okay. I'll be fine, really. Can I pay…"

She flushed the toilet, which muted the rest of her words.

Jack wasn't sure what prompted his next move. He entered the bathroom and bent down beside her. A washcloth hung from the towel rack and he turned on the water to wet the cloth. He pulled her head up and rubbed the washcloth over her pale face. As he did so, he noticed a dusting of freckles on her nose. Except for frequent trembles, she lay against him with her head on his chest when he wasn't supporting it.

He removed the knotted scarf that dangled from the end of her hair and used the brush from the sink to remove straw and dirt from the gold, red, and brown strands. He pulled the hair away from her face and ran his hand over the thick, silky mass. Her soft moan stopped his hand in mid-stroke.

He rinsed out the cloth and cleaned her arms. She was going to have one hell of a headache in the morning.

The thought produced only a trace of exasperation.

"Ms. Modine?" he whispered against her hair. "You're dehydrated. If you get some water in you, you'll feel better."

"Okay," she said through chattering teeth. With eyes still closed, she added "…had the flu, ran out of pain meds, thought whiskey might help. Stupid, huh?"

A vague light dawned. She played the game all drunks played during their addiction, making excuses, like his father and his ex.

The knowledge didn't help. He wanted to work up a stronger resistance to this woman and hoped his inability to do so was unrelated to her physical appeal. Maybe all those years of family counseling had finally paid off. Yeah, that was it, the counseling.

He helped her stand and tried to steady her as they walked from the room. She stumbled twice which made him pick her up and carry her down the hall to a bedroom. He placed her on the bed and moved to a dresser in search of a nightgown or T-shirt, anything to replace her dirty clothing. He didn't linger in the lingerie drawer, except to pause when he found a black lace thing tucked underneath the whites and pinks. He buried it deep and pulled out a worn flannel gown that had seen better days.

She lay where he had left her. Her eyes stayed closed as he sat down next to her.

"Ms. Modine, I brought you some nightclothes. Can you change into them by yourself?"

She gave the barest nod.

"I'll go out to the barn to check on the mare and foal one more time. I'll come back to make sure you're okay."

She nodded again. He turned at the door to look at her. All the urgent care clinics were closed by now. It would be the hospital emergency room or nothing. He'd see how she was when he returned.

Chapter Four

Cheyenne felt like she'd been dragged twenty miles on the mud flaps of her brother's eighteen-wheeler. She swore as long as she lived, which didn't seem to be much longer, to never again use alcohol to treat the flu.

It registered on some level of her benumbed brain that Dr. Carter was still nearby. His kindness confused her, him being an asshole and all. She made a brain note to thank him before she died.

Her thoughts came slow as she scratched off the items on her list of responsibilities. Dinah and the foal were fine, so she didn't have to worry about them. The school horses had all been fed and watered for the evening. John Michael, her part-time stable help, was scheduled in the morning to do the necessary chores so she didn't need to worry about those. Now, all she had to do was take off her clothes and settle the bill with Dr. Carter. Maybe not in that order.

First, though, she'd take a short nap.

\*\*\*\*

Jack slipped into the kitchen and listened for sounds—snoring, not retching. He'd given her ten minutes. With any luck, it was more than enough time for her to change and get into bed.

He filled a glass with cold water and walked down the hall to her bedroom. With careful movement, he entered the room to find her jeans half off and bunched down around her knees. She lay back on the bed with the nightgown clutched against her stomach.

"Cheyenne," he whispered and placed the glass on the nightstand, the clink of the glass making her eyelids flutter. Damn, she looked like the living dead and he wondered if she was even lucid.

"I'm taking you to the emergency room."

"No," she protested and struggled to sit up. "No, please, I…"

Her eyes filled with tears.

"Shhh," he said as he sat down next to her. It was simple to subdue her and he placed his hands on her shoulders to ease her back onto the pillow.

"I'll be fine," she said, the words so quiet he almost didn't hear them.

"Okay," he said, with some doubt. She was sick but he wasn't going to take her if she didn't want to go. "I'm going to help you get ready for bed. No arguments."

To his surprise, she handed him the gown.

Jack tried not to touch her as his fingers fumbled with the buttons on her shirt. Slowed by his exhaustion and the distraction of the strange evening, he wasn't able to stop her when she drifted forward. To make matters worse, her head fell under his chin and his knuckles pressed against her breasts as if they were glued together.

He froze, unable to extricate his hands from their impossible position. If he worked his hands from between their bodies, he wouldn't be quick enough to break her fall backward. Or she might just collapse into his lap…*Jesus*, he'd better not think about that now.

She adjusted her head, which brought her lips in direct contact with his skin. Her warm breath gave him goosebumps.

His fingers flew down the last four buttons as the backs of his hands rubbed against her softness. Surely it wasn't natural for a woman this slender to have breasts this lush. With an immediate flash of insight, he knew when he died this would be the torture the devil chose for him—a pair of beautiful breasts he'd never be allowed to fully touch on a semi-conscious woman!

By the time he got her nightgown on and pulled the sheet over her, his hands shook as if he had palsy. He wiped his wet palms on his shirt and took a moment to gather himself. Just when he thought the situation was under control the ache in his groin laughed at him.

*Roadkill, soggy noodles in the sink drain, mashed earthworms on the sidewalk...oh, yeah, the earthworm visual seemed to work.*

He waited a minute more and invited the tiredness to wash through him, to extinguish the last remnant of lust. Just one more thing to do before he left. His medical bag was on the kitchen counter, and he dug out some pain meds. A vision of his California King mattress floated through his mind as he walked back to the bedroom and woke her.

"Cheyenne, here are some pills to help you feel better. Drink as much water as you can to wash them down."

When she opened her mouth like an obedient baby bird, he dropped the pills in and tipped the glass up to let her take three decent swallows. He put the glass on the nightstand and watched her collapse on the pillow. She was as still as stone, which made him rethink leaving.

"I'm so cold." Her voice was hoarse and weak.

*Okay, that did it.*

"I know." He reached for the quilt to cover her. "I'll

stay for a few minutes until you go to sleep. You'll feel better in the morning."

Jack returned to the bathroom, got into the shower, and stood under the hot spray for about five years. He refused to wait, smelling like refuse. He dried his hair on a yellow towel with a duck embroidered on it, then slipped into the jeans and T-shirt he'd brought from the truck. He pulled an armchair close to the bed and stretched his legs out on the mattress, careful not to disturb her. It took him less than a minute to fall asleep.

\*\*\*\*

He awakened second by slow second, his arms tight around the pliant body fitted against him. With drowsy pleasure, he rubbed his erection against the soft butt. When he opened his eyes the early morning sun illuminated the room and his dull gaze drifted to the bottom of the bed.

A white cat, its blue eyes filled with disapproval, stared back. Not unusual for a feline, but, damn, it wasn't his cat.

The full implication of his position jarred him into action. He quickly slipped off the bed only to have his left calf cramp with the sudden movement.

He hobbled across the room and thought about her reaction had she found him beside her in the same bed. Sometime in the early morning hours, his need for real sleep and the ache in his shoulders had driven him to the beckoning empty space of the big, comfortable mattress. Somehow, his body had snuck underneath the quilt. At least the sheet had separated them, to his great relief.

Why hadn't he left after his shower? Hell, it was too late for self-recrimination. He needed to get his ass on the road. With any luck, she'd sleep through his departure and save him any further involvement. He didn't care if alcoholism was an illness. He cared even less about being politically correct. So what if his exhausted body had betrayed him? He'd lusted for the wrong woman before. In other words, not his first rodeo, but damn if he ever planned to participate in this event again.

Somewhere in the house, a clock chimed eight. Jack scraped his hands through his hair, scratched out a note, and left it on the kitchen table. He rushed to his truck, distracted as he buckled on his watch, and almost collided with a tall, skinny red-haired kid pushing a manure-laden wheelbarrow.

"Whoa, bud, got a license to drive that thing?"

"You the vet?" the kid asked as he nodded toward the words on the truck door.

"One and only." Jack cleared his throat when the kid's look drifted to the house.

"Your boss is a little under the weather. You might want to check on her before you leave today."

A wad of tobacco shifted from one freckled cheek to another as "Red's" attention drifted back to Jack.

The boy's face split with a wide grin.

"I reckon I could do that."

The kid pushed the wheelbarrow toward the barn, with an expert spit as he walked away.

Jack climbed into his truck and as it idled down the driveway, he smiled at Dinah and her stiff-legged foal in the pasture. Daylight showed the farm was clean and well-kept. He stopped at the end of the drive to check traffic and saw a wooden sign he'd missed last night. It read "Red Fox Farm, Cheyenne Modine-Owner, Riding Instruction, Children Welcome."

He shifted in his seat. It'd be a rainy day in hell before he let someone like Ms. Modine teach *his* kids how to ride.

Chapter Five

Cheyenne opened her eyes to bright sunlight. Luckily, she had moved to the driver's seat of her brother's semi, but the weakness lingered as if she had driven all night. In seconds, recollections of the previous evening roared to life. Every thought collided, like bumper cars at an amusement park during a six-year-old's birthday celebration.

Her meeting with Jack Carter, the foal, her drinking, his help—oh, crap, her *nightgown*—made her want to dive back into sleep. Instead, she placed the pillow over her face to muffle her groan.

She peeked into the corners of the room and listened. He was gone. Her last memory was when he handed her a glass of water to down some pills. Even if he hadn't been all that nice at first, he had gone above and beyond to help her. She recalled some surprising gentleness when she'd lost her cookies—on his boots, and *yuck,* her kitchen floor. She hated to think what *that* looked like this morning.

It was time to get up and face the music. She slid from the bed and lined up her day. First, she'd clean up the puke in the kitchen, take a shower and check on Dinah and Little D, as in *dammit, give me your foot.* Later, if she was up to it, she'd make a trip to the clinic to pay her bill. She'd rather suck a lemon than see Jack Carter again but she owed him for saving her mare and foal.

The floor seemed to move as she staggered to her feet. For some reason, the question of his marital status popped into her mind. Someone that hot was either married or gay. He hadn't worn a ring but lots of vets didn't due to the handsy nature of the job. Last night he had stared at her like he was attracted, which told her he wasn't gay. She was certain her gay friends would agree then shook her head to clear it of these useless thoughts.

Her unsteady legs carried her to the window where she looked for John Michael. He was there dependable as usual. Her decision to hire him had been a good one. Of course, Uncle Lyn recommended the kid so the decision had pretty much been made for her.

"John Michael," she called as he exited the barn with a hose in his hand. "How are Dinah and the foal?"

His gaze searched the house and landed at her bedroom window.

"Hey, 'Shy', you feeling better?"

Cheyenne stiffened.

"Just fine," she lied. "Why?"

"Well, when that vet left this morning, he said I might want to check on you 'cause you was feelin' poorly."

*This morning? He left this morning?*

She turned toward the bed and saw an indentation in the pillow. No Bubba fur covered the pillowcase which meant her cat hadn't made the dent. Cheyenne ignored the heat that raced through her. Just a residual effect from her fever, she thought, but she wasn't totally convinced.

"I'm okay, John Michael. Thanks for asking. How are Dinah and the foal?" she repeated and hoped to change the subject.

"They're good. That why the vet was here?"

"Yes, John Michael."

Cheyenne gave up and left the window. The hot shower might help unlock her jaw. Dr. Big-Shit Carter had seen her naked and slept with her. Great. Just great. When she saw him again she'd ask if it had been as good for him as it hadn't been for her.

She forced herself to visit the kitchen. She'd rather shovel manure from fifty Clydesdale stalls than clean up puke. To her surprise, the floor was clean when she got there. A place near the table was a tad shinier than the rest of the fake brick tile but that was it. Okay, so he'd seen her naked, slept with her, and cleaned up her puke. Maybe it was time they set the date.

Her attention drifted to a piece of paper on the table. The handwriting was nearly illegible, but she managed to decipher a few words. He told her to send payment to the Bourbon County clinic. Of course, he'd want to make sure he got his money. But what really surprised her was the comment he had emptied the whiskey bottle in the barn. What an arrogant jerk. He had no reason to trash her whiskey. Cheyenne swore she'd mentioned her flu and it was Daddy's bottle. When she and Billy packed up all his things after his death last year, they'd found it wrapped in an old copy of the Lexington Herald in the tack room. It had sentimental value even if she *had* made a dense decision to drink it while sick.

She wadded up the note and threw it across the kitchen. It landed short of the garbage can. He wasn't going to get away with this. At the very least, he owed her a bottle of booze.

Her mind clear, her purpose remotivated, she knew the sooner she got this over with the better. She'd thought about nothing but him since waking up and it wasn't productive. Once she set him straight and paid her bill, she'd forget the whole abysmal episode. There were more important things to do like making her riding school profitable. To hell with profit. She'd settle for breaking even.

The shower helped to order her thoughts and even improved her strength. Her temper still simmered but had cooled to a degree. If she walked into his office with her hair on fire, he'd have the advantage, which was a no-no in her book. She suspected, with the slightest encouragement, Jack Carter might be a total Neanderthal. Exactly the sort of man she despised—arrogant and rich—which gave her more than enough reason to stay as far away from him as possible.

Her childhood in Richmond, south of Lexington on the outer edge of the big, world-famous horse farms, had exposed her to plenty of his kind. Her daddy, a lifelong horse trader, knew all sorts of people. Members of the privileged class often called upon Walker Modine to do this and that, whenever it involved horses. He was a fair and honest man, and they trusted him to make the best deal but the *friendship* ended there. When she remembered their aloof, patronizing attitudes toward her father, her anger flared.

Daddy had said "that's just the way those folks are" but she had taken it personally and hated their smug superiority. Cheyenne never forgot her roots. To this day, she steered clear of anyone with pretensions. She'd just bet "ole Doc Carter" was full of them.

No doubt her fifty-acre farm with two barns and white frame house wasn't quite up to his usual standards. Let him go back to his multi-million dollar showplaces with their gold-plated tack room toilet fixtures. There had to be another competent vet in the area to take care of her animals.

After she was through with him today, he'd be just a bad memory.

\*\*\*\*

By mid-afternoon, the Equine Medical Center had finally returned to normal. Mike Blake and Win Barrington, Jack's partners, covered for him the first hour but joked about his unusual tardiness. His secretary and sister-in-law, Janie, had phoned everyone including his parents when he didn't show up for work on time.

That meant most of the morning was shot for Jack since he had to call everyone back to reassure them. Gray's only comments concerned the sex of the mare's owner after Jack filled him in on some of the previous night's events. Jack made no mention of the alcohol. He figured the woman had a right to choose how she wanted to ruin her life.

Only when Jack brought up the evening polo practice did his partners let up on the jokes. Polo was the one topic guaranteed to take their minds off everything. He knew that, of course.

"Jackson," Janie said, her voice loud over the speakerphone. "Gray's on the line. You got the time?"

"I'll take it." He punched a button and dialed back the volume. "Hey, didn't I just get done talking to you? I'm busy so make it quick."

Gray snorted.

"I guess that means you don't want to know Annie Oakley was just here to pay her bill."

"Oh."

"That's all you've got to say? In that case, I'll just

sign off…"

"Are the mare and foal good?" Jack jumped in, not sure why he did.

"Yes. Did I mention she wanted directions to your clinic?"

Jack stopped rifling through the papers on his desk.

"Here? Why? Did she have a problem with the way I handled things last night?"

Did she know he'd stayed all night or spent most of the night in bed with her? Surely she hadn't discussed the details with Gray. Jack hated being put on the defensive, especially in a situation like this. After all, he'd shown remarkable patience given her irresponsible behavior.

"No, she just asked if you were hung like a stud. I, of course, had to break the bad news and tell her you couldn't find yours with a magnifying glass…"

"Christ, Gray, what in the hell did she say?"

Jack buried his head in his hands while Gray slapped his thigh over his comedic timing. The loud slaps bounced off the walls of the office and Jack reached over to lower the volume again.

"Gray?"

"Aw, shoot, Jack, I'm sorry. You asked for it, bud."

Gray noisily blew his nose and chuckled.

"Ms. Modine didn't understand our payment system. When I tried to explain the clinic bill, she wasn't having any of it and insisted you should get something for *services rendered*…"

Gray's voice cracked but he didn't lose control this time.

"…so I suggested she come to your office and discuss it with you. Just wanted you to be prepared."

"When did you talk to her?"

"About twenty minutes ago. She was anxious. I figure she'll be there soon. After she left, I realized I might have met her a long time ago. Her father was a horse dealer down near Richmond. My dad bought my sister's first horse from him."

"When was this?"

"Caught your interest, did I? About fifteen years ago. We drove down on the recommendation of old moneybags, Lyndon Tyree. Lyndon said Walker Modine could put Sally on a levelheaded horse, if there is such a thing, and give us a good price, too. If I remember right, Cheyenne, her brother, and Mr. Modine were all there when we arrived. Cheyenne rode several horses for Dad. She was about twelve or so and a great rider for someone so young. Remember the big red roan Sally took her first lessons on? Well, that's the horse we bought. Sally even took him to college with her. Ms. Modine certainly has fulfilled all of her early promise."

Jack pondered Cheyenne's connection to Lyn Tyree. Lyn sponsored the charity polo match every year and Jack's team had played in the match for the past eight seasons. Jack wondered if Lyn knew about Cheyenne's problem with alcohol.

"Lyndon Tyree sent you down there? That must mean he knew the Modine family well."

The line from the front desk buzzed again.

"Look, bud, you sound busy," Gray said. "I'll let you go. Keep me posted."

"Yeah, thanks for calling."

Jack signed off and answered the other line.

"Yes, Janie, what's up?"

"Jackson, there's a Ms. Modine here to see you,

about a bill?"

Jack wasn't dense. He heard the note of inquiry in Janie's voice. Thank God Win and Mike were out of the office.

"Send her back," he said and rose to open the door as the sound of boots echoed down the hall.

Chapter Six

Cheyenne heard the latch click. Her heart pounded and she decided it must be the leftover anger. On her drive from the clinic, she'd worked up a good head of steam.

Her steps slowed when she found him at his office door. He shoved his hands into the pockets of his jeans and she tried to center her gaze on his right ear. Checking a man's ears for hair tufts was a guaranteed turn-off for her. The trick stopped foolish fantasies.

When she didn't find any, she refocused on his clothes. He wore one of those soft knit shirts in pale green. The short sleeves hugged his biceps. He didn't wear socks with his scuffed deck shoes. She found dark hairs on the tops of his feet and tried to work up an aversion, to no avail.

She lifted her gaze, disappointed with her inability to find anything more to dislike about Jack Carter. Unfortunately, looking at him all clean and shiny in daylight didn't help either. She sniffed in disdain.

"Dr. Carter," she said, her greeting formal.

"Ms. Modine," he said, matching her formality. "Any headache from your overindulgence last night? You seem to have recovered from your *illness.*"

She squared her shoulders. If he picked up on her frigid gaze he didn't show it.

His lips curved in a slight but cynical smile, which

was the last thing she expected. She had practiced her eat-shit stare on men. Until now, it always worked. Billy said she could freeze-dry coffee beans with the look.

"Yes, I have. I need to discuss my *illness* with you."

The accusation didn't leave his rich, brown eyes.

He gestured to a chair and walked behind the desk to sit down as if he couldn't get far enough away. Little did he know everything he'd just done doubled her need to incinerate his monied ass until he begged for mercy.

\*\*\*\*

His foot jumped as she looked around at his cluttered desk, his polo trophies, the wall of windows overlooking the paddocks, and the small refrigerator covered in scribbled drawings.

He wanted her to stop licking her lips.

"I know you're busy, so I'll make this short," she began.

He hopped out of his desk chair and moved to the refrigerator to hide his hungry gaze.

"Mind if I have a drink? It's turning out to be another scorcher and I'll be out for most of the afternoon."

"Of course not. Go right ahead."

He pulled out a soda and opened it. Her fingers tapped a rapid beat on the arm of the chair. He took his time crossing back to sit down, then swallowed a long drink before he looked at her. She sat with an ankle resting on the opposite knee. Her elbows barely touched the arms of her chair like she wanted to leave, yesterday.

He smiled at the glare she tried not to show. His suspicion was right. She didn't like his knowing she had a booze problem.

"I want to thank you for your...help, last night," she

said, her words curt. "Not just with Dinah, but with everything. I apologize if I put you in an uncomfortable position."

*Damn.* He hoped she didn't mean his raging morning erection.

"I certainly didn't help things by drinking as much as I did. Regarding my *illness*, I had the flu for about three days, I'd run out of Ibuprofen and made the mistake of using whiskey to blunt my aches…"

Jack laughed, unable to stop himself. Her mouth fell open as she stared at him.

"Look, Ms. Modine, I'm a vet. I get paid to treat horses, and I was happy to help Dinah. Is everything okay with her and the foal?"

"Yes, but…"

"Then I think our business is finished, don't you?"

Jack stood, irritated as hell. The flu story was asinine but, suddenly, he wanted to believe her. Like a bolt out of nowhere, his body had turned traitorous. Last night when he was dog-tired it was easy to dismiss any wayward lustful urges. Today it wasn't that simple. He hated his continued temptation, especially now.

She stood as well, but not to leave.

"Not just yet, *Dr. Carter*," she spat his name and her eyes shot sparks in his direction. "I'm not sure what your problem is, but I've got some ideas, and all of them are less than complimentary. I didn't appreciate your high-handed disposal of my whiskey, and I'll look for a replacement in the near future…"

"I'm sure there's another stashed somewhere in the house."

"Another stash!" she sputtered. "You arrogant son of a…"

She checked herself but the danger in her expression flashed a warning. When she spoke again her voice had dropped to a hiss.

"I'm leaving now, Carter. Before I do, I'm paying my bill. I prefer not to leave any loose ends where you're concerned because it will be a rainy day in hell before I ever call you again. How much?"

She reached into the back pocket of her jeans and pulled out a checkbook. When she grabbed a pen from his desk, her stare demanded his compliance.

Fascinated, his gaze had roamed over her body while she raged. He couldn't help it. Somewhere in the last few seconds his lust-induced stupor had won out over his disgust. The trite phrase 'you're so beautiful when you're angry' played over and over again in his head. He'd examined every perfect physical detail of her face, from the freckles at her hairline to her silver eyes, straight nose, and healthy pink lips. She wore little makeup to distract him from his thorough inspection. Her long hair was in a braid that hung to the middle of her back and the humidity had created wispy curls on the sides of her heart-shaped face.

"Dr. Carter. How much?" she insisted. Her chest rose and fell with her aggravation, and of course, he noticed.

He finally found his voice.

"Ms. Modine, I volunteer my time at the clinic. I work there as a favor to Gray—Dr. Benson. He's an old friend. He doesn't really like horses, so I and a few other equine specialists donate time to give the less wealthy horse owners in this area access to decent animal care."

Two bright dots of color flared on her cheeks. She straightened and slapped her checkbook against her thigh. When she bent over his desk and scribbled on a check, the sun from the window lit the red strands in her hair.

"Here." She ripped the paper from the book. "If you can't accept it for last night, take it and apply it to some other *poor* person's account—at Dr. Benson's clinic, of course. I'm sure none of the clients in this practice need it."

She reached over and stuck the check under his lamp, then started from the room before he could react.

He called her name when she got to the door.

She turned with a slight smile.

"Goodbye, Dr. Carter." She looked straight through him. "Oh, and by the way, I know you stayed the night. Be grateful I'm not in a litigious mood—at the moment, that is."

She slipped out the door with Jack three steps behind her when Janie's voice intervened.

"Jack, there's an emergency over at Peabody's. The foal out of Grand Slam you delivered last week has a deep gash on his front, left pastern, with some blood loss. Can you go?"

"Yes, dammit, tell them I'll be there in ten minutes," he yelled across the room.

"Yessir!" Janie replied, clearly insulted.

Jack knew a moment of contrition as he rushed to leave.

Chapter Seven

The white pick-up came to a dust-flying stop in the parking lot of Danny's Pub. Cheyenne yanked open the driver's side door then shut it and slapped the steering wheel. She was too angry to enter the bar and act in a reasonably friendly way. She needed a drink since she was still dehydrated, but she wasn't about to touch alcohol for at least a year and it had nothing to do with Dr. "Big Shit" Carter and his ridiculous accusation.

Two men stepped from a truck parked next to hers and one of them noticed her. She rolled her eyes when he winked, which made him laugh before he headed inside the building.

She tried to calm down but her thoughts refused to move away from the vet from hell. Instead, she invented a whole new process to describe exactly where he needed to insert a specific anatomical part. She was even more infuriated about the confirmation of her initial impression. He was a conceited, rich snob, raised in a privileged environment, who donated his expertise to poor people like herself, only because it pumped up his ego.

And he thought she was a drunk! Cheyenne slapped the wheel again, shook away the pain in her hand and swore Jack Carter was enough to make anyone want to drink—*heavily*.

If she was going to get Dr. Jackass out of her head

for good, she needed to satisfy her curiosity and there was only one person who might help her solve the problem. She pulled her cell from her purse and dialed the number.

"Yes, Lyndon Tyree, please."

She heard him juggle the phone when he came on the line and said hello.

"Lyn, it's Cheyenne," she said in response to her old friend's greeting. "How are you?"

"Cheyenne, how nice to hear from you. I'm about as fine as an eighty-year-old, arthritic geezer can be. How about yourself?"

Her anger slipped a notch. Lyndon proudly injected his age into every conversation.

"I'm doing okay, Lyn." She wasn't okay but that was something he didn't need to know. "Keeping busy with the farm, trying to get my business on a firmer footing. I wanted to thank you again for recommending John-Michael. He's a reliable, hard worker."

"Yes, he's a good boy. Just needed a break. I talked with him a few weeks ago. He speaks highly of you, too."

She cringed. Hopefully, this morning's situation hadn't changed John-Michael's opinion.

"When are you coming to see me again?" Lyndon asked and tried to sound gruff. "You've been back in Lexington for three months now and I've only seen you twice. That's not nearly enough for me."

"I'm sorry, Lyn. With my riding classes and all the farm chores, I sometimes don't know if I'm coming or going. Feeble excuses, huh?"

He gave an exaggerated sigh.

"Oh, all right. I guess I just don't realize how busy you young people are these days. Seems like technology

44

should do more to free up your time instead of keeping you busy with all that social media crap. I confess I'm not as into that stuff since I retired."

"You're retired?" she teased. "You host the charity polo match every year, you spend several hours counseling at the small business association office, you teach a business management course at the university. What have I missed? Daddy talked all the time about your many responsibilities." She slapped her forehead. "How could I forget your lifelong goal to breed the perfect polo pony?"

They both laughed. She wouldn't find him at home if she did visit more often. He had his finger in so many pies it was obvious he'd invented pies.

"Lyn, I had to call a vet last night to help Dinah foal. I wonder if you know him," Cheyenne asked when they stopped laughing.

"What's his name, my dear? I know a few," he said.

"Jack Carter."

"Jackson Carter? Of course, I know him. Highly respected, not to mention an excellent polo player. His team will play in my charity match this August, as a matter of fact."

"What's his background? Is he from this area?" she interjected. Lyn's obsession was polo and once he got started, she'd never get him off the topic.

"Why, yes, he grew up here in Lexington. His father was the Commonwealth's Attorney for many years before he retired last year. His brother is an attorney, too. Works in the same office their Daddy did. I seem to remember Jack, Jr., that would be Jack's daddy, wanting Jack to follow in his legal footsteps, but Jackson always had a strong will to forge his own path. He spent time in the Navy before he went to vet school. He comes from a fine, old Lexington family. Did he take good care of Dinah?"

"Uh, yes, he seemed competent. Old money?"

"Yes," Lyn drawled. Cheyenne heard the wheels turn in the man's brain.

"Why the interest, Cheyenne? This seems to go beyond finding a good vet for your animals."

"Just curious," she replied. "I had no quarrel with his veterinary ability, but I'm not sure I liked his attitude. Seemed like an arrogant, rich..."

"There you go again," Lyndon chided. "I thought your years away would mellow you on the subject of the haves and have-nots in Lexington. You were always far too sensitive for your own good."

"It's hard to forget how they treated Daddy, Lyn," she said. "I know he didn't care, but I cared for him, and it was sad to watch."

"Well, my dear, I hate for you to waste your energy on all that negative emotion. Jack Carter is one of the least pompous men I know. Besides, what difference does it make? Unless, of course, your interest goes beyond his skills. He's a good-looking man and single. I understand many women find him attractive."

She snorted into the phone.

"Now, Cheyenne, that's not very ladylike."

"Maybe that's because I'm not *ladylike*." She smiled at the ancient term. "Besides, I could never be interested in someone like Carter and I'm sure he'd say the same about me. We're too different."

"Hmm, well, perhaps, but like I said, your questions seemed to go beyond the professional," Lyndon commented, before he switched subjects. "How is the business going?"

Cheyenne thought hard about her answer. Lyn would help in a minute if he knew her financial situation. He didn't approve of a diet of peanut butter crackers and Ramen any more than she liked eating them but she was determined to do this on her own. Besides, she wasn't about to ask a friend or family member for a loan when she had no idea when or if she could repay it.

"I'm doing okay," she repeated. "I think I told you I talked with the director of the Speech and Hearing Center about a class for their kids. It seems a shame not to use my signing skills when riding therapy would help them."

"I understand your need to reach out to these kids, Cheyenne, but will that pay the bills? Didn't you say you wouldn't charge them your regular fee?"

Lyn was gentle but his reply carried a warning. He hadn't become a millionaire by ignoring the bottom line.

"I'm hoping the word-of-mouth advertising might produce some results. I have that dressage demonstration at the Horse Park in two weeks, which should also bring in more business," she added and waited for his approval. His next comment floored her.

"Jack Carter could help. He's, of course, very connected in the horse world."

"Lyn, please! Don't go there. I wouldn't ask Carter for help if…if…" she sputtered with indignation, unable to complete her thought at such an objectionable idea.

"Okay, calm down." He chuckled before he continued. "I'm convinced you don't like the man so let my suggestion die a natural death."

"I certainly hope so," she said. "And don't worry about me or my business. It will be up and running in no time."

*Hopefully, before I'm forced to travel over to the UK campus to sell my body to nineteen-year-old college boys.*

"If you say so, dear." He didn't sound convinced. "Just be sure and come to me if you need help. I can spare some cash. Rolling around naked in my mountain of hundred dollar bills every evening isn't as exciting as it used to be."

Cheyenne cracked up. She suspected that had been his intention.

Chapter Eight

The next day found Jack palpating mares at Kingston Farms, not far from Red Fox. He was on his last mare, his thoughts on Cheyenne in spite of himself when he realized something was wrong. The mare hadn't moved but his eyesight blurred. He leaned back against the wall and made a valiant effort to keep his breakfast down. The stable attendant who held the horse's head glanced back in concern.

"Doc Carter, you don't look so good. You wanna stop for a minute?"

"Yes, that might be wise, Jed," Jack mumbled as he tried to straighten up. "Where are the facilities?"

"Down the aisle on the left. Take your time. I'll be here when you get back."

Jack had just turned the corner when Jed called out, "The stomach flu has been going around. Hope that's not what you have."

****

He'd recovered enough by Sunday to join Ben and Janie and their three kids for dinner. As usual, the house was alive with shrieks and laughter. The two boys tore up and down the long hallways on their new hoverboards, while three-year-old Lea helped her father cook dinner.

Ben, his younger brother, worked six days a week but he reserved Sundays for his family. Since Janie worked part-time at the clinic and was responsible for the kids during the week, Sunday was her day to rest. Jack spied Janie in the middle of the pool, resting on a flamingo float with a book.

When Lea crawled into Jack's lap, his attention went immediately to the little girl and she rubbed her hand over his jaw.

"Scratchy." She giggled.

Her fascination with Jack was fodder for numerous family conversations.

"Give Uncle Jack 'five', Lea," Ben said as he stood at the sink and washed potatoes.

Lea held out a flattened palm for Jack to slap, then made him do the same. They laughed together when she slapped him, twice, and Jack was once again overcome with envy. These feelings had gotten out of hand since Lea's birth, so much so that Janie and Ben chastised him daily for spoiling her.

Lea slid to the floor to play with the pots and pans she had scattered about.

"Careful, Jack, your indulgence is showing again." Ben joked.

"Hell, I can't help it. She's too d-a-m-n cute," Jack said as he watched her.

"Well, why don't you make one of your own, then? You have all the necessary equipment, even if it isn't as big as mine."

Lea banged a wooden spoon on the pots and sang a made-up song about puppies.

"What about Elaine? You two still on?" Ben asked when Jack didn't respond to the timeworn gag.

Lea's curly brown hair was similar in color to Cheyenne's and once again, Jack's thoughts strayed. He snapped to attention when Ben barked his name.

"Bro, wake up. What about Elaine?"

"What about her?" Jack replied. "I haven't seen her in a month."

"I guess that answers my question," Ben mumbled. He placed the potatoes in the oven, dried his hands, and turned to face Jack. "Is there something you want to talk about?"

Jack took a sip of his soda and stood to walk to the window that looked out over the pool. He smiled at Janie's lethargic paddling.

"I don't know," he finally said.

When Ben didn't respond, Jack looked back and laughed at his brother's frown.

"It's a woman. I feel stupid asking my younger brother for advice about a woman especially since I taught you everything you know."

"Who better to ask than your happily married brother? I think I might have done something right," Ben said. "C'mon, what's up?"

Jack rolled his shoulders to ease his mid-back ache.

"I met her a few days ago. I *may* have made the wrong assumption about her. We had words. I'm curious…"

"And?" Ben prompted when Jack didn't finish his thought.

"And what?"

"Explain 'wrong assumption'. What kind of words? Why are you curious?"

Ben fired off questions like the prosecuting attorney he was.

"She has a riding stable east of here called Red Fox, out past Only Chance. Her mare was having foaling problems and I was at Gray's that night, so I went. It was late. I'd had a long day. When I got there she was drunk, and I assumed she had the habit. Now I'm not sure."

Jack gripped the soda can so tight it cracked. At Ben's smirk, he continued, "Hey, give me a break. You lived in the same house when Dad was drinking himself to death. You're not much more open-minded about it than I am."

Ben raised his eyebrows but remained silent.

"So, we had a bad start. Her excuse was she'd had the flu and was treating it with whiskey. I ask you, who uses hard liquor to help them with the flu? When I got the mare and foal taken care of, I found a half-empty bottle in the barn, and during a moment of insanity, I poured it out. She had gone to the house to get her checkbook and when she hadn't returned in a reasonable amount of time, I went looking for her. Found her worshipping the porcelain God and weak as a kitten."

He didn't mention the vomit on the kitchen floor. Ben would carry that information to the end zone.

"How many times did we see Dad in the same condition? Anyway, I stayed with her and left early the next morning."

"Whoa, Jack!" Ben remarked, a clear accusation in his voice.

"Hell, no." Jack swore. "What kind of bastard do you think I am?"

"Daddy, what a bat turd?" Lea asked, her innocent eyes wide in her round face.

Jack looked at Ben, and mouthed "Sorry."

"It's nothing, honey." Ben crouched down and put his hand on her head. "Why don't we all take a walk in the backyard while dinner cooks?"

Outside, they put Lea on a swing and headed to a picnic table.

"Okay, continue. You were just getting to the good part," Ben said when they sat down.

"There was no good part if by good you mean lewd," Jack insisted. "She said she had the flu. I didn't believe her because drunks are always in denial, as we both know. But she was alone and no matter how she'd gotten into that condition, I, well…I don't know. I couldn't just leave her, could I?"

Ben didn't answer. He seemed to understand Jack didn't need one.

"Anyway, as I was saying before you made your vulgar insinuation, I left early the next morning. She was still sleeping. I thought that was the end of it but apparently I was wrong."

"Wait," Ben interrupted. "That was the morning Janie called me at the office, right?"

"Christ. She called you, too?"

Ben came to his wife's defense. "She was worried about you, Jack. She thought you were in a ditch somewhere, mangled in the twisted metal of your truck."

"Okay, okay. Sorry. Yes, that was the morning. Now, will you let me finish the da…darn story?"

"Please, continue."

"She came to my office later. She wanted to pay me for my services. As I said, we had words. I was, uh, rude. She got really pi…angry and left the office. I tried to stop her but I had an emergency call."

"Hmmm." Ben laced his fingers behind his head and leaned back against the tabletop. "Let me guess. You called her a drunk based upon a first impression."

It sounded even worse when Ben said it.

"You always did have a knee-jerk reaction to booze misuse," Ben went on. "Yes, we were all affected by Dad's problem but it affected you more. Why do you think she's not an alcoholic, now?"

"I don't know for sure. However, yesterday was the first day I could get out of bed after a bout with the flu," Jack said.

"Ahh." Ben studied the leaves of the tree overhead. "Why are you so curious about this woman?"

Jack mumbled his answer.

"Speak up, boy," Ben said in a perfect imitation of their father.

"She's gorgeous, for one thing," Jack said.

Ben's laughter echoed across the lawn.

"You make that sound very undesirable."

"In this case, it is," Jack replied with irritation. "I refuse to be in lust with a woman who has a drinking problem. Look at my track record. I'm not traveling that road again, ever."

"Why don't you just ask her out? Put her in a social situation and see what happens. Maybe you'll get your answer."

"I told you. We had words. Her words included *rainy day in hell*. I think that means she won't go out with me."

"Yeah. Okay. Strong words. You might have a problem."

Ben appeared to ponder the situation.

"She has horses. You do horses for a living. Do you know someone in the horse world who knows her? Someone who could fill you in on her habits?"

Jack slanted a look at his brother.

"Lyndon Tyree," Jack said.

"There you go. Tyree knows everything about everyone in the horse business. What'd he say?"

"We're playing phone tag. I haven't talked to him yet."

"You're in the charity match next month. You'll see him then. Can't it wait?"

"I'd prefer not. He's usually in demand that day. The chances of me getting him alone are zilch. Besides…"

Jack stood and paced around the picnic table. Ben watched him but it had become too difficult to explain all his feelings to his brother.

"Besides?" Ben prompted.

"I'm feeling some confusion, some urgency. Can't put my finger on it. I just need to, uh, know."

"Feeling some discomfort in a certain erogenous zone, eh? This woman must be Lana Martin, Julie Sutherland, and Amanda James all rolled into one."

"Amanda James?"

"Yeah, that Victoria's Secret model back when we were teenagers. You used to have wet dreams whenever she came on stage."

Jack swore under his breath, so Lea didn't hear him.

"It was Manda Hart, ass wipe. You never could keep your model goddesses straight."

While Ben's chest shook with muted laughter, Jack sat back down and put his elbows on his knees. He stared at Janie in the pool, not really seeing her.

After a minute, he said, "She got tears in her eyes when the foal was born. I'm so used to the business-as-usual, blasé attitude of those in the racing world. It's been a while since I've seen a client cry over anything but horses that can't run."

"Uh oh. A gorgeous woman who loves horses with

55

a possible drinking problem," Ben intoned in a voice of doom.

"Yeah, da…darn it."

"Jack, do me a favor, bud. Swear when you're around me, just don't do it around the kids. You're giving me a headache."

Chapter Nine

Cheyenne hurried through lunch, a delectable combination of cereal and chocolate milk, to get ready for her first class of kids from the Speech and Hearing Center. There were only six but it was a start, and she wasn't about to turn it down.

She had designed the riding classes just for them. Giving the children confidence was far more important to Cheyenne than the financial gain. Uncle Lyn wanted her to focus only on the money at this point which made her question, not for the first time, her decision to run her own business. Still, when Daddy died and left her the farm, she took it as a sign. She needed to return to her first loves, horses and riding. A riding stable seemed the best choice.

Her thoughts scurried with the blare of a horn from a very large truck. She swallowed the last of the cereal and hurried to the window over the kitchen sink.

"Hey, Shy," her brother's voice boomed from the driveway.

She grinned and waved as she walked outside.

"Lord, Modine, can't you tone it down a little," she said with affection. "I may be able to sign but I prefer not to use it for myself until I'm ninety."

"Bitch, moan, bitch, moan," he said. "I'm just happy to see my little sis. My natural exuberance gets away from me and makes me want to holler."

Billy Modine alighted from the cab and scooped Cheyenne up with a bone-crunching hug. Then, for good measure, he twirled her around until she shouted through her laughter to be put down.

"Yeehaw!" he yelled when he planted her back on the ground.

"Coming back from a job?" She squinted up at him, his face so like her daddy's. The pinch of gathering tears made her look away so he didn't notice.

Billy put an arm around her shoulders and walked her to the porch swing where they both sat down.

"Yeah, brought a few horses down from Chicago and stopped in Louisville to pick up a few more," he said. He pushed his John Deere hat to the back of his head and exposed the dented hairstyle of a diehard cap wearer. As siblings, they shared the same texture and color of hair but the resemblance ended there.

Billy was tall and rangy, at three inches over six feet, almost a foot taller than Cheyenne. He had big, callused hands, a toothy, perpetual grin, and sky-blue eyes.

Cheyenne smiled at him. He always boosted her mood, probably because he believed the world was his.

"How are the sheik's horses doing this year?" she asked.

"Fair to middlin'. How'd you know I was haulin' some of his?"

"I have my sources," she said.

"You've been talkin' to Lyn, haven't you?"

Cheyenne dusted crumbs from her white shirt to avoid his alert gaze.

"Well, yes, but not about your hauling schedule," she replied, then changed the subject. "Are you going to the party after the charity match next month?"

"Probably. J.C. and I talked about it, figured it couldn't hurt business to mix and mingle with the upper crust for a few hours."

"How is J.C.?" she asked, more to be polite than from any honest curiosity.

J.C. Turner was Billy's partner in the horse transportation business they started six years ago. He was also Cheyenne's ex-husband. She was nineteen and he was twenty-two when they married. The marriage lasted one year. Cheyenne realized the mistake after six months, but they had parted friends. J.C. was a good man, just not the man for her.

Billy eyed her. "He's doin' well. Do I detect renewed interest?"

"Now, Modine, you know better."

"Can't blame a guy for hopin' since he's my best friend and you're my best sister." Billy straightened his long legs and stopped the swing. "You goin' to the party?"

Cheyenne stood up, suddenly restless, and gazed at her phone. She needed to get to the barn in five minutes to prepare for her class.

"I guess," she said. "But only because Lyn begged me. He seemed to think it would be good for my business to *mix and mingle* with *them*, too."

"Face it, sis, you gotta kiss a little butt in life." Billy joined her at the porch rail. A car turned into the driveway and drew their notice. "Just be glad Lyn didn't want us to start playing polo again so we could be in his match. I'm so rusty I probably wouldn't know which end of the stick to hold."

"Don't think he didn't ask," she said. "He thought since I'd played last year, I'd be eager to have a go once

I came back here. I used my business as an excuse not to play, which is the only excuse he would have accepted."

Billy grunted. "I hear ya. The man's obsessed with the game."

They watched the car pull up to the new riding arena as she and Billy walked to the truck. She told him she expected him to be available at the party when the burden of socializing with Lexington's movers and shakers became too much for her. He left her with some vague advice about bringing antacid to share.

She waved when he drove off and her mind returned to the match. Lyn had mentioned Jack Carter's participation before she'd cut him off. If Carter attended the after-party, she didn't want to be there. Somehow, some way, she'd come up with an excuse not to go, even if Billy was right. Under no circumstances would she ever consider kissing Carter's ass or any other part of his egotistical body.

&#42;&#42;&#42;&#42;

Jack slammed down the phone receiver. Lyndon Tyree had no damn business being this hard to reach. The old guy was never home. The one short conversation they'd had was cut short by a long-distance call for Lyn, something about a polo pony for sale in England. They'd only discussed the charity match. The subject of Cheyenne Modine was still a mystery.

Janie entered the office and caught his mutter.

"What was that, Jackson?" She handed him a file and grimaced when she stared at his desk.

"Uh, nothing. Is this the worming schedule for the yearlings at Kingston farm?"

He buried his head in the folder to stop her questions.

"Yes, and some more resumes for the part-time attendant job. Win said you get all the resumes before you leave for the conference. Are you putting those someplace special?"

"Just throw them on the corner there."

With an exaggerated movement, she placed two more folders on the stack already there, then sat down.

"Got a minute?" she asked. The innocence of her smile made him suspicious.

"Will you be attending the party after the charity match?" she asked with an expectant expression he knew well.

"Ah, hell, Janie, you know I hate those stuffed shirt affairs. Isn't it enough that I'm playing in the game? Lyn doesn't expect me to go to the party."

He stuck his head back into the folder.

She didn't take the hint.

"Jack, you know your mom and dad will be very disappointed if you don't stay. How long has it been since you've seen them? Oh, and by the way, Lea and the boys are coming."

"You're taking the kids?" He stared at her.

"Let me get this straight." She laughed and shook her head. "You'd consider coming because of Lea but not for your parents?"

"Well, maybe for Mom."

"Jackson, be nicer to your dad. He tries so hard."

Jack rose to leave for his appointment and stuffed the folder into his bag. He hated it when she used his parents for leverage, but her mention of Lea was downright audacious.

"I'll let you know by the end of the week. After I get back from the conference," he said.

Janie followed him out of the office, a sweet smile on her face. "That will be fine. I'll just call Mom and Dad tonight to tell them the good news."

"I'll let you know," he repeated.

Jack decided all his experience with women had disappeared. Lately, they'd been walking all over him.

****

He returned to the clinic two hours later to an uproar. Mr. Tibbles, an aging stallion, had arrived the day before due to another bout of colic. Apparently, the colic had lessened because Mr. T wanted out of his stall. Of the three vets and several assistants in the practice, Jack was one of the few who could get near him, but only on a good day. Today was not a good one for the old rascal.

As Jack strode down the aisle of the infirmary, the snorts and curses reached him first. Win catapulted from the stall shaking his left hand just as Jack got to the door.

"That damn horse almost broke my wrist!" Win sputtered and leaned against the outside wall, his chest heaving. More embarrassed than hurt, he turned to stand beside Jack as they assessed the animal. Mr. Tibbles back leg struck the wall with a thunderous thwack. He faced them and nodded his big brown head, in victory triumphant.

"He appears to be feeling better," Jack said.

Win looked down at his hand and slowly flexed his fingers.

"Are they all working?" Jack asked.

"Yeah," Win said and lifted his stethoscope. "I wasn't able to get close enough to listen, however."

Jack punched the button to the automatic door on the other side of the stall and watched Mr. T exit to the outside paddock.

"Let's give him an hour to work off some energy."

"Jack, Lyn Tyree is on the phone." Janie said from the wall speaker. "I know you two have been trying to reach each other."

Jack turned to leave but Win stopped him.

"Don't forget, we need to look over those resumes for the part-time attendant position. I don't mind interviewing while you're gone but I want to know your choice before you leave."

Jack held up a hand as he walked away.

"Yeah, yeah, we'll get to it soon. No worries."

He waved to Win and hoped his partner got the message. He didn't want to miss this call.

## Chapter Ten

"Pam-myyyy!" Cheyenne wailed into the phone. "You're not going to believe what just happened."

"Do tell."

Cheyenne winced at her sister-in-law's breathless response. Pammy was eight months pregnant and had gained fifty pounds with this third baby. Billy swore it was going to be a *big* boy which made Pammy swear they were never having sex again.

"Crap, girl, I just noticed the time. I shouldn't have called you now. Are you putting Jess down for her nap?"

Billy and Pammy lived in the homeplace in Richmond. Unfortunately for Pammy, the bedrooms were upstairs.

"No, no, she's been asleep for about fifteen minutes. It just takes me that long to maneuver my bulk down the steps."

Cheyenne heard a slight groan, followed by the crackle of the couch's plastic cover that her sister-in-law insisted on using when they didn't have company.

"Where's Doobie? In daycare?" Cheyenne asked as she rubbed the taped toes on her left foot.

"Yes, thank heavens. I don't know how I'd handle a three and five-year-old all day in my current Buddha condition. Oh, and by the way, it's Debbie now, not Doobie. She informed Billy and me two days ago that everyone said her name wrong."

Cheyenne managed a smile. Her oldest niece was a Cheyenne mini-me.

"What's your problem, darlin'?" Pammy asked in her down-home Tennessee accent. Ten years in Lexington hadn't put much of a dent in her mountain drawl.

"Dudley stepped on my foot, and I think my toe, uh, make that two toes, are broken," Cheyenne moaned. "Both of them hurt like hell. I can't even get my boot on."

"Billy told you to get rid of that big, dumb horse," Pammy scolded. "I don't care if he is your 'dressage' mount. He's too big for you, not to mention goofy."

Cheyenne smiled again at the way her friend pronounced *dressage.* It came out like "message" instead of "massage". No amount of correction worked. Pammy thought it was too stuffy a word for a backwoods girl.

"He's getting better," Cheyenne insisted. "Besides, this wasn't totally his fault."

Dudley had stepped on her toes as he shifted in his stall but she suspected the real damage came from her earlier, well-placed kick against the refrigerator. It had left a puddle the size of Lake Cumberland on her kitchen floor in the middle of the night. She wasn't about to share *that* information with Pammy, though, because her family would want to buy her a new refrigerator.

There was a way to get through this maze. She just hadn't figured it out yet.

"I'm sorry, Pam, what did you say."

Cheyenne pulled herself out of her funk to catch the last part of her sister-in-law's comments.

"I said I could send you some painkillers. I have some left from when I used to have my monthly misery, back in the dark ages. You should go see a doctor, but I know you won't," she chided.

Cheyenne ignored the doctor suggestion.

"That would be great. I was really just calling to ask if I could borrow some over-the-counter meds. But prescription stuff would work if you're okay with that. Can you spare, uh, four? I don't want to be greedy. Besides, someday, you too will have periods and suffer like the rest of us females."

"Oh, please God, that day better get here soon." Pammy laughed.

"Are you coming tonight with Billy and J.C.?"

Cheyenne tried to tug on her boot as sweat rolled down her spine.

"In this condition? You've got to be nuts, girlfriend. I spend every other minute in the bathroom. Don't you remember how narrow those stalls are? Besides, you're doing me a favor by getting 'love machine' Modine out of my hair."

Cheyenne fought off the "love machine" reference. It made her think about Jack Carter and she definitely didn't need that.

"Okay, so I'll send those pills with the guys tonight. Just remember not to drink any alcohol while you're taking them," Pammy said.

Another image of Jack Carter flared; this time as he'd appeared in his office when he called her a "drunk". Every muscle in her body tightened as the toe pain shot up her leg.

"Yes, Mommy." Cheyenne managed to stifle a groan. "I'll drink juice like a good girl."

****

Cheyenne drank juice. The bartender gave it to her

in a tall glass with a tiny, pink umbrella. Told her he had to dress it up, so the other customers didn't know it was just juice. She suspected he was flirting but since she was surrounded by men—Billy, J.C., and John-Michael—he shrugged when he handed her the drink and went back to the other barflies.

Billy fished the pills Pammy had given him out of his back pocket and handed them over.

"She said not to take them with…"

"…alcohol," Cheyenne said and swiped at the finger he stuck in her face. The capsules he gave her were definitely a prescription drug, but she'd never had reason to use anything like it. Her periods were tolerable and as regular as night followed day.

Since her foot pain hadn't let up, she used the water fountain in the hallway near the restrooms. Taking a prescription pain pill at the bar with her fluffy little drink, while the whole room watched, wasn't her thing. Besides, the horse people at the steakhouse tonight might send her some business. No need to encourage any other unfair assessments of her character.

Cheyenne lifted her head from the spray of ice-cold water, blotted the dribble on her chin with the back of her hand, and turned to find Jack Carter glaring at her. A wave of heat climbed her neck and she hated her body's traitorous reaction. The frisson of physical awareness startled her enough to issue a verbal challenge.

"Slumming, Dr. Carter?"

His gaze darkened. "I see your addictive personality isn't limited to just booze."

"And just what do you know about my personality, Doc? We've met twice, not counting tonight, and for that small favor I'm immensely grateful."

His jaw was set as he studied her. They stared at one another and when he didn't respond, she made a move to pass. As she angled around him the pain in her foot caused her to stagger against him. He caught her elbow, and she glanced up at him. Furious didn't begin to describe the look on his face.

"I suggest you not complicate your life more by combining prescription drugs and alcohol tonight. You don't seem too steady on your feet as it is."

She jerked her arm from his grasp and left him in the hall.

\*\*\*\*

Jack took a minute to rein in his temper before he headed back to the table he, Win, and Mike occupied near one of the front windows. Seeing her here tonight twisted him in knots and it hadn't helped that he'd caught her taking a drug at the water fountain. It was like waving a red flag in front of a bull—her being the flag and him being the bull.

He wasn't sure why he cared. And she was right. He didn't really know her. They were virtual strangers. Sure, she'd vomited on his boots, he'd touched her breasts and slept with her but they were merely acquaintances.

*She's a grown woman and not my problem. Let her make her own stupid decisions. Given my history, I'd be an idiot to get any more involved with her.*

But, damn, what a waste. Lyn Tyree, as astute as he was, had no idea what was going on. The old man had spoken highly of her and their long friendship. At one point Jack even caught a hint of matchmaking in Lyn's words, which was when Jack cut the man off in mid-sentence.

Jack made his way back to the bar area. The planets

must be out of alignment or something. The odds of seeing her here tonight were minuscule yet here they were. Yes, the steakhouse was a hangout for the horsey set, but he and his partners had been way too busy to keep up their monthly outing tradition. The only reason they'd stopped by tonight was a grueling polo practice that had put all of them in a very thirsty state.

It was a typical Friday evening at the bar. Jack scanned the crowd as he threaded his way through the horde. She was surrounded by three men and Jack recognized the red-haired kid as her stable help. The other two hovered over her as if they couldn't get enough of her.

"Son of a bitch," he mumbled when he noted her fingers wrapped around a glass with a little umbrella sticking out of it. Take away the umbrella and it appeared to be his father's choice of poison. The old man drank screwdrivers to the exclusion of everything else with the belief that vodka left no liquor smell on the breath. Jack clearly remembered the odor of adulterated orange juice instead.

She threw her head back, laughed, and hugged the man in the John Deere hat. The other men at the bar watched her like fish eyeing a baited hook.

Jack looked away when he realized he did the same. *This isn't my problem.* Maybe if he repeated it enough, it might sink in.

He averted his gaze from the bar as he zigzagged through the bodies to their table. Then he made the mistake of glancing back.

"Hey, Doc Carter! How ya doin'? It's me, John-Michael, from Red Fox Farm."

The red-haired kid waved his arms to get Jack's

attention.

Several people laughed, and Jack felt all eyes on him. He gave up and made his way to the bar, unable to ignore John-Michael and hurt the kid's feelings.

"John-Michael, Cheyenne, didn't expect to see you folks here," he commented and pretended he hadn't already seen her. He didn't miss the way her fingers squeezed her glass.

"Doc Carter helped Dinah foal last week," John-Michael explained. "What brings you to the steakhouse, Doc?"

Jack was tempted to mention "slumming" but he didn't.

"My partners and I drop by when we get time."

As Cheyenne's silence lengthened the man in the John Deere hat held out his hand.

"Dr. Carter, I'm Billy Modine and this is J.C. Turner. It appears you already know my sister and John-Michael. You'll have to forgive Cheyenne's rudeness. She's been up north for a few years and just came back to town. We're trying to teach her the southern way again but it's not easy, her bein' so bullheaded and all."

"So that's what it is." Jack shook Billy and J.C.'s hands.

The two men exchanged glances, which made Jack unsure if they simply acknowledged her stubborn nature or the tension between her and him. Everyone but John-Michael seemed aware of it. The kid babbled on in ignorance.

"Dinah and the foal are doin' real well, Doc. You should come out and see the little guy. He's growing like a weed, isn't he, Cheyenne?"

"Yeah, a weed," she mumbled.

Her full attention now centered on the hole in the knee of her jeans. A few seconds of silence followed before the bartender cut in to take Jack's order. Reluctantly, he gazed at Win and Mike, who sat at the table and stared in his direction. Win held up two fingers.

"I'll have a soda and two light beers," he replied. He watched Cheyenne sip her drink with her index finger holding the umbrella against the back of the glass. Her hair was loose tonight, something he hadn't noticed in the hall. His hand flexed, an instinctive movement he tried to ignore.

The bartender came back with the drinks.

"Well, it was nice meeting you all. Maybe I will stop by and see that foal, John-Michael. At no cost to you, Cheyenne."

Her lips tightened when he turned to go. So that guy in the hat was her brother…

"See somebody you know, Jack?" Win smirked at Jack's return.

Jack slammed the beers on the table.

"Next time get your own damn drinks," he grumbled.

He sat down as she left her stool and headed back to the hall. Jack wondered if she was taking another pill. The uncomfortable tightness in his groin continued as he silently repeated his new mantra—something to do with *not my problem.* He continued to watch as she rounded the corner and disappeared from sight.

Chapter Eleven

Billy studied the vet as Cheyenne walked away. He recognized the hungry gaze. His sister affected most men that way, usually unaware of the havoc she caused. There was something going on between these two, though. Billy hadn't seen his sister's composure this badly frayed in a long time.

"John-Michael, what's going on between Cheyenne and the vet?"

The kid hurriedly crunched the ice cube in his mouth and gurgled an answer. "She thinks he's uppity. Other than that she hasn't said much. I think she must like him a little, though. He stayed with her the night Dinah foaled."

J.C. whistled softly as he and Billy swapped incredulous looks. John-Michael scanned their faces and blushed beet-red.

"Damn. Maybe I shouldn't have said…"

"Yeah, bud, I don't think I'd mention it to anyone else." Billy grinned and filed the information away. Never knew when something like that might come in handy.

\*\*\*\*

Cheyenne flipped the latch on the stall door and wished like hell she hadn't taken the damn pill. A little pain might help curb her extreme need to hit the metal partition, hard, until either the door or her hand gave out.

The man was insufferable—an A grade, one hundred percent raving, total jerk. Not only did he think she drank to excess, but he also implied she was stupid enough to abuse drugs and alcohol at the same time. And the way he watched her as she sipped her juice made her feel like a criminal. She slumped down on the edge of the toilet seat and smacked the flush button. Exactly what she'd like to do to Jack Carter—smack him and flush him.

She should march back out into that room and tell him, in front of everyone, what a fool he was.

No, maybe she should find his truck in the parking lot and let the air out of all four tires. A sneak attack.

She elbowed the flush button again and imagined his pinhead swirling and circling, around and around and around.

"Hey, wash goin' on over there?" a drunk voice in the next stall said.

Cheyenne cringed, unaware someone else was actually in the restroom with her.

"Sorry. I've got a floater."

"Oh, okay," came the amiable reply. "Don't'cha just hate it when that happens?"

Cheyenne fought a smile that threatened the good head of steam she'd worked up over Dr. "Jack-ass."

The occupant of the other stall flushed and left without washing her hands. Hopefully, the woman wasn't an employee of the steakhouse.

The interruption hadn't erased Cheyenne's plan for getting back at Carter. In seconds, she tossed out the other ideas—too juvenile, too temporary, too minor. She needed something big and unforgettable to satisfy her need. Even more important, she wanted to embarrass him in front of his kind.

Lyndon? The charity polo match? She mulled it over. There were several obstacles if she wanted to achieve the best result. She hadn't played since last year and had little time to get in shape by next month, not to mention there might be no opening on the other team. She didn't even know who the other team was. Lyn's past formula had included some British guys. If they were the opposing team this year they wouldn't arrive until a few days before, yet another negative.

She had two positives on her side, however—Uncle Lyn and she was a damn good horsewoman. Lyn called the shots with the charity match; it was his money, and he had a far-reaching reputation in the polo world. If he let her play she'd work out with an area team until the other team arrived. It wasn't the best idea, but it was possible. And yeah, if it meant skewering Jack Carter, she might consider it.

Cheyenne savored the moment when he found out a woman could beat him at his own game. She closed her eyes to watch the fantasy play out. The crowd was record-setting under a hot August sky. Sun reflected off the windshields of the fancy luxury cars with their super-powered engines parked in a distant lot. From the tailgates, genteel, upper-crust Lexingtonians dined on cold chicken and Brie. The sigh of champagne corks resonated over muted talk of "the market" and the latest vacation at Oracabessa Bay, a well-known playground for the rich and famous. An unknown player rides onto the field and all attention turns to the mysterious figure. The crowd gasps as the player's helmet comes off and long, luxurious curls float in the breeze.

The restroom door creaked open.

"Shy, get your butt back out to the bar or we're leaving you here to find your own damn way home," Billy yelled through the door.

Cheyenne tabled her dreams of retribution and started to leave the stall. For good measure, she reached back and hit the flush button. It was music to her ears.

\*\*\*\*

The next day, Cheyenne and Lyn sat on his veranda and viewed the two front pastures of his farm. Lyn had lived on the beautiful property for fifty years and all his good memories lingered in the expansive rooms and lengthy hallways of the sprawling antebellum home. Fortunately, Lyn had Gabe, his house attendant, to assist him as he aged. She hoped Lyn stayed here for at least the next twenty years.

He took a sip of his Mint Julep, swallowed with obvious enjoyment, and held the glass up in invitation.

She shook her head, settled back into the wicker chair, and fidgeted with her earring.

"I have a proposition for you. I wonder if it's too late to change my mind about playing in the polo match."

Lyn sat forward in his chair faster than a dog chasing a squirrel.

"This year's match?"

"Uh, yes."

"Why? And maybe more important, why now?"

Cheyenne decided to give him a partial truth. If she told Lyn she sought revenge for the way Jack Carter had humiliated her—twice—he'd think she was petty. Part of her recognized the pettiness. She didn't attempt to analyze whether she sought retribution against him or his class; mostly they seemed to be one and the same. Besides, it unsettled her to view them as separate.

"I've been thinking about the positive aspects of being in the match," she said finally. "It would be another good way to get my name out there. I can display my riding abilities to a group of people, who, dare I say, can afford to give their kids riding lessons."

"And?"

"Isn't that enough?"

"I suggested the very same thing when you first came back. You said you didn't have enough time to devote to the needed practice. The match is only four weeks away after all."

*Crapola. Either I tell him the truth or give him an equally compelling reason to make him believe me.*

She walked to the front of the veranda and studied the smoky wisps of fog that had settled over the grass.

"My refrigerator bit the dust." She turned to face Lyn, so she didn't feel like a coward. "My finances are tight. I need to give my business a shot in the arm."

She pointed a finger toward him at the same time he opened his mouth to speak.

"I don't want a loan. Don't even suggest it."

He closed his mouth and sighed.

"Then this idea doesn't have anything to do with Jack Carter playing on the other side?"

They made eye contact. Because he didn't pursue the loan idea, she didn't curb her answer.

"I can't say I wouldn't gloat after my team beats his," she bragged.

Lyndon threw back his head and chortled with glee. One knot in her spine loosened. Making him laugh was a positive.

Gabe chose that moment to enter with refreshments. Without waiting for Lyn to say anything she poured herself tea and fixed a plate of cheese and crackers for her host. Lynn loved it when she made herself at home and she'd play any angle if it put him in a conducive mood.

"Gabe, Cheyenne has an interesting idea." Lyn eyed her as he picked up a cracker. "She seems to think she can get herself in shape in time to participate in this year's charity game. What are your thoughts?"

She kept quiet as she waited for Gabe's answer. Gabe had given Lyn some very astute investment advice once and it was common for the employer to ask the employee's opinion on a wide range of topics.

"Well, Mr. Tyree, both of us can see she appears to be in fine shape."

Gabe displayed a brilliant set of white teeth when Lyndon laughed in agreement. At the same time, heat rushed through Cheyenne all the way to her sore toes.

"If Cheyenne thinks she can be ready by the date of the match, do you trust her commitment?" Gabe continued. "I seem to remember your appraisal of her riding ability as quite favorable."

Cheyenne mouthed "thank you" when Gabe turned to go.

"Of course, it would cause quite a stir if word got out that a woman was playing when you've never had one before." Gabe's voice carried from the hall. "Might even sell more tickets."

His footsteps faded as he disappeared into the cavernous house.

"Getting awful full of himself in his older age," Lyn mumbled with a definite spark in his eyes.

She had started to feel positive vibes, but his next comment floored her.

"Jackson's clinic is searching for a part-time attendant to look after the infirmary animals. The pay is good and you've got all the qualifications. If you won't accept a loan from me, I could write a recommendation for you."

For a second, Cheyenne was robbed of speech. In the next second, she was even more astonished to find she actually wanted to consider the idea. It must be the vision of the cooler loaded with ice that now sat in her kitchen where the refrigerator had been.

"I don't think that's realistic, Lyn," she said. "It's evident Dr. Carter and I don't like each other."

When she imagined Carter's reaction to Lyn's letter of recommendation, she stifled a laugh. The one feeling she was unable to explain was the tide of disappointment which came out of nowhere, disappointment that had little to do with money.

"It's my understanding the hours are ten p.m. to six a.m., just a few nights a week. I doubt you'd see any of the vets during those hours."

She chewed her bottom lip.

"Lyn, not even a recommendation from you could make Jack Carter hire me," she said.

"Might give you some hints on how to beat him at polo," Lyn said as he ignored her point.

He appeared to weigh her reaction but said nothing more. He ate a second cracker while she tried to reason with herself. Surely, she'd find another part-time job with hours as perfect as those—and they were perfect. She'd rearrange her class hours to suit the work schedule—no, no, it wasn't for her.

"I don't think so, Lyn," she said. "I can help the team win without taking a job in Carter's clinic. But for me to help the team win, you have to let me play."

Chapter Twelve

She secured Lyn's permission to participate in the match. An hour later, Cheyenne entered her kitchen and slid to the middle of the floor in another puddle of water. This time the puddle was filled with ice cubes and bits of Styrofoam. It was deja vu and she was cursed.

Bubba stared at Cheyenne from a dining room chair. He licked his paw and showed no guilt over the white bits that clung to his wet stomach fur. She now realized the cooler had become the latest victim of Bubba's search to find the perfect claw-sharpening post.

She pulled her cell from her pocket before her thoughts gelled.

"Lyn, you can send the letter of recommendation."

****

Frantic, Jack stuck his head into the front office. "I can't find the damn flash drive with my conference notes."

He'd torn apart his desk minutes before but the drive was nowhere. Janie gestured at him like a mad woman with the phone at her ear.

"Take these." She waved papers in his face before she covered the mouthpiece. "The notes are on the top if you don't find your drive. The others are resumes. I'll be back as soon as I get off the phone."

"My plane leaves in two hours." He grabbed the papers as she turned away. "It takes an hour and a half just to get through security."

She flapped her hand in dismissal and he stalked down the hall.

Back in the office he dumped the notes into his briefcase, loaded the resumes on the desk pile, and stared in amazement. Calling his desk a mess didn't do it justice.

Janie popped in two minutes later as he clawed through the mess. The look on his face must have stopped her from saying "I told you so".

She picked up a few papers that had drifted to the floor and placed them on the resume pile.

"Well, don't just stand there. I still need the drive."

Her mouth worked as if she fought laughter.

"What?" he said.

She pointed a tentative finger to the floor behind his desk.

"What's that laying on the rug? The shiny thing with the cap."

Jack turned the air blue with curses as he grabbed the flash drive and threw it into the briefcase with his laptop and all the other junk. He lunged for the door as he called out last-minute orders.

"I'll be back late on Friday. Don't forget to tell Ben to check on my animals. The neighbor's teenage daughter is feeding, watering, and walking but I'll feel better if he checks on them, too." Jack stopped and turned. "Give Win those resumes. The one on top seems the most qualified."

He looked at her. "Am I missing anything?"

Janie smiled as she advanced and poked a finger in the wrinkle between his eyebrows.

"Nervous?" she asked.

He let out a pent-up breath. "As hell. I've never presented a workshop before. Just don't tell anyone. I have a hard-core image to uphold."

"You'll do fine." She chuckled. "You're a good vet and an entertaining speaker."

When she kissed him on the cheek, he gave her a look of apology.

"Sorry about yelling before."

She flapped her hand. "I'm used to it. Now go."

He squeezed her shoulder and veered toward the door.

"Oh, Jack," she called out as he strode down the hall. "You'll find a folder in your briefcase compliments of your brother. Let the record show I had nothing to do with it."

He had no time to hear her explanation.

"I'll look at it on the plane," he said and left.

****

Jack planned to kill his brother when he got back. Ten minutes after the plane departed, he opened the folder Janie mentioned and found it filled with Cheyenne Modine's life story. Ben's note on the front read "you can thank me later" which made Jack want to wring the little shit's neck. If his brother hadn't collected the information Jack wouldn't be reading it now against his better judgment.

He sipped his drink as his gaze stopped here and there to absorb the pertinent information. She'd spent no time in a treatment center for alcoholics, had no psychiatric consults or unexplained stays in a hospital, no visits to a hypnotist or an Alcoholics Anonymous group, no o.v.i.'s—no indication of a drinking problem. Still, she was plastered the night her mare foaled and her flu excuse was bunk. Then she'd pulled a prescription pain pill from a plastic bag at the steakhouse. Two or three other pills rested in the bag, she looked guilty, and she'd staggered against him.

He closed the folder. This information proved nothing and he refused to give her the benefit of the doubt. The issue of alcohol abuse was too sensitive for him, and if she was stupid enough to bring drugs into the mix...

Jack rubbed his temples in exasperation. She didn't appear stupid and deep down, he recognized she might inflict major damage if he let her get too close.

The folder lay there like a taunt. Hadn't he decided against even a casual relationship with Cheyenne Modine? If so, there was no reason not to read the rest of the information.

He opened the file again and pushed back his seat. For the next hour, he had no place to go but the toilet and he needed a diversion from his conference presentation. He picked out the page copied from her high school yearbook and made an attempt to relax.

\*\*\*\*

Cheyenne rushed through her chores to work in dressage practice for her demonstration at the Horse Park next week. If she timed it right, she'd manage a solid hour before her one o'clock class arrived.

Dudley was her mount for the demonstration. Daddy had purchased him ten years ago when Dudley had proven himself a "dud" on the track. His lack of speed didn't hinder him in the dressage ring, however. He moved with grace and coordination and had an excellent temperament in spite of what Pammy thought of him. And, yes, his big foot hadn't helped the condition of her toes, but she had forgiven him.

He was anxious to work. She laughed at his whinnies and head nods as she pulled him out of the stall. After she tacked him up, they walked to the outdoor ring and she used a fence rail to mount. His sixteen hands and her five foot three didn't match but they were in perfect tune when they rode the test.

She thought ahead to the Tuesday night polo practice. Lyn had contacted a local team of older players who now played for fun. They were thrilled to find a fourth since one of their players had recently retired and moved south. Her use of Lyn's ponies in the practice games gave her the advantage since Carter's team only rode Lyn's ponies for the charity match. At this late stage, Cheyenne welcomed any help, no matter how minor.

When the practice finished Cheyenne hosed Dudley with lukewarm water and hooked him to the hot walker to cool off. She ran to the house to clean up and ate a stand-up lunch before her kids arrived for the most enjoyable class of the week. The Speech and Hearing Center had called after the first lesson to tell Cheyenne the center van was bringing the kids from now on since the lesson had been so beneficial.

She stood at the kitchen window and took one bite of her banana, the only item on her lunch menu. When the phone rang, she almost choked. It was Carter's clinic number. She cleared her throat in time to answer and managed to schedule an interview for the job. She was in shock at the speed of Lyndon's recommendation but even more so over Carter's acceptance of her application.

The van pulled in when she hung up the phone. Her

hands still shook at the prospect of seeing Jack Carter again. Then, she had no more time to think about anything but the happy smiles of the kids as they ran and jumped their way to the barn.

\*\*\*\*

Cheyenne arrived early for her interview at the clinic on Wednesday morning. The previous night's grueling polo practice made her allow extra time to get ready. As she sat in the reception area listening to phones ring and staff chatter, she was unable to ignore the murderous ache in her arms that a hot shower and the last of Pammy's pain pills hadn't managed to dull.

An eerie calm accompanied her as she drove to the interview. If she didn't get the job, she'd try the Speech and Hearing center. They had an available temporary position to fill in for summer vacations. Still, the hours at the center weren't as ideal as the clinic hours. She refused to think about the other reason she wanted the job, the reason which had nothing to do with money.

The blonde behind the desk glanced over again. This was the fourth time in ten minutes. Cheyenne shifted position to inspect her clothing but detected no fashion faux pas.

"Ms. Modine?" the blonde said. "Can you fill out this brief legal form while you wait?"

The woman gave her a friendly smile as she pushed a clipboard across the counter. Cheyenne retrieved the form and realized she had seen the blonde before on the day she'd lost most of her good sense during a blazing hissy fit.

She noticed the other woman at the back desk also stared at her.

Something strange was going on here. Either she

suffered from paranoia or the possibility of facing Jack Carter again distorted her perception of everything.

Cheyenne attempted to dredge up the anger from the steakhouse incident. Anything was better than an attack of nerves. It amazed her she was able to identify the feeling since she so rarely suffered from man anxiety. Still, her sweaty palms seemed like a sure sign.

She completed the paperwork, took it back to the blonde, and studied her nameplate. It said "Janie". Cheyenne wondered if her previous visit was the cause of all the speculative looks. She hoped no one here today had a one-sided view of the confrontation especially if it affected whether she got the job.

*I want this job.* The realization hit her like a proverbial ton of bricks. Cheyenne checked her moan but Janie noticed.

"Everything okay?" Janie asked.

Cheyenne smiled and tried to hide her embarrassment.

"My horse stepped on my toes last week. Sometimes they answer back when I lean the wrong way."

Her toes really didn't hurt anymore, but she kind of wished they did. The pain might offset her shock over the discovery she *wanted* the job.

"Go on back and sit down. The form looks fine. Can I get you aspirin or something? We've all been stepped on here and we keep a large bottle on hand just in case."

Cheyenne shook her head.

"Thanks, no. I hate to admit it but before the horse stepped on my toes, they connected with my dysfunctional refrigerator in a more or less direct kick. The pain reminds me I need to keep my body parts from making contact with large, inanimate objects."

A tall, angular man with reddish hair popped his head around the corner and interrupted their laughter.

"Hey, you lowly minions, get back to work," he said with mock sternness. "We don't allow fun on company time."

"Minions! I'll have you know we're all minionettes here, Mr. King Who Never Sleeps." Janie handed him the paperwork and gave Cheyenne a warning look. "These vets. They're all unyielding taskmasters. Think very carefully if he offers you the job."

The vet smiled as he came over to shake Cheyenne's hand.

"Ms. Modine, I'm Win Barrington. I'll be interviewing and hiring for this position."

He guided her down the hallway. They passed Jack Carter's office on the way. It was empty, the desk even more disorganized than the day she'd seen it. Oddly, she experienced a curious letdown at this turn of events.

They entered Dr. Barrington's office, which was as clean and organized as Carter's was disorderly. The only clutter in this office was the full-size horse skeleton which stood along one wall. Dr. Barrington gestured to a seat at a large circular table, sat down on the other side, and tossed the application onto the table's shiny surface.

"Ms. Modine, I'll be honest with you. You are obviously the most qualified candidate for the job. My two partners and I agree, and with Lyn Tyree's high praise, we'd like to hire you. When can you start?"

Chapter Thirteen

Jack's high followed him home. The conference had been a huge success and the summer afternoon upon his return was a rare blend of low humidity and bright blue skies. He was headed to the office for the weekly Friday night barbecue, hungry for Janie's secret burger recipe. Jack knew the secret, of course. Two words—Worchester sauce.

He hung his arm out the window as he maneuvered the big, four-wheel drive through late Friday traffic into downtown Lexington. When he turned onto Water Street, he decided to swing by the Commonwealth Attorney's office to see if his devious little brother was up to no good.

He dialed Ben's cell number. It started to ring as he spotted a familiar wine-red SUV pull out into traffic two cars ahead.

"Carter here."

"Hey, bro butt. I'm going to wring your neck for putting together that folder."

"Folder? What folder? Who is this?"

"Don't get cute with me. I'm still an inch taller, two years older, and ripped. Also, I've got your back fender in my sights at this very moment."

Ben's head jerked to the rearview mirror, and he waved.

"Hey, did you just get in from the conference?"

"Don't try to change the subject."

"What subject?"

Jack was familiar with this routine. His brother had honed it to a fine art by the age of sixteen.

"You knew I couldn't resist the folder but it didn't work."

"What do you mean? It was a gold mine of information. You can now be reasonably assured she doesn't have a drinking problem."

"It doesn't prove anything. Like a million or so other lushes she just hasn't gotten caught yet."

Jack heard Ben's heavy sigh.

"Your pig-headedness is Guinness Book of World Records size. I think you need more counseling or something. This woman might be…"

"No might about it, bro. I can't take the chance. Too many other eligible, *sober* women in this town. That's why I called Elaine while I was in St. Louis. She's coming tonight. You *are* going, aren't you?"

"Uh, yeah. You called Elaine?"

Jack's attention snagged on Ben's peculiar intonation.

"Yes, she's meeting me there. Why?"

"Oh. Nothing. The last time we talked, though, you mentioned you hadn't seen her in a month".

There it was again. Jack couldn't quite describe it but a wariness lingered in between Ben's words.

"Janie said you have a new weekend attendant."

Jack was too preoccupied trying to guess what his brother wasn't saying to make more than a cursory comment.

"Yeah, I talked with Win yesterday. He said he hired the one we all agreed on. What exactly do you have against Elaine?"

"I don't have anything against Elaine. I don't think you two are a good fit but she seems like a fine person."

"What do you mean we're not a good fit? And what in the hell does *she seems like a fine person* mean? She is a fine person or I wouldn't be with her, would I?"

"Whoa, Jack. Calm down, bud. I simply made an observation. Look, I've got to stop at the deli here to pick up some drinks. I'll see you at the clinic."

The line went dead right before Ben's car pulled into the market parking lot. Jack promised himself a talk with Ben tonight over burgers and potato salad. Suddenly he had an itch tied to a hunch that his little brother's stilted words were the poison weed that started the rash.

****

Ben stopped his car and waited until Jack's truck drove out of sight. He dialed the clinic number and waited for someone, anyone, to answer.

"Mary, it's Ben Carter. Is Janie around?"

Mary, one of the staff assistants, answered in the affirmative.

"I need to talk to her right away."

It would take Jack another ten minutes to reach the clinic. Ben hoped it didn't take his wife as long to come to the phone.

He heard her breathing before he heard her voice.

"Sorry, hon, I was flipping burgers." She paused for a moment to catch her breath before she spoke again. "You'll never guess who's here."

"Elaine."

"Did you just read my mind?"

"No, Jack told me. He's on his way." Ben checked the time. "We have about four minutes before he shows up so I'll make this quick. Is Ms. Modine there yet?"

"Yes, but Ben, what about Elaine? I thought you told me she and Jack weren't a thing anymore."

"That's not important right now, babe," he said. "Didn't you say Jack had agreed with Win and Mike about hiring Cheyenne for the position?"

"Er, yes. Why do you ask?"

"Based partly on Tyree's recommendation, right? Jack actually said to you or the guys that she was his first choice?"

"Well, no, that's not exactly what happened. Right before Jack left, he gave me the stack of resumes and said the one on the top seemed the most qualified." She paused. "Uh oh."

"What? Is Jack there?"

Ben heard the disbelief in her voice when she continued.

"No, I just remembered something. Monday was so hectic here. I was on the phone arguing with the drug supplier. Remember, I told you they shorted us on our order. Anyway, while I was on the phone Jack came in, absolutely wild because he'd misplaced his flash drive with the notes for his workshop. I handed him the two last letters for the position, he went back to his office, I finished with the call, and went back to help him find the drive, and, and, oh, my, I hope I'm not right about what I'm thinking."

"Tell me."

"I picked up some papers from the floor in front of Jack's desk and placed them on top of one of the piles. You know how, well, you know what his desk looks like."

"Did my perpetually disorganized brother say he'd

read the papers?"

"Uh, I don't know. What I do know is the one on top was from Lyndon. He has that distinctive letterhead," she said with some hesitation. "Something else I'm wondering about is whether Win told Jack which candidate he hired…"

She said something else but not to him.

"Janie? Honey? What's going on?" Ben asked.

A muffled conversation followed but none of the words were clear.

"Ben," she whispered. "Jack just got here. What do I do?"

Ben backed out of the parking lot with a new appreciation for power steering and quick acceleration.

"Damage control," he said. "Try to get to Win before Jack does. If you can't, find the nearest cover and duck. I'm on my way."

If his conversation with Jack today was any indication, his brother had not approved they hire Cheyenne Modine. Janie would take some of the responsibility for the confusion with the papers but Ben knew it was mainly Jack's fault. His brother's habit of leaving messes was legendary. The last time Ben had seen Jack's desk it looked like the dunes of Los Alamos, after the test.

Ben's main concern was for his wife, however. He was prepared to be her human shield against his brother's hard-to-arouse but nevertheless impressive temper. Whatever happened, Ben just hoped he got there in time. He certainly didn't want to miss any of the fireworks.

Chapter Fourteen

The clinic was impressive. Dr. Barrington had given her a brief tour after the interview. Tonight, Cheyenne received the expanded version from Mary Donnelly, one of three assistants in the practice. Mary was young, smart, and talkative. Cheyenne already knew the girl's life story, and they'd only seen the surgery and x-ray room so far.

From a covered walkway connected to the main front office, they entered the large u-shaped barn which housed recuperating horses and those under watch for various ailments. When Mary started on her love life, Cheyenne decided the best way to get the information she needed was to nod and question Mary regardless of her current topic.

"My boyfriend, Jeff, is pre-vet at U.K., too," Mary said as she switched on the overhead lights.

"How many stalls does this entire building have?"

"There are thirty altogether, ten in each section of the 'U'. These first ten can be used for foaling, and measure sixteen by sixteen. As you can see, we only have three occupied at the moment since it's somewhat late in the foaling season."

Mary stopped near a stall that held a chestnut Thoroughbred mare and pointed to the plastic covered chart held to the stall door by a metal bracket.

"This is Lady-in-Waiting's information. She's due

next week. Every attendant is required to enter anything unusual about the stall occupant after each watch. I proposed the idea of a corresponding chart at the front desk based upon Jeff's suggestion," Mary said. "The vets liked the idea and put it into effect last year."

Cheyenne nodded. Jeff sounded like Mr. Perfect!

"Of course, if something happens on your watch that appears to need the doc you contact whoever is on call, twenty-four/seven."

Cheyenne remembered to nod. "How do you decide what situation needs a vet, aside from the obvious emergency?

Mary laughed. "I call them if a horse farts. The docs never get mad. These animals are too valuable. Jeff is very jealous that I get to take care of such fine horseflesh."

Cheyenne studied the restless mare in front of her. The horse's tail was in constant motion.

"Is Lady always this high-strung?"

Mary leaned against the stall wall. "Pretty much. She's been here about four days. This is typical. She prefers being outside in the paddock, but the vets want her in at night."

They walked two stalls down where another mare snoozed with her broad backside turned toward them.

"Jeff and I are going to start an equine clinic after we graduate."

Cheyenne scanned the chart on the door.

"What's Alley Cat's story?" she asked.

"She's old and her owner is a neurotic foreigner with too much money. She sent Alley here to be bred and to foal. In her younger days, Alley went to the Olympics and won a few medals for England. She's a sweet old girl."

The horse turned at the sound of voices before she resumed her position and shut her eyes. Cheyenne tried to ignore the Olympic reference and hoped the topic left her brain during the rest of the tour.

They turned a corner into the gelding area of the building. The five occupants weren't all Thoroughbreds. Cheyenne counted two Standardbreds, a Quarter Horse, and a Shetland pony. The last area of the U held the stallions with three in residence. Mary warned Cheyenne about Mr. Tibbles when he gave them a fierce nod as they passed.

"I told Jeff I'd be late tonight since I'll be staying to break you in. Do you think you'll need me past midnight?"

Cheyenne's thoughts lingered on the Olympic mare. All it took was one mention and she had to fight the only childhood dream which refused to die. Several seconds later she managed to answer Mary's question.

"I'll be fine. All I need is a little instruction with the video cameras in the front office, and you're good to go."

They exited the back doors and headed to the tree-shaded area where the barbecue was in full swing.

Several more people had joined the group while Cheyenne and Mary took their tour. Cheyenne was amazed at the number of people the clinic employed. It wasn't the largest equine practice in the area but it appeared to be thriving and popular.

"Oh, look, Doc Carter is here." Mary's glance slid to Cheyenne. "Our resident Greek God," she whispered behind her hand.

Cheyenne smiled but said nothing. Since she had accepted the job, her earlier anger at his ignorant assumptions had lessened. Her strong need to beat him at polo remained but if he was willing to approve her hiring, he must have realized the error of his rash judgment. It'd be interesting if he tried to apologize tonight. All in all, the evening looked better than she thought possible.

****

"Jack, my man, hear you knocked them dead at the conference."

"Standing room only." Jack shook Mike's hand as he joined the group. He spotted Elaine at the grill with Win. She'd cut her hair since he'd seen her. He tried to recall what they'd done the last time they were together. Some kind of golf outing and he'd only gone because it was an event to raise money for Shriner's Hospital For Children. It had been her idea because he hated golf.

"What happened here this week? Any problems while I was gone?"

"Nothing we couldn't handle," Mike said with a smile. "Quite a few females asked where you were. Jan from the yearling barn at Three Rivers seemed especially disappointed when I showed up instead of you."

"Jan?" Jack waved at Elaine to let her know he'd arrived.

"Yeah, the tall brunette with the legs up to here." Mike put his hand chest high.

"Oh, that Jan. The one with the tattoo of…"

"Right, just above her…"

"Yeah, kind of hard to miss," Jack said, amused. Elaine headed toward them at the same time he noticed Mary and another woman leave the barn.

"We hired the new weekend attendant," Mike said. "There she is now with Mary. Janie thought it would be a good idea to have her here at the cookout to meet everyone. After I saw her, I graciously consented to take Win's place on-call this weekend. For some reason, he said no."

Mike chuckled. "I'll introduce you. Jack? Hey, Jack?"

It *was* Cheyenne. Ten seconds after she and Mary left the barn, he knew. What he didn't know was *how* in the *fricking hell* they'd managed to hire *her?*

He passed Elaine, unable to trust himself to speak to her in a reasonably friendly tone. He ignored the greetings from the other staff as he plowed his way through the lawn chairs to the grill.

"Win," he hissed. "We need to talk—now."

Win stared at Jack and the burger he flipped fell unheeded to the ground.

At the same time, Janie rushed up, and Win recovered enough to hand the spatula to her.

"No, don't give it to Janie." Jack looked around. "Lisa, get over here and watch the food. Win, Mike and Janie, come with me."

An unusual quiet fell over the group as he strode away. In the background, Mary's voice carried through the air. "Hey, what's up?"

They reached the back door to the office just as Ben entered the front door.

"You." Jack pointed at his brother. "In my office."

He left them without another word, certain they'd follow, or risk being vaporized by the meteor about to explode in his brain.

Chapter Fifteen

Mary finally left a few minutes past midnight. Cheyenne sat in front of the monitors and listened to the night sounds of the quiet building. The muted boom of the air conditioner sent another whoosh of coolness through the rooms. So far, her only drowsy episode had been around ten when Mary raised the topic of the cookout for the third time.

Apparently, it was unusual for Doc Carter to show his truculent side to his employees. Since it was the only side Cheyenne had seen, she hadn't been at all surprised. A disappointment, maybe, but not a surprise. In the three hours prior to the start of her new job, Cheyenne knew Jack Carter wasn't about to apologize.

She was curious about the woman Elaine. The woman's expensive designer sandals and stylish jacket highlighted her wealth. When Carter and Elaine stood together, they looked like a Town and Country ad, except when Carter glared toward Cheyenne. She was certain Town and Country didn't allow their models to glare.

Cheyenne made a point not to look their way again for the rest of the evening. She wanted to enjoy her food. The leftovers now sat in the lunchroom refrigerator. Maybe now she could eat in peace without people buzzing over their boss's odd behavior. More importantly, the absence of Carter's venomous gaze meant the remaining food wouldn't taste like road kill.

She looked at the cameras. As soon as she checked on the mare in stall two, she'd run, not walk, to the lunchroom.

Cheyenne wasn't convinced Lady's restless behavior was normal. When she got to the stall she left the overhead lights off and took a flashlight into the stall with her. Mary had told her not to enter the stall but that was so much bull in Cheyenne's opinion. How was it possible to check on an animal from several feet away separated by a wall and iron bars?

She whispered as she approached the mare and placed a hand on the horse's rump to signal her approach. Lady shifted her weight and turned to watch Cheyenne. The churned bedding and a depression in the center of the stall indicated the horse had rotated in constant circles.

Cheyenne stood at Lady's head and did her horse whisperer routine so the horse could adjust to her presence. When the horse calmed she moved to the mare's shoulder and bent over, to direct the light between the horse's back legs. Milk seeped from the mare's bag and her pelvic ligaments had relaxed. The mare gave a half-hearted kick toward her belly with a back foot. Lady's foal was about to arrive. It was time to call Dr. Barrington.

The number on the chalkboard by the door was almost illegible but Cheyenne checked it twice and copied it, before she headed to the lunchroom. She stuck the food in the microwave and dialed the number with a plan to eat outside the horse's stall after she made the call.

She heard a sleepy, gravel-voiced "hello" and her reply stuck in her throat.

"Hello." The voice was more insistent this time and she had to answer.

"This is Cheyenne," she said. Had she copied the number wrong? "I'm trying to reach Dr. Barrington."

"I'm on call tonight. What's the problem?"

His cold voice made her shiver, but her anger kicked in and she quickly overheated. *Great.* Now she knew what a hot flash felt like. She'd use the heat because she refused to let this jerk with his alcohol derangement syndrome get to her. This job was paying for her new refrigerator, and she wasn't about to return it simply because she worked for one idiot.

"Lady-in-Waiting is going to foal tonight. I thought you might like to know."

"She's not due yet."

Cheyenne counted to ten and rubbed the muscle that twitched at her temple.

"Since you're there and I'm here you might want to allow for the possibility I'm right. It's up to you what you do with the information," she said.

He didn't hide his curse.

"What's she doing?"

He said it like she was the dumbest creature since God made rocks and the insult was too much for her.

"She's practicing her Lamaze breathing and timing her contractions. What do you think she's doing?"

She hung up before he fired her. It didn't matter, of course. He'd fire her anyway. She wondered if the store would pick up the refrigerator.

The plate of food in the microwave had cooled so she reheated it for another minute. She'd eat the food or hoard it but she wasn't about to throw it out. It might be the last decent meal she had for a while.

When the plate finished heating, she took her small carton of milk and walked back to the stall. Lady now circled, with intermittent pauses to nip at her belly or pee before she started to walk again. Cheyenne sympathized with the mare. The pain in Cheyenne's butt was scheduled to arrive any minute now.

She munched on her hamburger and thought about the recent path her life had taken. Her return to Lexington to start her business had been a reasonable decision. She might have built a smaller riding arena and purchased fewer school horses, but she had embraced a "be prepared" philosophy. Yet if she hadn't committed herself to so much debt the pressure to take this job wouldn't have existed.

Cheyenne finished her burger and chastised herself for arguing the facts. She had no control over the matter. The minute Carter walked in he'd fire her. Yes, he'd goaded her, and his judgment had been unfair from the start. Still, he had all the power and she had none.

Lady gave a hearty groan and sank to the floor. Cheyenne looked at the clock. It was almost twelve-thirty. She'd check on the other horses and then come back to wrap the mare's tail and wash her down. Since she was about to lose her job, the rule to stay out of the stall wasn't important. She planned to do what was needed and to hell with Jack Carter.

The other horses were asleep. Even Mr. Tibbles hadn't moved from his head-down posture. She stopped to look at him as he rested. The slight sway of his back showed his age but he was fit with outstanding confirmation. Even his advanced years seemed capable of giving her the ride of her life. The thought of not seeing him again after tonight stayed with her as she walked back to the foaling barn.

Chapter Sixteen

Win's exact words had been, "We give her a one-month trial. I refuse to fire her based upon a vague feeling you have regarding her fitness for the job."

"She was recommended by *Lyndon Tyree*, Jack," Mike added. "We couldn't ask for a more trustworthy source than Lyn. She more than fits all the requirements for the job." He gestured toward Jack's desk. "We thought you had approved her, too."

If Jack hadn't seen the damn file, his hope that she had a criminal record might have given his partners a good reason to rethink her hiring. As it was, the information in the folder showed nothing but a person of good character with life-long horse experience. With Lyn's letter and Cheyenne's physical appeal, Jack knew why Win and Mike thought she was heaven-sent.

"I don't have a choice here, do I?" he said. "We agreed on majority rule when we started our practice and I've been outvoted. I'll abide by the decision but I'm not happy about it."

Win stood up. "It's settled then. Now let's get out there and eat."

Jack put up a hand. "Wait. I'm taking call duty tonight and every other night she's here for the next month. You two have any problem with that?"

"Jack, for God's sake, you just came back from a week-long conference," Win protested.

"I'm the one who has the doubt. And since when have either of you wanted to be on call at night?"

Win and Mike looked at each other. Mike shrugged and said, "I don't care if you don't."

Win gave a dismissive wave and turned to leave. "Do what you want."

\*\*\*\*

Jack drove to the clinic with a hundred thoughts in his head. His anger with himself lingered from the earlier meeting in his office. Had his desk been more organized, they wouldn't be in this situation in the first place. The bad feeling between him and Win had never happened in their long friendship, and it was all because of a woman who was little more than an acquaintance.

She drove him crazy. Since that first idiotic night at her farm, he had ricocheted between active hostility and the purest lust he'd ever known. He recognized the situation for what it was—the danger of repeating the mistakes from his earlier life which gave him little control and no confidence in his judgment.

His truck headlights illuminated the front door of the office as he came to a stop. He turned off the engine and listened to the sounds of late evening. The clinic sat a quarter mile back from the road but he heard the occasional noise of a car engine. The cricket chirps were more a comfort than an irritation.

He left the truck with everything and nothing on his mind. Still, it was time to observe just exactly how a horse practiced Lamaze.

The overhead lights were off when Jack entered the foaling barn. Cheyenne carried a flashlight as she walked around the mare and whispered something too low for him to understand. He wasn't surprised to find her in the stall. She seemed fearless even if it was against the rules. When he found himself admiring the trait he erased it from his thoughts.

He made enough noise to let horse and human know he was there but kept it to a minimum. Mares about to foal were touchy creatures. Too much noise and light hindered the process.

She looked up as he slid open the door, stepped around him, and was on her way out when she said quietly, "Two hours. Tops."

Jack shook his head, and replied, just as quietly, "We need to talk about clinic rules and why it's wise to follow them."

He thought he heard a sniff but she was out the door and he had a horse to examine.

****

The monitors in the office gave her a good view of the stall as he checked the horse. They didn't pick up everything, but they were an adequate replacement in between the checks. His routine was sure and unhurried, and his love of his profession was evident in the way he rubbed the horse's neck and stroked her ears. The horse responded by lying down.

He left the stall and slid the door bolt closed. For a few seconds, he disappeared from view before he popped back onto the camera.

"You were right," he said. "She's ready. Make me some coffee."

Cheyenne's jaw dropped as he disappeared again. He knew she watched him. She jumped when he came back and said, "We're still going to talk about those rules."

She smiled, betrayed by her sense of the absurd.

They disliked each other and she was about to lose her job after one shift. How was she able to find humor at a time like this? She turned away from the camera and tried to remember where she'd seen the coffee machine.

Ten minutes later, she handed him the coffee.

"Do you want me to stay?" she asked. He sat on a folding chair outside the stall with paperwork spread across his lap and looked up as he reached for the cup.

"No," he said, with his typical assessing gaze. "That's not necessary."

She nodded and turned to leave.

"Cheyenne?"

*Here it comes. Goodbye, refrigerator, decent meals, and the truck tune-up I've already put off for far too long.*

"I don't want you in the horse's stalls when you're here by yourself. It's too dangerous."

She hadn't expected that. Her surprise made her turn and ask, without thinking, "You're not going to fire me?"

"Why would I do that?"

"I hung up on you, for one. Two, I was impertinent."

She dug her own grave, but something in his expression goaded her.

"Of course, you were rude, but that doesn't necessarily excuse my insubordination," she added.

He watched her while he sipped his coffee.

"I was rude?"

"Yes, you were definitely rude."

"I guess I can't fire you then, since you seem to think I asked for it—insubordination, that is."

He stopped smiling. "Just don't give me any other reason to fire you. There are certain things I won't put up with. I'll be watching to make sure you don't bring one particular habit to work with you."

She turned away and stomped down the aisle, unable to talk without shattering glass. It didn't matter anyway. Words didn't work with him. She'd have to prove him wrong and planned to spend the rest of the night figuring out how. Cheyenne refused to believe she wasn't up to the task. After all, she was a Modine.

Chapter Seventeen

A day later, Jack stopped at Red Fox Farm and pulled up behind a van from the Speech and Hearing Center. Several kids and adults climbed out, all of the kids dressed in identical black boots, and riding hats. He figured this meant she was here.

He followed the group through a door, into a lounge with a view of a covered riding ring. Stalls lined one wall of the ring and it appeared all the horses in those stalls were for the class. Jack spotted Cheyenne at the opposite end of the barn where she helped a small child tack up her horse.

He noticed Cheyenne's breeches fit like a second skin and his throat turned dry. Thankfully, a pop machine in the corner offered him a lifeline.

Around three a.m., within minutes of Lady giving birth to a filly, Jack convinced himself he needed to come back to check on Dinah's foal. After all, he'd mentioned it to John-Michael at the Steakhouse. What he hadn't done was tell Cheyenne before he left the clinic.

When he said goodbye, she was washing out the coffee machine in the lunchroom. Her response was a soapy hand lifted in acknowledgment.

He might have told her then, maybe, but she'd displayed numerous signs she didn't give a damn what he did.

His attention came back to the ring, and he noticed

a small boy and his mom now struggled to place a saddle on a round, chestnut pony. The saddle slipped off the other side of the animal and the boy slid under its belly to retrieve it. Jack took a sip of his pop and smiled as the two of them laughed.

When he refocused on Cheyenne she signed rapidly to the little girl near her. The information in Ben's folder mentioned her work as a speech therapist on a Native Reservation in South Dakota. It seems she had contacted the Center to offer riding lessons to their clients and he thought the idea both smart and practical.

Had it only been yesterday when he'd lost his temper over Win's decision to hire her? Today, as he watched her with the children, he realized his reaction might have been too over the top. He wasn't able to forget her inebriation but seeing her here helped him make peace with her presence at the clinic for the next month.

Cheyenne turned and strode toward the lounge. When she saw him through the window, her eyes narrowed and she wheeled into the room.

"Whoa, stop." He raised his hand before she did the Ninja thing and wrestled him to the ground. "I came by to check on Dinah and her foal."

The straight line of her mouth relaxed a bit but she said nothing, which told him she wasn't convinced of his good intentions.

"I got the impression you said that to John-Michael for effect."

Jack wondered if her voice could get any cooler.

"No, it's something I do for all my clients," he said. Of course, this was the first time he'd extended the service to include those he treated from Gray's clinic.

"What do you charge for this visit?" she asked.

"I think I mentioned there was no charge. Would you like names and phone numbers to verify that?"

She shook her head but her eyes betrayed her. "No, I'll take you at your word. Now, if you'll excuse me, I have a class to teach."

She walked back out into the ring, and he left to check on Dinah and the foal. He was bothered by the way she said, "I'll take you at your word." Her clouded gaze told him she was disappointed with his explanation.

He preferred her mad, for some reason. After he was finished with the horses, he'd return to watch her lesson, just to give her another go at him.

**\*\*\*\***

The parents all leaned against the ring when Jack rejoined them. Cheyenne willed herself into meditation with his return. She didn't want to cheat the kids by letting her attention drift. Within a minute, she recognized her meditation skills had deserted her.

She didn't believe his visit today was a coincidence. He came to check on her, not Dinah or Little D. He wanted to catch her drunk or something equally as ludicrous.

Her signing took on new energy. She signed everything as she stood in the center of the ring while the kids walked and trotted around her. The lesson was almost over when she saw him leave. She swung her arms to release the knotted muscles. What she really needed was a long soak in a hot tub and another nap before she returned to work tonight.

As she said goodbye to the kids and turned the horses out for the afternoon, her mood took a downward slide. Last night's sleep deprivation and her few hours of rest this morning had been filled with edgy dreams. There'd been a polo field and her horse had gone lame. She'd taken Mr. Tibbles out for a ride, Carter had caught her and accused her of riding drunk. She woke up but fell immediately back to sleep, plagued by visions of him making love to Elaine. Cheyenne reawakened drenched in sweat, unable to clear her head of the picture they made. When she thought of them together, now, she got an immediate headache.

She entered the tack room to make sure everything was in proper order when a voice from behind made her jump.

"I thought you were gone," she said and turned around to face him.

He lounged against the door frame with his arms folded across his chest.

"I was in my truck looking over my schedule, waiting for everyone to leave. Thought you might want a report on Dinah and the little guy."

She needed a distraction and turned back to look at the tack hanging from the wall pegs. If he moved closer, she'd have to bury her nose in a saddle to mask his come-on scent.

She moved a bridle from one hook to another.

"Cheyenne?" His footsteps told her he had the nerve to come closer.

"Yeah. How are they?"

"Everything looks fine," he said. "You might want to think about not breeding Dinah anymore."

"Why?"

Cheyenne's guilt over the accident that resulted in the new foal returned but she didn't need a warning about Dinah's age from him.

"How old is she? Early twenties?"

"Yes, in that range. Is she okay?"

"She's in good shape. Just a little too old for another foal."

"Okay," she said.

"I'm leaving now."

She started to look for another bridle to relocate but noticed he hadn't moved.

"Uh, thanks for checking on my animals."

"Sure, anytime."

*You can leave now, Carter. I don't want a normal conversation with you, of all people.*

"Cheyenne, turn around."

When she didn't, he hooked a big, warm hand around her upper arm and forced her to turn. His touch was firm, and he didn't remove his hand when she faced him.

"Yes?"

"Do you charge those kids for their lessons?"

The sound of buzzing flies grew louder. *Damn.* Why'd he ask that question? He really needed to take his hand off her skin.

"Yes."

"The same thing you charge others?"

Hesitation. "No."

If he didn't stop touching her she was going to drip all over the floor. The muscle in her arm twitched and she started to shift back but his gaze weakened her intent.

His eyes searched her face with the same heat he tried to hide in all their previous meetings. A hint of it even surfaced last night when they discussed her impertinence. She knew her return look reflected his.

Thank God he broke the connection with his next

question.

"Okay, so what's the difference between you charging those kids what I assume is a lower rate and my not charging for my services at Gray's clinic?"

The irritation in his voice revved her up and she pulled her arm from his grasp.

"A great deal of difference. I charge them something so they can retain their dignity. You, on the other hand, are motivated by the strokes you receive for bestowing your expertise on the poor, unwashed masses…"

He stepped back and glared at her.

"What do you know about my motivation? And where in the hell do you get this bullshit?"

He just didn't understand. His kind never did.

She left the room without looking back. A warm, bubbly bath called her name.

## Chapter Eighteen

Jack simmered all the way home. He told himself he should never have gone and promised never to do it again. He flexed his hand, the one still warm from her silky skin and fought against the attraction, an attraction that continued in spite of every effort he made to deny it. If he didn't figure this out soon, he was in deep trouble.

To take his thoughts in a different direction, he thought ahead to his evening with Elaine. The benefit was for a charity the clinic sponsored, to raise money for a local chapter of the Make-A-Wish Foundation. Elaine knew he was a sucker for kids, and he agreed to attend even though he sincerely disliked wearing a tux, hobnobbing with the power elite, and listening to the latest gossip about the city engineer's wife's liposuction.

To be fair, they weren't all that shallow. He just wasn't ready to differentiate at the moment.

He entered the house and his dogs slobbered with joy before they did their dance to go outside. Why they couldn't use the doggie door was an issue of continuing confusion. Nonetheless, he watched them cavort in their version of canine heaven through the deep yard bordered by mature shade trees. Over the privacy fence, Jack made eye contact with the Zimmermans next door. They were having another casually chic outdoor dinner party on their lantern-festooned patio. He waved and headed to the shower when he realized he didn't feel all that neighborly.

He needed to move. This place was his ex-wife's style, a transitional in an upscale development surrounded by other transitionals that looked just like his. He'd call a realtor on Monday. A smaller house, more land, away from the upwardly mobile 'burbs. The dogs would love a small farm about the size of…Red Fox.

*Aw, hell.*

Just like that, the woman he couldn't stop thinking about took over his thoughts, mainly because she hadn't really left them.

He worked the soap and himself into a good lather. The poor, unwashed masses? She said it as if he was one of *them*—that is, the type he'd be with tonight. He assumed the booze had already fried her brain.

Buck, his black lab, jumped into the shower and stopped Jack's fitful contemplations. It seemed the animals used the doggie door after all. He smacked the big, furry rump and reached over to turn off the faucet. Buck exited the shower and shook, flinging sprays of water everywhere.

"Hell, Buck, get out of here," he yelled. "You're making a bloody mess!"

Jack wrapped a towel around his waist and headed for the bedroom. It was the only room in the house he liked. Big enough for a king-size bed, plenty of shelves for his books, and the dogs, a fireplace, and a decent size skylight in the vaulted ceiling; he practically lived in this one room.

But the rest of the house was a downer. He was definitely calling a realtor on Monday. It was time to move, for the dogs.

\*\*\*\*

Cheyenne had read Mr. Tibbles' chart for his current stay and the two other occasions when he'd been sent to the clinic, all due to colic episodes. Three times over the last two months were suspicious. His colic always cleared up after they brought him in. So far, the detailed notes told her they hadn't determined a cause.

She noticed he always became symptomatic on a Thursday, not on a regular basis but twice last month and once this month. She knew his stomach troubles were tied to the farm, which made her decide to take the farm tour. If she figured out the cause of the colic, she was on her way to making Carter choke on his absurd assumption that she was a drunk.

First, though, she needed to sweep the barn aisles. The other part of her plan was to kill Carter with kindness. Every time she saw a chore undone, even if it wasn't her responsibility, she'd do it and make herself indispensable. The continuous activity might even help her stay awake. Tonight she found it much harder to keep her eyes open especially while she sat in the office.

Maybe she'd bring her headset and listen to music while working. A little FGL was guaranteed to keep anyone alert—alert and hot. No, she needed to rethink FGL. Their hotness only fanned the flames higher.

Hadn't she mentioned to Pammy that her sex life was on hold until her business became solvent?

"Why are you sweeping the floor?"

"Holy shit!" She dropped the broom and twisted around. "Why do you…"

*Oh…my…God.* Her stomach sank. He looked like a combination of every sexiest man alive from the last twenty years. Suddenly, she didn't hate tuxes. The darks and lights were perfect—his dark hair, the pristine white of his shirt, the black satin lapels of the jacket against the brilliance of his smile. If ever a man was made to wear a tuxedo it was Jack Carter.

Life was so unfair.

She was so shallow.

"Why do you…" She made an effort to pick up her previous train of thought but failed. She was also unable to stop her stare. As usual, she took refuge in sarcasm.

"Don't tell me. You've been nominated for an Oscar and decided to try out your look on the horses."

"What?" He looked confused so she pointed to his clothes.

His shoes were a fashion statement if she ever saw one. Instead of black, patent leather lace-ups, he wore mud boots. Somehow, he made it look right, because, well, this was Hollywood, and he was the sexiest man alive.

"I know. You weren't allowed on the wedding cake until you changed your boots."

He finally got it and gave her a sheepish grin.

"I had to wear this. It was for a good cause."

She reminded herself he was here to check on her, to catch her doing something unprofessional. It wasn't right that the air shifted around them as they exchanged stares, the same shift like the one in the tack room earlier. Nope, she wasn't going there.

Apparently, he'd been somewhere with a female companion. Elaine? Men like Jack Carter didn't attend functions stag. A spurt of jealousy shocked her into activity.

She picked up the broom, shoved it into a corner, and walked back to Mr. Tibbles' stall, desperate for a distraction.

"What's going on with this guy?"

"Don't change the subject. My brother does it all the time so I'm familiar with the maneuver."

"What maneuver?"

She had to think of something else if Mr. T wasn't enough to erase the magnetic tug of the way Carter looked, smelled, stood, spoke, and stared. He surrounded her and it made her mad, and weak, and tingly. In about a second she was going to wrap her arms around his warm strong body. She might even lick his throat.

"I want to know why you were sweeping the floor. We have a crew that cleans the place. I know this because we get a bill every month for their hard work."

His voice sounded closer. All her focus stayed on the horse while Mr. T's gaze concentrated on Carter.

"I like to keep busy," she said. "What about Mr. Tibbles' colic?"

*Please tell me about his colic. Please don't come nearer. Please, please, please help me out here.*

He wrapped his hand around a stall bar two inches away from her fingers. It was the same hand that had encircled her arm after her class.

"We haven't been able to figure it out." His voice was husky and his pine-scented body heat radiated around her. "We know it has to do with something at the farm, but both Win and I have been there, talked with the manager, walked around the barn and pasture, and found nothing out of the ordinary."

When she didn't respond, he asked, "You haven't been in his stall, have you?"

"No, I haven't been in his stall," she said, with more sass than was necessary. He needed to move away so she could breathe.

She was swamped with disappointment when he stepped back.

"What do you have to eat around here?" he asked, and she watched him walk down the aisle toward the office.

\*\*\*\*

He was insane. He'd left a lovely woman at a prominent social event at the Lafayette Club, where they served real food, to munch on Oreos while he did paperwork in his office.

Something was very wrong with this picture.

It was one a.m. on a Sunday morning. He should go home. The stacks of paper on his desk were in proper order. All that was left to do was to get everything in a folder and into a filing cabinet. He pulled out his cell to take a pic. He hadn't seen his desk this clean in three years.

God, he hated paperwork. But he didn't totally trust technology. Computers crashed or got viruses right when you needed them. Therefore, he had paperwork, lots of paperwork.

He heard the noise of a vacuum in the hall and swore under his breath. *She* was his reason for being here. He wanted to catch her with booze on her breath. He wanted to strip her naked and lick her into a writhing frenzy. He wanted to make her mad enough to quit. He wanted her hands in his pants—immediately. He wanted to know why she left that reservation in South Dakota and came back to start a riding business.

He did?

"Do you want me to clean up those wads of paper on the floor around your trash can?"

"No, dammit." He spun around in his chair and pinned her with his stare.

"What did you mean when you referred to 'the poor unwashed masses'?"

She gave him a look he recognized—the one that said "Oh, please, how can you be so dense?"

He stood up.

"I want to know what you meant. Unless, of course, you don't know what you meant. You have this habit of not completing your thoughts."

"I know what I meant," she said. "I just can't believe you didn't."

He leaned over and put his hands on his desk. "Well, I don't so enlighten me."

She slipped her hands into her pockets and seemed to think about her answer. Or maybe she debated whether to answer at all. With her, he never knew.

"Where did you go to school?" she asked.

"Vet school? Cornell. Why?"

"What about high school?"

"Sayre School, here in Lex. Why?"

"The Sayre School is private. Cornell is—what— ranked one of the top five vet schools in the nation, with a hefty tuition most can't afford."

He almost understood where she was going with her questions. "You're trying to tell me my privileged upbringing has something to do with my volunteer work at the Bourbon County Vet Clinic, right?"

She stepped closer.

"What make of watch are you wearing? What kind of car do you drive and I'm not talking about your truck. Is your tux rented or do you own it? Have you ever wanted for anything in your life?"

His gaze searched her face.

"This isn't really about me, is it? When I was six years old, should I have told my parents I wanted to go to a public school? When I was accepted at Cornell, was the wiser choice a school of less academic merit? And why didn't I shove this watch in my Dad's face when he presented it to me upon my graduation from Cornell?"

Her eyes reflected anger and a variety of other emotions. He refused to apologize for being born into affluence though there had been times when he chafed at the expectations associated with wealth and privilege. He didn't consider himself above anyone else but it was clear she thought he did.

"I didn't expect you to understand."

She sounded indifferent, which increased *his* anger.

"You think my primary reason for volunteering at the clinic is to stroke my ego—an ego resulting from the arrogance of the upper class, of which I happen to be a member."

"Yes." Her answer was unequivocal. Now he was the disappointed one.

She was the first to look away. "I have to check on the horses."

When she left, he stooped to open his bottom left drawer. He pulled out Ben's folder, slipped it into his briefcase, and thumbed the locks into place. Until now he'd never given any thought to the briefcase, an Asprey, with his initials embossed on a brass plate near the handle. It, too, had been a gift, from Ben. Jack knew his brother had chosen it for its good looks and durability. But did any of them consider cost a factor in the purchase of such an item?

In the front office, he checked the monitors. She

stood at Mr. T's stall and talked to the horse as if he understood every word. Jack thought about her hands on the bars of the stall when mere inches had separated their bodies. He'd fought with himself to move away from her body heat and the warm, fresh flower scent that floated around her.

He grabbed the bag of Oreos and popped one into his mouth. He hoped the chocolate smell was strong enough to erase her scent. Then he wrote her a note to tell her he had left.

Tomorrow he'd look at the folder again to fill in the blanks. He suddenly wanted to know a great deal more about this woman.

Chapter Nineteen

Hunter Glen Stables was one of the newer breeding facilities in the Bluegrass. It was smallish with only three stallions and enough stalls to hold thirty horses. The main buildings included a large broodmare barn, a stallion barn, and a barn to house the yearlings.

The farm tour was held every Wednesday afternoon in the summer and was the only link Cheyenne could see to Mr. Tibbles' stomach problems. She knew it was a long shot, but she was an expert at finding minuscule needles in a mountainous haystack.

Her plan to make Carter shove his privilege up his ass, or maybe to change his mind about her had sounded great last night. The first aspect of the argument had fallen through, however, when Carter made his God's-gift-to-women appearance in the perfect tux, a tux that covered an equally perfect body. Then he had to confuse the logic by making her trot out the "rich" issue.

She stayed back as the group of tourists moved down the wide aisle of the stallion barn. The barn manager was a big, thirtyish, born and bred Kentuckian, judging by his accent. While he discussed the stallions' bloodlines, she took the time to note the barn conditions.

It was bright and airy, with skylights over every stall. The aisles were clean, the stalls a good size, and in a good state of repair. The grounds were spotless. As Carter had mentioned, nothing appeared out of the ordinary. She wondered how specific she could get with her questions without alerting the manager's curiosity.

She stood outside Mr. Tibbles' vacant stall. There were no signs of cribbing, a frequent cause of colic, and a common habit of high-strung horses. No toothmarks dented the wooden sides of the stall. The clinic notes said the vets had checked Mr. T's teeth for unusual wear. Still, she'd check them again, just to be certain. The bedding in the stalls was treated, shredded newspaper, which almost no horse wanted to eat. Each stall had its own paddock, and she hadn't noticed any of the board fences damaged by a wood-eating horse.

She followed the group to an occupied stall. Music Man, the young stallion in the stall according to the brass plate on the door, had his nose buried in a feed bowl.

"Mr. James?" She raised her hand and walked closer to the front. "What's the feeding schedule for the stallions?"

"Ma'am?" He looked up after slipping a few slices of apple into the stallion's feed.

"How often do you feed the stallions?"

"Oh, that varies, ma'am. In summer, we feed grain twice a day, in the morning and early evening. We feed hay mid-day, and late at night."

She examined the horse while he ate his grain. It was one-thirty in the afternoon.

"This guy must have a different schedule." She smiled and gave him a wide-eyed look to soften the inquisition in her tone. Her experience told her it worked with most men.

Mr. James was no exception. He smiled back.

"No, ma'am. When we have tours, we change the schedule a little. The stallion we keep in the barn for the tour gets an added meal."

The look on the manager's face turned to condescension. Up until then, she kind of liked his easy-going manner and round, open face.

"See, ma'am, stallions are hard to handle, especially if they don't get their exercise. We try to keep them occupied during tours with food since they spend part of their day inside."

*Men.* She nodded to show she understood his patient explanation. Good thing her nod hadn't taken the direction of a head shake. She just hoped he didn't make the mistake of calling her "little lady".

"What kind of exercise do the stallions get? If they're hard to handle, are they hard to exercise?"

"Well, no. We have experienced staff here and they know what they're doing. All our stallions are ridden every day, and they get a lot of pasture time. I was just speaking of the stallions we keep in on tour days. We rotate our three stallions. This week Music Man is inside, next week is Mr. Tibbles, and then Adonis. On the day a stallion is inside, we feed them on a different schedule, and they get less exercise, but it's only for that one day. It doesn't bother them any."

She thanked him and walked to the back of the group. It wasn't much, but she was fairly sure it did bother one. With Mr. Tibbles' age, a change in his feeding/exercise schedule might create stomach problems. Add in apples and other treats from the manager, and the possibility increased to probability.

Cheyenne left the tour and walked back to her truck. Her fun was over for the day. She needed to practice for her dressage workshop again, and she had polo practice after dinner. Making the time to take this tour had been all about Carter's comeuppance. She wasn't naïve enough to think he'd fall at her feet and profess his undying gratitude. It'd be a notch in her belt, though, if she figured out the reason for the old stallion's colic. All part of the master plan.

****

Jack had an idea, but he needed to persuade Janie and Ben to go along with it. He'd ask Janie first because he was a polite, well-bred individual of the upper class. After Janie said yes, as he knew she would, he'd work on his brother. Ben owed him because of the folder; the same folder Jack carried with him as he strode down the hall to the reception area.

He rounded the corner.

"Janie, get Gray on the line. What's wrong?"

Jack stopped short at his sister-in-law's expression. Her pale face was a distinct contrast with the bright red top she wore. He hadn't seen her that pale since her pregnancy with Lea when she'd barfed hourly for the first three months.

"That was Mary." Janie hung up the phone. "Her mother's been in a terrible car accident and isn't expected to live."

"Aw, crap." He sat down. "That's bad. Is there anything we can do? Give blood, anything?"

Janie shook her head. "She said her family's already done that. She comes from a big, extended family. I told her to take all the time she needed, and to call us if…if…well, if."

"Yeah," he said because he didn't know what to say. He looked at the folder in his lap. Cheyenne was one year old when her mother died in a car accident. He wondered what was worse—never knowing a parent or losing them later when the bond was stronger, with all the good and bad of that situation.

"They live in Louisville?" he asked.

"Yes," she said with tears in her eyes.

"Call Marty Boyd. His brother, Mark, is an orthopedic surgeon at U. of L. hospital. See if Marty can find out what's going on and have him call me, asap."

Marty was an old friend from the Navy. Jack hadn't seen him since their ten-year reunion, a few years back, but they called each other every season to practice their curses and discuss the latest Jack Reacher novel.

Jack headed back to his office, slapping the folder against his thigh. His thoughts scattered, for a moment going blank on what he held in his hand. When he looked down, he stopped the slaps.

Back at his desk, he called the front office.

"Janie, who's filling in for Mary?"

"Oh, uh, no one, yet." Her quiet answer told him she was still in shock.

"Let me handle it," he said. "Just call Marty, then call Gray and ask him to call me, sometime today. Tell him to call my cell if he can't get me here."

He tried to reach Cheyenne, both her cell number and landline, but she didn't answer either number. Her recording said, "Red Fox Riding Stable. Leave your name and number. I always return my calls."

His message was "Cheyenne, it's Jack Carter. We've had an emergency here at the clinic and we need your help. Call me at the office or on my cell."

Jack suspected she was busy with a class or working with her horses. He'd like to see her ride. Gray had talked about how good she was, even as a child. He pictured her on a horse, dressed as she was for her lesson last week—

snug beige breeches hugging taut thighs, black riding boots, a white sleeveless, high-necked blouse. Had her hair been braided, or down, the way it was the night at the steakhouse? When he thought about her hips rocking with the motion of the horse, he had to stop. His Cheyenne fantasies were already far too dangerous.

Thankfully, the phone rang with perfect timing.

A distinctive honk carried over the line before Jack spoke.

"That you, Gray?"

"How'd you know?"

"I'd recognize those clogged nasal passages anywhere. Allergies acting up?"

"Yes, dammit. My allergist switched my meds and said it would fix all my problems. It fixed me all right. I've slept fourteen of the last twenty-four hours, some of those sitting upright at my desk."

"It might help if you told him you have up close and personal contact with dog dander."

Gray sneezed. "Are you nuts? He'd throw the book at me."

Jack shook his head. His friend was such a wimp when it came to doctors. Gray's allergist was one of the best in Lexington, stood five feet tall, had a well-known temper, and talked with a heavy accent Gray didn't understand. Yet Gray refused to switch and always defended the man.

Jack waited until Gray blew his nose before he posed his question. "I wanted to talk to you about Cheyenne Modine."

"Ah, little sure shot," Gray said, and Jack heard the smirk in his friend's response.

"Yeah, well, we just hired her for an attendant

position last week and I need a little background information."

"Hired her? What position?"

"Remember the kid, Sean Davis, recommended to us by the Job Partners Association?"

"Oh, yeah, the little reprobate with the sticky fingers, and a yen for two-hundred-dollar jeans. You had to let him go, huh?"

"Actually, he let himself go, by not showing up for his shift. Cheyenne replaced the kid."

"I told you not to hire him. I don't care if the JPA director and your dad are old friends."

"The kid had good instincts with horses. He worked at the track for two years and I got a good report from the trainer Davis worked for. Davis seemed competent."

Jack stopped when he realized he defended his decision, not the kid's reputation. "You're right. Probably wasn't the best move I've made, even though Win and Mike were okay with the hiring, too. Anyway, about Cheyenne…"

"I don't know if I can help you much there, bud. I haven't seen her in years, except for that brief ten minutes she was here about the bill. Besides, we only saw each other twice, way back when."

"What about her home life?"

"Her home life? How does that relate to her competency to do the clinic job? That *is* why you're calling, right?"

Jack ignored the dig. He wasn't exactly sure what he wanted Gray to say. Something along the lines of "she had her little girl scout uniform on, and I overheard her pledge never to abuse alcohol for as long as she lived" might have been good, though.

"Just tell me your general impressions. Was her father reputable in his dealings? What kind of place did they have? How did they seem together?"

Gray was silent for a minute, except for his wheezing. "Did you talk to Tyree? He'd be able to tell you much more than I can."

Jack pressed the speaker button and sat back in his chair.

"Lyn sent a recommendation letter. He's why she got the job in the first place."

Jack didn't expand on the situation, since it involved his basic inability to keep his desk organized.

"Is there anything at all you can tell me?" he asked.

"Let's see. I remember the farm was small and clean. The house was a red brick, two-story. My dad said Mr. Modine was fair in his prices, and honest, but I think I already mentioned that. There was no pressure to buy. Modine assured us the horses were vet-checked, but Dad could bring in his own vet if he wanted."

Jack heard the tapping of a pencil from Gray's end. "The family seemed tight. Come to think of it, I didn't see a woman around...you know, a mom or wife. Cheyenne was a real tomboy. Rode a few of the horses bareback, without shoes, until Mr. Modine told her to put on boots. She did what he asked without complaining. I think she and her dad were especially close."

"Hmmm." Jack rubbed his bottom lip. "Okay. Thanks for the info."

"I didn't help much, did I?" Gray said. "Still, it might make a difference if you'd tell me the real reason why you're asking."

Jack frowned. "Who says I didn't."

"Did you?"

"No."

"At least you admitted it. I'll call you back if I think of anything else."

"Sounds good. Hey, one other thing. Do you have anyone working for you who might need more hours? Maybe Chris?"

"Chris? I don't know. Why?"

"One of our attendants had a family emergency. We need immediate help. It would be evening hours—a temporary thing until she returns. I'm guessing two or three weeks."

"You certainly are having your share of staff issues. I'll ask Chris. He's in later. I'll call you back as soon as I wake up. Right now, I feel another nap coming on."

Gray hung up and Jack's thoughts remained on Cheyenne. In truth, she hadn't left his mind at all since last Friday night. And when she did, it was only to move to other areas of his body, like a submarine about to deliver a sneak attack.

Something or someone had to give. He hadn't been this turned on since...uh, never.

He checked his cell for Elaine's number and clicked off. He didn't want Elaine. He wanted...

"Cheyenne's on line one, Jack," Janie said over the intercom.

He answered and turned off the speaker, so no one overheard the conversation.

"Hi," he said.

"Hi."

Her heavy breathing sounded like she'd been riding, or—no, no, he couldn't go there.

*Where have you been? How are you? I apologize for being rich. Meet me for dinner later? Tell me you're not a drunk and make me believe it. Shit.*

"Mary's mother has been seriously injured in a car accident, in Louisville. We need someone to take over part of her shift. Are you interested?"

"I, I, uh…" she paused. When she spoke again, her voice trembled. "How serious?"

"I didn't talk to Mary but the initial report doesn't sound good."

"That's, it's…of course, I'll help in any way I can. For Mary."

He hated to hear the tremor in her voice. Were her thoughts about the possible death of a fellow worker's mother in a car accident tied to the death of her own mother?

"I know you have your own business to consider. What hours work best for you?"

"I can do Tuesday and Thursday evenings. Six to ten?"

"Yeah, that's good." He thought fast. "Mary sometimes goes out on calls with us, if we need extra help. At your convenience, can you go if needed?"

It was a bald-faced lie. Mary begged the docs to go out on calls for the experience, but they never needed additional help. There were always enough workers at the farms to take up the slack.

He was pathetic.

"Yes," she said. "I can do that, sometimes."

"Good," he said. "Thanks."

He'd done an about-face, reluctant now to hang up. This was the first non-combative conversation they'd had. It was great and he really was damned pathetic.

"How's Mr. Tibbles?" she asked, out of nowhere, which saved him from making an ass of himself.

"He's doing well, the old devil," he said with a smile. "We'll probably turn him loose on Friday, then cross our fingers we don't see him again, except in the breeding shed."

"Is he good at that?" she asked.

"Oh, yeah. Gives new meaning to the word 'stud'."

He thought he heard her laugh, but Janie's voice interrupted.

"Jack, Marty Boyd is on the line."

"Cheyenne, I have to go. I'll see you tomorrow." He paused. "Thanks again."

"Sure."

When the call ended, he ran his hands through his hair. Pathetic didn't even begin to cover it.

Chapter Twenty

It was the day of her dressage demonstration at the Horse Park and Dudley was in the middle of his extended trot when she surveyed the crowd. Jack Carter stood at the far end, and he was hard to miss. Apparently, he didn't need to wear a tux to distract her.

What was *he* doing here?

With effort, she redirected her attention back to the test. His presence was a surprise, but her mind had been so full of him, along with the call about Mary's mother, that the surprise seemed almost...belated? It was as if, in the back of her mind, she'd expected to see him.

Or maybe it wasn't really him. She moved Dud into the canter pirouette, out of sequence, just to be sure.

Okay, she was positive now. His broad shoulders and upright stance were dead giveaways. He watched with total concentration, just like at the picnic last week. Or maybe not. Then, his expression had been a glare. Now, his look showed complete focus, on her.

It was unnerving and somewhat flattering. Surely he had seen dressage before.

In fluid collection, she sent the horse into a half-pass. Amazing—she'd spent so much time in the pirouette she was dizzy. Thank God her horse hadn't allowed *his* attention to wander.

Three teenage girls cast furtive glances in Jack's direction. He seemed not to notice. Did that mean he really hadn't noticed, or did it happen so much he was used to it?

What was she thinking? Of course, he was used to it. This was Jack Carter.

She and Dudley made a left and crossed the arena at a trot. When they turned, the place where he'd stood was empty.

****

Well, now he knew and wished he didn't.

She rode as if she and the horse were one. Yes, that was the purpose of dressage. Horse and rider perfectly synchronized, in movements of flawless execution, as if all the rider had to do was think the cue and the horse performed. Still, did she have to be so fricking seductive while she did it?

He walked across the grounds to the parking lot. If it weren't for those three girls, he'd still be torturing himself with the image of riding with her, on the same horse, and they weren't exactly concerned with flying lead changes. His mind conjured up something straight out of a dark historical romance, in the Olde English countryside, where the highwayman comes riding—come being the pertinent word here—while his lady love sits in front of him on a big, black steed in full gallop.

His erotic thoughts took a dive when he'd noticed the teenage girls. What was it with teenagers these days? Christ, he was old enough to be their father.

His original goal was to stay until Cheyenne finished, to tell her Mary's mother had improved. He knew she'd want to know.

Jack decided to tell her tonight.

His attention caught on the Rolex that hung from his rear-view mirror. Speaking of fathers, Dad would hose him if he ever found out the watch was on the mirror and not on Jack's wrist. For a moment, Gray's comment on the relationship between Cheyenne and her dad filtered through Jack's head. He wished he'd been as lucky, but he realized Cheyenne might see it differently. At least he had a father *and* mother in his life.

He pulled out of the lot, already late for his next appointment. To reconnect with the positive, because Mary's mother had improved, it was time to revive his plan. He wanted Janie and Ben to have the Friday night barbecue at their house. There, he'd be able to watch Cheyenne in a social situation away from work in a less restrictive environment.

Damn, it was bold, it was original, and it was his brother's idea, which meant Ben would go along with it. The guy loved it when Jack took his advice—a brother thing, so to speak.

Jack was sure he'd hear about it for the next six months.

****

Cheyenne studied Mr. T for several minutes, talking to him as she did with all the horses. Sometimes she asked questions, or used what her brother called "baby talk". She purposely whispered even though no one was around to hear her. Of course, Carter had vowed to watch her like a hawk so she expected him to appear any minute now.

Mr. Tibbles had luminous, intelligent eyes and she thought he understood the intent of her words. His "come on in, friend" look invited her closer and she debated whether to risk it now or later. It was almost eight and since Carter wasn't here, she had better get to it.

To complete her investigation of Mr. T's colic

episodes, she needed to examine his teeth. Therefore, she had to enter the stall and break one of Carter's biggest rules.

She wasn't afraid of the horse, and he gave no indication he was upset by her presence. He didn't paw, snort, or flatten his ears when she stopped by. He intimidated a few of the other staff but that was more a comment on his gender. Stallions were difficult, but most horses with track experience, and stallions standing at stud were consistently handled. Her scariest encounters had occurred with abused or fearful horses. This horse held his proud head too high to be in either of those categories.

Cheyenne looked around and listened. No truck engine idled outside. With luck, she'd conduct her exam quickly and get out. It fit better with her plan to leave Carter's ire unprovoked.

\*\*\*\*

Jack stopped at Imperial Hunan on New Circle Road, ordered enough food for two, and headed back to the office. He hadn't eaten since noon and it was past time for dinner. Late calls were typical in his business and today he'd made the situation worse by his detour to the Horse Park.

Upon arrival, he grabbed the three bags of food in one hand and shouldered open the back office door. Cheyenne wasn't around, of course. He smiled to himself as he placed the food on the counter. She was probably polishing paper clips, or in the barn with a magnifying glass looking for the one out-of-place piece of straw that marred an otherwise immaculate facility. He noticed she liked to keep busy and wondered if her high metabolism extended to anything else. No, not yet. First, they would eat, then they had a few things to work out before they got naked.

But, good God, it had better be soon.

In the last few days, his knee-jerk reaction to her drunken state the night Dinah foaled had transitioned from a felony to a misdemeanor. Jack was also ready to explore different explanations for the prescription med scenario. The lack of evidence helped. She hadn't come to work drunk. Tyree said nothing about her abusing alcohol. The Speech and Hearing Center sent kids to her riding stable for lessons. For those reasons, he had reached the point where he was willing to listen.

Hell, who was he kidding? All she needed to do was look him in the eye, make the sign of the cross, and say, with her delectable pink lips, "Jack, I swear I don't drink or do drugs" and he'd fall to the ground, and lick her boots.

He almost laughed out loud at the woeful vision.

After he unloaded the cartons from the bag, the smells of fried rice, egg rolls, and sweet and sour chicken filled the room. When his stomach growled again, louder, he noticed the time. It was 8:10 and he needed to find her. He froze when he examined the monitors.

She stood in Mr. Tibbles' stall.

He smacked open the double doors and sprinted across the passageway through the mare's barn. Lady's new foal jumped when Jack flew past. If Cheyenne was still alive when he got to the stall, he was going to give serious consideration to killing her.

He rounded the last corner in the stallion barn and shouted her name. Mr. T pivoted, and his powerful hindquarters flung her body hard against the wall. Like a sack of potatoes, she collapsed on the stall floor and disappeared from sight.

\*\*\*\*

Cheyenne regained consciousness as Jack Carter's hands moved down her arms in a clinical way. Had she been able to breathe, she might have requested he stop his examination. Except for the bump on the back of her head, some pain in her shoulders, and the breathing problems, everything else worked. Still, she didn't open her eyes while his hands tested her legs with the same gentle pressure. She must have a brain injury. Otherwise, she'd be able to deny how much she wanted him to touch her.

He eased off her boots and rotated both her ankles. Her painful gasps for air eased and she almost groaned with pleasure when his warm fingers encircled her foot. He paused, which made her peek toward her feet. He stared at her taped toes, clearly visible through her thin sock.

She shut her eyes again and he moved to her other leg. His curses stopped, finally. Maybe, if she kept her eyes closed long enough, he'd get over his anger and allow her to explain her presence in Mr. T's stall. Then he touched her side, under her breast, and her eyes flew open.

He was furious.

Okay, that might be an understatement. His dark brown eyes were now a murderous black.

When he stood, she lost her better judgment.

"Go ahead. Curse," she said. "It'll make you feel better."

Good grief. Was that her voice? She sounded like Minion Bob. Either that or the bump on her head had destroyed her ability to hear.

He jammed his hands into his pockets and started to pace, his eyes on his feet like he counted his steps.

She watched him walk the same path for several seconds.

Finally, he stopped and pointed his finger at her.

"You, I, if…"

He glared at the ceiling and called it a bad name.

"I'm sorry I…yelled." He bit off every word but still didn't look at her.

"Yeah, I'm sorry you yelled, too. That was so stu--"

His scowl shut her up.

"I'm sorry I went into his stall," she mumbled, even though she knew his shout caused Mr. T's abrupt movement. She might think about the "don't go in the stall" rule, later.

"Can you sit up?"

"Why? So you can get a better angle with your right hook?"

"Don't tempt me," he warned, but she saw the barest hint of humor in his eyes.

He put his hand down to help her. She hesitated, then slid her hand into his.

Chapter Twenty-One

When he touched the lump on the back of her head, they argued about going to the hospital. She won, so Jack filled a plastic bag with ice and tied it to her head with a dishtowel. It must have been the knock on her head that made her consent to eat the food he'd brought. It was barely warm when they sat down at the table behind the reception desk.

"I'll pay you back for my share," she said as she cut into a pot sticker.

He had his mouth full, so he shook his head.

"I insist," she said.

He swallowed. "No, consider it part of the apology."

"But you bought the food before—"

"No." He stared her down.

She popped the potsticker in her mouth and made a face.

"You look like a Sikh." His gaze lifted to the towel.

She put her hand up to the ice pack and shifted it back over the bump. It slid to the side again. "It's my braid."

She untied the towel and laid the ice pack on the table in front of her. As if by habit, she pulled the end of the braid over her shoulder, removed the elastic tie, loosened the braid, and threaded her fingers through her hair.

He watched every movement. When she tossed her

head and hair fell over her shoulders, he stuck his hand into a cup of duck sauce. Before she noticed, he wiped his fingers with a napkin, while she replaced the ice and towel.

"Need any help?" he asked. If he stood behind her, he wouldn't have the mind-boggling view of her breasts as she raised her arms to tie the towel.

"No, thanks. I've just about got it."

She put her arms down and he refocused on her head.

"Now you look like that singer who always wears weird head gear."

"Gee, thanks, I think."

He tried to concentrate on his plate of food. Numerous pieces of the Cheyenne puzzle weren't in the folder. He wanted to ask her to fill in the blanks, but it was too risky, with the most significant risk being her discovery of the folder.

"You didn't kill Mr. Tibbles or anything, did you?"

She had turned to view the monitors.

"Kill?"

"Yeah, you know, like that old movie about the mob, where someone put a horse head in bed with the movie producer who pissed off the Corleone family because the guy wouldn't cast the godson of the boss."

He smiled. It was the longest sentence he'd heard from her, aside from the nonsense about his privileged upbringing. It figured it had to do with horses.

"No, but I thought about hog-tying him while I dragged you out from between his legs."

Her egg roll stopped midway to her mouth. "Oh."

"He's not dangerous," she said, after a bite and swallow.

142

Jack sat back in his chair and folded his arms.

"No? Tell that to Win the next time you see him."

"I will," she said. "I have an idea about the cause of his colic."

"Who, Win? He's been known to suffer from a little acid reflux, but I don't think he'd call it colic."

Her face split with a sarcastic grin.

"I'm talking about Mr. Tibbles. Do you want to hear my theory or would you rather have the horse back here in a few weeks with his fourth episode in two months?"

Because he was more ticked that they couldn't find the cause of the colic than about her attempt to play vet, he said, "Please, by all means, Dr. Modine, give me your ideas."

He took it as a minor miracle that she didn't rise to the bait.

"I think it has something to do with the farm tours at Hunter Glen."

"Why?"

"Mr. Tibbles' symptoms always appear on a Thursday. They have their farm tours on Wednesdays. They rotate their three studs for the farm tours, leaving one in the barn each week to allow the tour groups to see a stallion up close. For that one day, the horse in the barn is on a different schedule, both for feeding and exercising."

He considered what she said, unwilling to fully accept the idea until he checked it out.

"How do you know all this?" he asked.

"I've been around horses all my life. I'm not—"

"Okay, settle down." He leaned forward and rested his elbows on his knees. "I meant, how do you know about the farm tours?"

She looked away. "I took the tour yesterday. I like Mr. T and I thought it'd help if I checked things out."

He studied the muted flush on her cheeks and the slight increase in her breathing. He tightened his clasped hands and fought the urge to pull her against him, to kiss the stiffness out of her. His urge had nothing to do with her desire to help Mr. Tibbles, although that was commendable. It was the mix of pride and vulnerability and fire and guts, and the damn rag on her head. It was her pink, moist lips and the fact that she disliked his wealth and upbringing and...

"Are you an alcoholic?"

"What?" Her glance narrowed with disbelief.

"Do you have a problem with alcohol?" he repeated, unable to let it go, even though sparks darted from her eyes.

To hell with the sparks. He'd committed himself, and he wanted an answer.

She opened her mouth, her indignation front and center.

"Just tell me," he said.

Her mouth made jerky, little movements like she wanted to spit. He watched her struggle before she leaped to her feet and shouted, "No!"

He dropped his head and closed his eyes when she stomped off. She was halfway out the door when she flew back to grab her boots.

"Stop," he ordered, unsurprised when she didn't.

She smacked the door frame with her exit.

He followed her out. They weren't finished, not by a long shot.

\*\*\*\*

*Asshole! Jerk! Idiot!*

She fumed all the way down the aisle, unable to stop and put on her boots because of her anger. All that mattered at this point was her need to get as far away from him as possible. He'd ruined a perfectly good conversation—even though she didn't really want to converse with him. Still, she *had* come up with a reasonable idea for Mr. T's stomach problems.

The load of ice shifted on her head as she raced through the barn, faster now when she heard him call her name, in the same self-important tone he'd used in the office. The footsteps behind her quickened and she broke into a run, the escape door only a few feet away.

She didn't make it. His hand grabbed her elbow and swung her around. Her boots thudded against his leg before she dropped them to the floor, and her ice towel dislodged, hurling cubes in every direction. Drops of cold water dribbled down the back of her top.

They stood and stared at each other.

"I believe you, dammit!"

She tried to peel his fingers from her arm, but he tightened them.

"Fine," she hissed. "Since this is the third time I've told you, you have my undying gratitude. Now, let…me…go!"

"No, not before I explain." The pain in his eyes stopped her struggle. She'd never been able to refuse anyone who showed that kind of vulnerability. The look battered her into consent, for a reason she refused to examine.

"Okay," she said. "Explain."

He released his hold on her arm.

"Put your boots on." He picked them up and handed them to her. "If you're busy with your boots, you can't run away from me."

She huffed down on a hay bale and started with her left foot.

"My dad had a drinking problem," he said.

"And I look, think, talk, act like your dad." She pointed two fingers, like a gun, at her forehead. "Oh, hey, wait. I *am* your dad!"

She stood up and held out her hand.

"Son, it's real nice to meet you after all these years," she said in a deep voice.

He didn't shake her hand, and his lips tightened. Finally, he stared her into submission, and she sat back down to attend to her feet.

"I fail to see what that has to do with your ignorant assumption that I'm an alcoholic," she mumbled as she struggled with her boot and the tightness of her jeans. She needed to rethink her country cowboy look, especially when she was, uh, agitated.

"My dad's problem makes me hyper. I've tried to develop a more chill viewpoint, but I don't quite have the hang of it yet."

She looked up at him, exasperated. "And this applies to me *how?"*

He put a hand on the back of his neck. "My ex-wife also had the problem."

It was on the tip of her tongue to say "with you as her husband, I can see why" but she didn't. She wasn't that heartless, and he sounded so honestly confused and disgusted with himself that she couldn't fight the tug of sympathy his admission triggered.

"I couldn't believe you were drinking whiskey to help with flu symptoms. It sounded like one of the lamest excuses I'd ever heard and believe me, I've heard them all."

She refused to share her financial problems with him. Telling him she hadn't had the money to purchase an eight-dollar bottle of generic pain meds was too damned humiliating. He wouldn't believe her anyway. He lived on planet bountiful, while she drifted in the galactic vapor of living paycheck to paycheck.

He crossed his arms, a gesture she now recognized.

"I'm sorry," he said, his sincerity clear. One side of his mouth inched upward and his mesmerizing dimple reappeared.

A shiver of something—fear, jitters, a passing haint—wiggled its way along her nerve endings. Her experience with men was broad enough to recognize lust in all its forms. His eyes promised far more and she fought further speculation on how it might be between them. Her nipples hardened and heat gathered between her legs, but she managed to tame her body when she pulled every bad memory of his type out for review.

She bent down to work on her jeans again and prayed he hadn't detected the reckless hunger inside her every time their eyes met. Still, her fingers refused to cooperate, unable to move the fabric even an inch up her leg.

He walked over, crouched down, and waved her hands away. When he ran his fingers under the hem of the jeans at the back of her leg, his touch turned her body into one big goosebump.

"If you didn't wear your jeans so damned tight, this wouldn't be a problem," he said, the tease in his words contradicted by the heavy tone in his voice.

"Until tonight, it wasn't…" She leaned forward to smell him but jerked back when he looked up. "…a problem."

"It's a problem for me," he said. She recognized the real meaning in his words and knew it had nothing to do with how she put on her boots or the tightness of her jeans. His intense gaze pierced the murky haze of need that was about to pull her under.

"I know," she whispered.

The air shifted around them.

"Open your legs," he said, no give in his tone.

She did what he asked without questioning why.

He moved close. The inseam of her jeans rubbed against tissues swollen with need.

"Put your arms around my neck."

His fingers dug into her thighs as she linked her arms behind his head. His gaze roamed her face, and she noticed the unsteady rise and fall of his chest. His body emanated stark urgency, but he didn't move.

He wanted her to close the gap. She eased into him until her lips hovered an inch away from his, inhaling him in with every tortured breath. He finally broke.

"You're driving me insane," he said as he brought his mouth to hers.

The kiss was unyielding like he wanted to absorb her. The excitement was one degree short of unbearable when he moaned and plunged his tongue into her mouth, wringing her out with his need. She clung to him until he flattened his palms on the stall wall behind her head, and she climbed his body.

Everything around her faded into a vast, open plain, overwhelming every last bit of her resistance. His lips dipped and coaxed, bit and slid, while she worked loose the buttons of his shirt. Her fingers sank into the warm, silky hair and hot skin on his chest and stomach. Her nails raked over his nipples, and he jerked in response.

He ripped off her top and threw it on the floor. "Christ, don't you ever wear a bra? Never mind, what am I saying."

His hands covered her breasts, and she arched against them. His thumbs flicked her nipples into rigid points, and she whispered "please, please" as he lowered his head to use his mouth.

But his mouth never made it. He reeled back and dragged her to her feet. He thrust her top toward her and she saw his fingers fumble as he tried to button his shirt.

"What's going on? I don't understand," she said, frozen in place.

"Put your top on," he ordered. He stopped, grabbed her top back, and worked it roughly over her head.

"Someone's coming. I saw the lights bounce off the window. Don't ask me how I noticed."

She turned toward the window while he helped her push her arms through her sleeves. He yanked down the hem.

"You can tuck it in yourself. I don't have the willpower to do it for you."

Stunned and confused, she unzipped her jeans while he stared at her, his smile distracted and hungry. He slipped his hands into his pockets, and she realized he hadn't recovered yet either.

"We're a sorry-looking pair." She snapped her jeans and shook her arms to redirect the circulation away from the over-sensitized areas of her body.

He reached for her but dropped his hands. "Shit, the cameras."

She began to comprehend the enormity of their actions when someone walked around the corner and called out, "Doc Carter?"

Chapter Twenty-Two

"Chris!" Jack ran an unsteady hand through his hair.

"Dr. Benson said you need some help. Told me to stop by on the off chance you'd be here."

Chris walked toward him as the kid noticed the ice cubes scattered over the floor. When his glance shifted to Cheyenne the look on Chris's face was obvious. He studied her like a puppy with his first chew toy, and Jack knew why.

Her hair fell in waves over her shoulders, her nipples stood out like headlights, and her normally pink lips had deepened to rose red in high summer. Add those signs to the off-kilter way she gazed into the distance, and Jack knew he needed to do damage control. She was *his* chew toy, he saw her first, and he didn't share.

"Chris, this is Cheyenne Modine. She's one of our attendants."

She pulled herself together, somewhat, put her hand out, and said, "Hello, Chris. Nice to meet you."

Chris gave an audible swallow and nodded in dumb silence before he wiped his hand on his jeans and shook her hand.

"Will you be training me?" he croaked.

Jack slapped him on the back and said a little too loudly, "She's new, so I'll train you myself. Let's start now."

With a firm hand on Chris's shoulder, Jack nudged

the kid back up the aisle.

"Cheyenne, you can go home. We'll take it from here," he called out. "I'll see you tomorrow."

"Now, Chris, the first rule I need to mention is to never go into a stall when you're here by yourself."

\*\*\*\*

Every rag rug in the house hung on the line, absorbing the mid-summer heat that reflected off the white frame farmhouse. Equipped with a sturdy broom, Cheyenne was more than ready to pound the shit out of them, starting with the shades-of-green oval, a goodbye present from her friends on the Res. She was certain they'd understand her need to pummel something.

Right as she reared back for her first good whack, a car horn blared from the driveway. The pop of gravel followed and signaled the slow approach of a white SUV. Cheyenne shaded her eyes, dropped her broom, and ran toward the car. Her sister-in-law waved and yoo-hooed as she struggled from the stopped vehicle. Cheyenne reached the car in time to catch a flailing arm and give Pammy the momentum to eject her bulk from the driver's seat.

"What's up, girl?" Cheyenne surveyed the back seat and found it empty. She straightened and placed her hands on her hips.

"Don't start," Pammy said. "I had to wait for Big Jeans Modine to go to work this morning before I could even get out of bed. He's been sticking to me like white on rice, breathing down my neck every time I leave the house."

She pinched Cheyenne's arm. "So you just back off. I'm gonna go nuts if I can't get out every now and then."

Pammy slammed the door and they walked to the

front porch, with Pammy's tummy leading the way.

"Where are the girls?" Cheyenne asked.

"Momma took them for a week. I'm sure they'll come back with new computer games, dirt under their fingernails, begging for ice cream every other minute."

Cheyenne automatically fit her hand under Pammy's elbow to help her up the porch steps. With like minds, they sat in the porch swing as if the movement had been choreographed. The chain on the swing creaked in response to their slow rhythm.

"Want something to drink? Iced tea, pop, juice?"

"No, hon, thanks. I'd have to pee. If I don't drink I can go five minutes between urges."

*Urges.* Cheyenne did a mental grimace and wished Pammy hadn't brought up *that* topic. She'd spent a miserable, sleepless night tossing and turning with wanton thoughts. In between, she'd been angry and humiliated at his abrupt dismissal, with equal irritation over her inability to resist him. The insurmountable obstacle between them still existed, even though he, of course, gave it no import. He'd apologized and for him, that was enough.

"Cheyenne?" Pammy touched her arm. "Where'd you go, girl?"

Cheyenne wrapped her braid around her hand and tugged to clarify the muddle in her mind, or at least rescue her from going under in a rocky river of doubt.

"Sorry. I've got a problem that's giving me fits."

She stood, unable to tolerate the lulling motion of the swing.

"What is it, sweetie? Is it, uh, related to money?"

Cheyenne blinked and turned. Pammy's face showed *uncertainty*. She wasn't sure about bringing up the subject, Cheyenne realized.

"No, I wish it were." It *was* related to money, but not in any way Pammy would understand.

Cheyenne's cell phone blipped—again.

"Is that your phone?" Pammy eyed her own shoulder bag to make sure it wasn't hers.

"Yes." She knew who it was. He'd already phoned twice—to apologize again for his boorish accusation, which wasn't his term, and to tell her the cookout was at Ben and Janie's house tonight. Her attendance was mandatory, he said.

She had two perfect excuses. She didn't know where they lived and they weren't in any online directory. Cheyenne wasn't about to call the office. She was too busy beating rugs.

Pammy's head cocked toward the front door. "The landline is ringing now. It's a man, giving you directions?"

Crap. Now she'd have to think up another excuse. Of course, if she didn't go, he'd show up later at the clinic, maybe under the pretense of watching her for signs of inebriation. Last night, after their discussion, he *seemed* to believe her, but…

Pammy patted the seat next to her.

"Come back and sit down. Tell me what's going on. I won't tell Billy, I promise."

Cheyenne plopped back onto the swing and debated the wisdom of telling anyone about Jack Carter.

"Is it something to do with that man at the steakhouse?" Pammy asked.

Cheyenne frowned at her sister-in-law.

"How'd you know about him?"

The night at the steakhouse, Cheyenne had made a

point of not saying anything about Jack Carter, especially to Billy.

It was Pammy's turn to play with her hair. "I think Billy might have said something, off-hand, of course. He said you spent so much time in the restroom you smelled like disinfectant the rest of the evening. Thought you might be avoiding that man—a vet, according to Billy."

Cheyenne got back on her feet.

"I wasn't avoiding him! Damn Billy. What else did he say?"

A knowing smile spread across Pammy's face.

"You like this man, don't ya?

"No, yes, no…" Cheyenne paced as she talked. "I took a part-time job at his clinic a few weeks back. He's my employer, that's all."

Even as she spoke, she recognized her non-truth. She could make a case for lust, but…

Dinah and Little D romped in the pasture as Cheyenne sat on the porch railing. Dudley dozed in the shade of the barn while his tail circled in lazy arcs to shoo away flies. As usual, the scene calmed the rough edges of her thoughts.

"Pammy, did Billy ever tell you about Daddy taking a job in the university maintenance department?"

"Yes, why? What's that got to do with the vet?"

*Nothing. Everything.*

"Did Billy tell you why Daddy took the job?"

"Not really. Billy just thought he wanted to see what it was like to have regular hours, a steady paycheck, and health insurance."

Cheyenne shook her head. "Daddy took the job because he wanted to send me to Atlanta, to a private high school, and the bank turned him down for a loan because he had no credit rating."

"That's when you lived with your aunt Sally," Pammy said. "Billy told me Walker caught you skinny-dipping in the farm pond one summer night and thought you needed some female guidance in your life. I always wondered if that was the whole story, though. Knowing your Daddy, and his laid-back attitude, I didn't think the punishment exactly fit the crime."

"Billy only told you half of it." Cheyenne smiled at the recollection. "J.C. was skinny dipping with me and we'd just emptied a blender of daiquiris, with rum we borrowed from Daddy's cabinet. I was fourteen, and J.C. was interested even then. Of course, I made the daiquiris and dared J.C. to strip and swim with me, which I told Daddy later so he didn't hold anything against J.C."

"You're giving me fuel to pester J.C., you know." Pammy chuckled.

"It'll take more than a lewd memory to get a rise out of that man," Cheyenne said.

"Damn, don't I know it," Pammy said. "What other motivation did Walker have for sending you south?"

"Well, Aunt Sally had no children, and we got along really well," she said, unable to voice some of the more unpleasant memories. "He bought Dinah for me to soften the blow. I trained her in dressage during my spare time."

She'd had a lot of spare time. Most of the other girls at the school were clique-ish and socialized with their own. Of course, Cheyenne's pride didn't allow her to make many friends, which made her realize later that part of the blame fell on her.

"Was it hard for you?" The note of sympathy in Pammy's voice made Cheyenne shift position.

"Aunt Sally was good to me. I had Dinah. But I

missed Daddy and Billy, especially the first year. Mostly, I hated to think about Daddy working at a job he didn't really like to give me what he said I needed."

Cheyenne paused again. Pammy didn't prod her to finish.

"He always said I needed more than he and Billy. He made it sound—at least I took it this way—as if he was thinking of my mother, not me." Cheyenne stood up and brushed the back of her jeans from habit. "I'd have been happier here."

She threw up her hands. "I guess I was hard to figure out because back then, maybe because I never had a mother, I wanted to stay with the family I did have. Daddy hated the university job, and well, I hated that he did it for me out of some oddly confused logic."

"Are you sure?" Pammy asked.

"Am I sure about what?" Cheyenne looked at her sister-in-law and noticed her shrewd assessment.

"Are you sure he didn't know you and that you didn't need more?" Pammy stopped the swing. "You came back from Atlanta and married J.C. within a year. Then you divorced a year later and started college. When you got your degree, you left for South Dakota. Now you're back to start a business with horses, just like your daddy."

Pammy hesitated as if she thought she might be on dangerous ground.

"Go on." Cheyenne didn't know if she wanted to hear more but she was too proud to cave to her fear.

Her sister-in-law looked at the porch floor and avoided Cheyenne's gaze.

"I'm not sure you're the type to be in business for yourself," Pammy said and glanced up. "Look at Billy.

157

He's as happy as a pig in mud, hauling horses from way up north to way down south, working on the truck engines to keep them in good running order, having J.C. as his partner, even doing the damn books. He loves it, every last tedious detail of running his own business, just like your daddy. Modine even whistles when he's doing his taxes."

Her eyes challenged Cheyenne but not in a bad way.

"I don't see much enjoyment in you. Yes, you love horses and riding, and kids, but you teach only five lessons a week. You don't want to spend any money on advertising, you built a much larger riding arena than you can afford, and you hired John-Michael because you have too many horses to take care of by yourself. Do you want me to go on?"

Cheyenne was stunned into silence. She wasn't sure how this conversation had taken such an abrupt turn and questioned if Pammy's hormones were to blame.

"I do love horses and riding, and being back here in Lexington. I gave a dressage workshop at the Horse Park and I'm participating in the charity polo match to advertise my business. You can tell Billy that, by the way. I built a large arena with the goal of growing into it, instead of having to add on in a few years. I'm just as capable of running a business as Daddy and Billy…"

Pammy put her hand up. "I didn't say you weren't capable."

"Well, then, what are you saying? I don't understand your point."

"You're not listening to me," Pammy interrupted with irritating calm. "I really don't see you being happy in your own business, and your personality has something to do with that. You're more tightly wired than Billy and your Daddy, which means you have a harder time adjusting to changes that come with being self-employed. You're too proud to ask for help when you need it, especially when it comes to managing money…"

"I manage my money just fine."

Cheyenne looked back out at the farm, afraid to see the compassion and understanding on Pammy's face.

"Whatever happened to your dream of trying out for the Olympic equestrian team?"

Cheyenne burst out laughing.

"*That* was a fantasy, not to mention totally stupid," Cheyenne said. "People from our side of the tracks can't afford to indulge in those kinds of dreams. It takes lots of money, money I certainly don't have."

People like Jack Carter rode in the Olympics, not people like her. She wasn't about to tell Pammy how the old Olympic mare at the clinic had reignited her visions. Just the thought of it hurt too much.

"Lyn once offered to finance your way to the U.S. equestrian trials."

"No! What is it with everybody all of a sudden? I can't go a day without someone suggesting I take money from this or that person. Am I incompetent and unable to support myself in the eyes of my friends and family? I mean, really, what is going on?"

Pammy stood with clumsy grace. She wasn't the least bit intimidated when she spoke again.

"I need to go. Billy comes home for lunch and if I'm not there he'll put out a BOLO."

She waited until Cheyenne looked at her.

"It's up to you what you do with your life. Some people get more satisfaction from knowing they can make a choice than from what they actually do when the decision is made. That *might* be you. I don't know. Billy and I just want to see you happy." Her gaze swept over the farm property. "You know, this farm is worth a lot of money."

Cheyenne gasped, unable to accept Pammy's unspoken suggestion. Daddy had left her this farm. It broke her heart to even think about selling it.

"Just consider the possibilities, Shy. What would make you happy."

Pammy reached over for a hug and Cheyenne hugged her back. She didn't watch her sister-in-law walk to the car. When she entered the house the phone rang, again.

Chapter Twenty-Three

If she didn't answer this time, he'd figure out how to carve fifteen minutes from a crammed schedule and stop by her place.

"Hello," she snapped.

"And a pleasant good morning to you, sunshine." When she didn't reply, he asked, "Did you get my messages?"

She sighed. "Yes."

"So you'll be there?"

She sighed again, louder. "What will you do if I don't come?"

*Combust. She'd better not have a date.*

"Why? Do you have other plans?" *If she had a date, he'd have to put a contract out on the guy.*

"No, but can I bring a guest?"

Okay. She was nervy enough to bring the poor idiot into the enemy camp. Of course, that made it easier for him. He'd blow the competition away himself and forego the hitman.

*Just where did she get off asking to bring a guest after what happened last night?*

"I noticed you had a guest last week—Ellen, was it? And Janie's husband was there, as well as the significant others of a few other employees."

Her voice dared him to object.

"Her name is Elaine." He cleared his throat and

added, "Sure, bring someone."

*But it's not going to be pretty.*

"Okay, good. I'll see you there around seven?"

"Yeah, seven. Don't forget your bathing suit. They have a pool and everyone will be swimming." At least he'd see some skin while he plotted her "guest's" demise.

When she hung up, it occurred to him this wasn't exactly the plan he had in mind.

****

Jack rushed home to shower, shave and let the dogs out before going to Ben and Janie's, only to discover fate conspired against him. He cut himself shaving. Buck dug a hole under the fence and was halfway to freedom when Jack caught him. Thoughts of Cheyenne and her guest hadn't left his mind all day and he was irritable and aroused at the same time. By the time he got to the cookout, it was half past seven and he had to park several cars down the street.

Gray's beige SUV was parked in the drive. The windows were smeared from his four kid's hands and his dog's tongues. Jack smiled and tried to relax.

The front door was locked so he rang the bell. Lea answered and plastered herself against his bare legs. She giggled when he picked her up and threw her in the air, then placed her on his shoulders while he walked through the house. Ben's head was buried in the refrigerator when Jack entered the kitchen.

"Daddy, Uncle Jack swinged me," Lea said, her hands grasping Jack's ears for balance.

Jack gave her a half-hearted toss before he placed her back on her feet.

"Is she here?" he asked his brother, who idly

munched on a carrot.

"Who?"

"Uncle Jack, swing me again." Lea pranced at his feet.

"Honey, go find Mommy." Ben walked his daughter to the patio door. "Uncle Jack and I are talking."

She left with a pout and Jack strolled to the window.

"You know who. Did she bring a date?"

*Crunch.* "Uh, yeah, they arrived around seven. Where have you been?" Ben handed Jack a napkin. "Here, you're bleeding…your chin."

Jack grabbed the napkin and pressed it to the spot on his chin.

"I got stuck at my last call, then I went home to shave and shower. The damn dog decided he wanted to roam and dug this huge hole under the fence…I don't want to discuss this. She really brought a date? Where in the hell are they?"

Jack scanned the entire backyard. He searched the small groups of people clustered here and there, but he didn't see her anywhere.

Ben pointed with his carrot. "See where Gray, Win, Mike, and Kathy's husband, Barry, are, over there near the pool, ostensibly playing cards?"

Jack shifted his gaze. "Yeah, I see them."

"Now look in the pool. Oh, wait, I stand corrected. Focus on the pool ladder. She's coming up. Jesus," he mumbled in mid-crunch.

Jack flattened his palm against the window. "Damn," he whispered as his breath fogged the glass.

Water streamed down her body as she emerged from the pool. They both stared while she stood at the pool's edge and towel-dried her hair.

"Wet agrees with her, don't you think?" Ben said.

Jack inhaled a tortured breath. "Hell, and I'm the one who told her to bring a bathing suit. What is wrong with me?"

Ben started to chuckle. "Look at Mike. I can see his hands shake from here. He'll never be able to deal."

*To hell with Mike.*

"What kind of fabric do you think that is?" Ben rambled on.

"Clingy." Jack groaned when she bent over to sort through a canvas bag that leaned against a chair.

Ben barked a laugh. "Will you look at that? Mike just sprayed the cards everywhere."

Jack swore as he moved to the door. "I've had enough." He stopped and turned, his hand on the doorknob. "Who came with her?"

Ben smiled.

"Your eyebrows are growing together."

"Ben," Jack warned. He knew he acted like a jealous jerk, but he'd spent the entire afternoon imagining her with some other guy. "Who came with her?"

"Lyn Tyree."

****

Cheyenne found the elastic band and put her hair in a ponytail. It was an automatic gesture. Everything she'd done after Pammy left that morning had been automatic. When she wasn't thinking about their conversation, her attraction to Jack Carter and the implications of that situation threatened her sanity. She wanted to enter Ostriche-ville and stick her head in the ground.

She stepped back to the side of the pool, sat down, and dangled her legs in the water. The air temperature hovered in the upper eighties. The smell of grilling meat filled the air and made her mouth water. Janie Carter drifted up in a floating Flamingo chair, with a drink mug in the armrest hole. The mug was one of those stainless tumblers with the blue and gold Kentucky Wildcat on the side.

"Do you bleed blue?" Cheyenne asked when Janie floated closer.

"No, but Ben and Jack do." She lifted the mug. "One of Jack's clients gave him a whole box of these, along with season tickets."

Cheyenne shook her head. It was on the tip of her tongue to comment about the impossibility of someone giving away tickets for Kentucky basketball when they were valuable enough to write into wills, but she didn't want to offend her hosts. Janie Carter seemed nice, even if she was rich.

"I know it's odd someone would give them away, but Jack has saved many a client's valuable horseflesh from certain death, and they're grateful."

"Yes, he seems very, uh, competent."

"He's better than competent." Janie's grin widened. "Of course, I'm a little prejudice."

Janie shaded her eyes as she looked toward Cheyenne. "He's attracted to you."

Cheyenne's feet stopped stirring the water. *And I'm attracted back.*

"We're very different."

"Does that mean you reciprocate the interest?"

"It means I'm uncertain the interest can survive if there's no common ground."

"That's fair, I guess," Janie said when her attention snagged on her two boys running at the other end of the pool. "Boys, walk," she ordered.

Ben's stern repetition of the order helped slow the boys down.

"I see more similarities than differences." Janie refocused on Cheyenne. "Although I'm not sure differences matter when it hits."

Her expression was enigmatic. Cheyenne was about to ask what she meant when Janie paddled closer and whispered, "He's here."

Cheyenne's gaze followed Janie's and she saw him immediately. He stood under a tree with Lyn, but his eyes were on her. His gaze was so warm she turned back and slipped into the pool. It was either that or let everyone see the evidence of her "interest" as it poked through the top of her bathing suit.

Janie had drifted back to the center of the pool, which left Cheyenne alone to gather her unruly reactions and stuff them into a deep, dark place. The splashes behind her caught her attention, and she grabbed onto it like a lifeline.

It was Lea Carter in her water wings. The little girl reached out for support, and Cheyenne lifted the child up without hesitation.

"Hello," Lea said. "Remember me? I'm Lea."

"Sure I remember you," Cheyenne said as they floated away from the side of the pool. Lea told Cheyenne that Ben and Bryan, her brothers, had squirted water at Lea earlier which made her cry. Cheyenne said brothers often did that to sisters but assured Lea when she was older, she'd be able to stop them.

"You're pretty." Lea locked her little arms around Cheyenne's neck as if they were BFF's. "Your eyes look like stars."

Cheyenne fluttered her eyelashes, which made the

child laugh as they floated into deeper water.

"Mommy doesn't let me go this far unless I'm with an adult. Are you an adult?"

"I'm an adult," Cheyenne assured her. "I won't let you go."

They drifted through the cool water and spun around like they were the only two in the pool. Eventually, they worked their way back to the shallow end, and Lea went to play a game of noodles with some other kids.

Cheyenne pushed off into the deep end again and stroked to the other side. Her fingers touched the rough ledge before she broke the surface. When she opened her eyes, Jack Carter stood above her.

"I see you're working a spell on my niece, too."

He bent down and put a hand in the water as if testing the temperature.

"Too?"

"You know what I mean."

Unfortunately, she did. The humid evening air took on a new heaviness as they studied each other. She was very much afraid her unspoken thoughts were as transparent as his.

"I sent Mr. Tibbles home today. I talked with the farm manager about either leaving the horse out of the rotation for the farm tours or keeping the feeding and exercise schedule the same. He said he'd give it a try."

She nodded. His acceptance of her reasoning pleased her, but she tried not to show it.

"I don't know whether to be happy or sad about Mr. T not coming back. I had this secret fantasy…" She stopped, and shook her head. It wasn't a good idea to share her fantasies with Jack Carter, even one as dry as her desire to ride Mr. Tibbles.

"Go on. Tell me." He sat down and slipped his feet into the water. His muscular thigh was a mere inch from her right elbow where it rested on the pool edge. She had the ridiculous urge to touch the silky hair on his legs, then sink down and come up between them, right where he had his hands loosely clasped.

"Go ahead," he said, his voice husky.

"What?" she asked. He'd followed the direction of her gaze. Stark desire now hardened his features.

"Your fantasies?" he said.

She pried her tongue from the roof of her mouth. "I, uh, wondered what it would be like to ride…" She forgot the horse's name. If he asked, she feared her own name might prove equally as elusive.

"Mr. Tibbles?" He eased his shirt off.

Cheyenne thought her mouth had been dry before. Last night, the dim light of the barn had given her an idea of his fitness. Seeing him here with nothing on but his swimming trunks gave her a whole new definition of fit. The hair on his chest and stomach grew in a T pattern and thinned as it disappeared into the elastic band of his trunks. His nipples were flat and the color of milk chocolate. She tried to look away when he sank into the water next to her.

"Thank God for the cool water," he said, just loud enough for her to hear. "If you don't stop looking at me with that 'eat me' message in your eyes, we're both going to end up in disgrace."

"I don't know what you're talking about." She fixed her gaze on the lounge chair in front of her and willed her heartbeat to slow.

"Yeah, well, then, you're delusional."

"Hey, you two." Janie floated up behind them.

Cheyenne turned in a flash. She was about to drown and it had nothing to do with water.

"Janie," they both said at the same time.

Janie's innocent yet perceptive gaze moved from Jack to Cheyenne.

"Is this a private conversation?" she asked.

"No, of course not," Jack said. "You're always welcome."

"Oh, good. Just wanted to let you know we'll be eating in about ten minutes. You two might want to think about grabbing some chairs in case there's a particular place you'd like to sit."

She looked at Jack as she drifted away. "Jack, Mary called. She wants to stop by in about an hour, for a few minutes—to talk to you."

He raised his eyebrows when Janie left.

"Mary's mother is okay, right?" Cheyenne asked.

"Yeah, you heard? I meant to fill you in last night but somehow got distracted."

She studied the way his body looked underwater when his trunks billowed up to expose the tops of his thighs.

He gave a pained curse before his hand hooked around the back of her neck. His lips came down on hers soft and sudden. For a brief second, she gave in to the need as their bodies floated together. His tongue slid over hers and he deepened the kiss. When she remembered where they were, she panicked and broke away.

Her dazed look was reflected in his eyes and expression. Everyone started to clap and whoop as if the home team had just scored a touchdown.

Cheyenne was mortified. It was either submerge or leave the pool altogether. She had a quick view of Jack's face as she hoisted herself up and stood. His eyes were closed in distinct annoyance.

She, on the other hand, wasn't able to tough it out. She wrapped a towel around her and escaped to the house as quickly as pride allowed. Lyn could find his own way home. The Cheyenne train was leaving the station ahead of schedule and wasn't about to stop at this crossing ever again.

Chapter Twenty-Four

Her wet footprints led to an upstairs bathroom.

"Cheyenne." Jack knocked softly on the door. "C'mon out."

He heard a muffled but definite "no" over the sounds of snaps and zippers.

"I'm sorry I embarrassed you out there. I don't know what happened."

He damn well knew what happened, but he refused to admit it to anyone but himself. He was seriously in lust and had been since five minutes after midnight on the night they met. Otherwise, how did he explain his totally uncharacteristic behavior? He didn't maul women in public and hated even the thought of anyone seeing him do it. He also kept his personal life private. Hell, at sixteen, when all his friends bragged about their sexual conquests, he'd stubbornly refused to join in. The only person he shared his woman experiences with was his brother and that only lately, in a very sanitized way.

He knocked again. "Cheyenne?"

"Go away."

Her tone was defeated and remote. If he made her angry, she'd feel better. The only problem with that method was she became a live wire when angered. Unpredictable, scary, fun, and exciting as hell.

He'd make her angry.

"Chicken," he taunted.

The door opened so fast he fell forward against her. She pushed him away and stepped around him before he found his balance.

He caught her in two strides. "I'm not going to apologize again."

"Fine."

"It's almost time to eat."

"So?" She turned the corner and headed for the stairs.

"Lea was asking about you a minute ago. She wants you to sit next to her."

*Then I'll sit on the other side.*

"Tell Lea I had an emergency and had to leave."

He stopped. "What about Lyn? He came with you, didn't he?"

She kept right on walking and was almost to the stairs when he called out, "You can't leave now. Everyone's expecting you."

She whirled around. "Well, I wouldn't want to deprive them of the pleasure of whispering and pointing and smirking, now would I? Jeez, I'm so cruel."

"They might whisper but they wouldn't smirk and point. They're too well-bred."

Oh, man, his ass was trash now. She screwed up her mouth and put a hand on her hip as she advanced.

"Meaning what?"

There was something here he needed to pay attention to, but his temper got the best of him. He hated it when his words were twisted into something he hadn't meant. He didn't talk in riddles; there was no room for misunderstanding. He didn't play those games.

"You missed my point." He planted his feet in the middle of the hallway to keep himself from moving nearer. He didn't need more distraction. "Did you have an arrested childhood or something? I was merely expressing what I know about my friends and family. If you leave, it would be a slap in the face of their hospitality, as well as an indication of a serious lack of manners and a poor upbringing."

She stalked toward him with murder in her eyes. "You've already established not everyone had the same kind of cushiony childhood you had! That doesn't mean the rest of us were raised in a barn!"

He dragged a hand through his hair. "I didn't mean that!"

"Jack!" Janie's voice interrupted from a room downstairs. "Mary's here. She'd like to see you."

His gaze didn't break from Cheyenne's when he answered. "Tell her I'll be there in a minute."

Jack studied the rigid set of her shoulders and debated how to make her stay. "You and I aren't through. Right now, I need to talk to Mary. I'll see you outside."

He didn't wait for her reaction. It hadn't been a command. Still, as prickly as she was, she might read it all wrong and leave anyway.

Her intent to twist his words was a puzzle and funny at the same time. She had turned into one of those gifts within a gift. Every time he opened one box, another one hid inside.

He wondered if he would ever get to the last box but figured he was just the man for the job. She'd become the adventure of a lifetime, and he loved nothing better than a challenge.

\*\*\*\*

Cheyenne hovered in the hallway outside the kitchen and listened to Jack and Mary's private conversation. She was on her way out, to tell Lyn she was leaving, but something about the tone of their discussion stopped her.

"How can we ever repay you, Dr. Carter?" Mary said, her voice tearful.

"There's nothing to repay, Mary. Win, Mike, and I made the decision together and we're happy to do it for your family."

Mary sniffed. "No offense to the other docs, but I know it was your idea. I was your helper elf at the Women's Shelter last Christmas, remember? I've observed your charitable tendencies up close."

Cheyenne peered around the corner as Carter cleared his throat.

"Just let us know if you need any other help," he said. "After your Mom gets here, I mean. I understand it will be a long recuperation, so don't hesitate to ask."

The look on Mary's face said it all. Vulnerable, filled with equal parts hope and fear, the girl nodded and smiled. Cheyenne had to blink back tears as she watched them exit the patio doors. Compared to Mary's situation, she now viewed the pool incident from an entirely different perspective.

She needed to express her sympathy to Mary. They didn't know each other well, but Cheyenne thought she might find some way to help the girl through the trauma.

When she walked outside, Cheyenne was relieved to find everyone gathered around Mary. She joined Lyn at the table set for dinner. He sipped a drink and smiled up at her.

"Forgive me for not standing, my dear. This old back isn't working very well today."

She waved off his concern and sat down next to him.

"That's the young lady whose mother suffered the automobile accident, I understand."

She nodded as she poured herself an iced tea. "Yes, it was bad. Mary's mother wasn't expected to live." She thought about what she had overheard in the kitchen. "I think her mother is coming here to Lexington for therapy."

"The UK Hospital has a decent reputation in the area of orthopedics." Lyn's hand moved to his back. "I've made some use of their expertise myself. Perhaps the family decided to bring her here for that reason?"

"Perhaps." The group broke up and walked toward the table. Jack's gaze found her but she wasn't able to read what she saw.

She refused to worry about the few curious stares directed her way. Mary walked over and thanked Cheyenne for covering her hours at the clinic.

Cheyenne squeezed Mary's hand. "Let me know if I can do anything else."

Mary's gaze drifted to Jack Carter. "I will but I think it'll be fine. It seems everything's been thought of already."

The food came to the table then and for several minutes the talk and laughter revolved around the mammoth size of the hamburgers, and whose idea it was to serve baby wieners in hot sauce from a fondue pot. It seems the vets thought the wieners were too weird for a down-home backyard barbecue.

"What I want to know is how in the hell you find buns to fit these things," Jack commented. He popped one into his mouth and smiled at Cheyenne from across the table as he chewed. She shook her head and tried to concentrate on her baked beans. This gathering was similar to one of Billy and Pammy's summer cookouts. If they started playing cornhole, she was in trouble since the line between the have and have-nots had already begun to blur.

Cheyenne knew Carter watched her even when she didn't look at him. Her irritation heightened when she realized she wanted to look at him, but it wasn't possible without everyone's notice. She gazed at her plate to find a bean smiley face in her potato salad.

"Lyn, what kind of food will you be serving at the after-match dinner?" Jack asked. "None of this mini hot dog stuff, I hope."

Cheyenne's nervous system flipped into overdrive. How much detail was Lyn willing to give about the polo match?

"So you'll be attending the meal afterward?" Lyn drawled.

"Uh, oh, he's got you there, Jack." Janie laughed.

When Jack frowned, Cheyenne wondered what was going on.

"Tell me you'll roast a pig or grill some ribs and I promise I'll stay to eat," Jack said.

"Good enough," Lyndon replied, delight evident in his expression. "I can even guarantee you won't be cornered by a certain council member this year. You know, the one with the bootlicking demeanor who can't understand why you don't want to join the political fray and suffer beside him in the city's governmental affairs."

Jack grimaced before he leaned back in his chair and studied Lyn.

"How did you manage that?" Jack asked.

"The gentleman in question is, unfortunately, out of town on business when the match is scheduled."

Jack laughed at Lyn's tone of regret.

"Of course, I chose the date upon learning of the man's scheduling difficulty," Lyn mumbled to Cheyenne, and she had to fight a smile.

Her smile disappeared with Jack's next question.

"Lyn, when will we know who the other team is? I don't quite remember this much secrecy in previous years."

"Worried, Jackson?" Lyn cast a sidelong glance across the table at Jack, Win, and Mike.

"We've managed to beat any team you've brought in, what, six of the last eight years?" Win remarked. "I doubt we need to worry unless it's the British crew again. They've given us a run for our money in a few games, especially when they play, uh, what's his name again?"

Win looked at Mike for an answer.

"Spike? Brute? Killer?" Mike shrugged his shoulders. "Strong, silent type with the broken nose."

"Y'all are thinking of 'Crush' McVey," Lyndon said, the playful glint back in his eyes.

"So, are the Brits the team we're playing against, Lyn?" Jack asked.

Cheyenne recognized Lyn's ploy and doubted Jack would be able to outfox the fox.

"I didn't say that, my friend. I was merely trying to help young Mike out with a name."

Cheyenne debated whether she might introduce a topic equally as interesting to Lyn. He'd promised her anonymity, but he wasn't above throwing out tidbits of enticement.

She froze at his next words.

"I can only tell you there will be a woman on the opposing team."

Everyone started to talk at once. Janie was excited, Win laughed, and Mike commented on a remarkable British family with three excellent female polo players.

Cheyenne waited for Jack's reaction and knew it wasn't going to be good.

Lea was in his lap and he covered her ears with his big hands.

"Dammit, Lyn, you old devil. You're fricking nuts if you think I'm playing against a woman!"

## Chapter Twenty-Five

Lyn's chuckles filled the cab when they left an hour later.

"I believe I've stirred up a hornet's nest," he said as he leaned back against the truck seat.

"Why do I get the feeling that was your intention?"

Cheyenne maneuvered the truck into the Friday night traffic near campus. Even in the middle of summer, with the student population one-third its normal size, the streets were alive with energy.

"All this potential," Lyndon said absently before his gaze returned to her. "It *was* my intention. I admit I had a premonition Jackson would react the way he did. He has something of his daddy in him. You know, an old-fashioned gallantry toward women."

"Seemed like sexist and chauvinistic to me."

She wanted to add something about Carter's caveman persona, but she didn't, which confused her. She wouldn't have hesitated two weeks ago.

"No, Jackson is neither of those things," Lyn said. "I really think he believes women shouldn't participate in arenas where their opponents are physically stronger, and therefore capable of inflicting the greater injury."

"That's all fine, Lyn, but what if a woman wants to participate, in spite of the physical disparities? It's her right to make the decision herself."

"I agree," Lyn said, without elaboration.

"Besides, this is polo. It's not totally a game of strength. A player has to rely on the agility of the horse, the accuracy of her shots, riding skill, and a whole host of other abilities which have nothing to do with how hard her muscles are. I hear Carter's played the game long enough to know those things."

"I agree again," Lyndon said. "You're a might vehement, my dear. Why didn't you join the discussion at the cookout? I've never known you to hold back on topics you feel this strongly about."

Cheyenne didn't answer. The truth was she didn't want any more attention after the pool debacle, so she'd kept her mouth shut. Carter was so arrogant in some of his opinions, a trait she attributed, once again, to his class.

On the other hand, she had begun to see other aspects of his personality, especially his charitable tendencies. He volunteered at the Bourbon County clinic, attended events in support of good causes, and was helping Mary's mother, in some way.

"Could your silence at the cookout be in any way related to the embrace between you and Jackson in the pool?"

She sighed but said nothing.

"I noticed that Jack tried to get your attention as we left," Lyn said. "I think he wanted to talk to you, but was unable to extricate himself from the ongoing conversation about the match."

Cheyenne's laugh came out a little too high to sound genuine, and even she noticed it.

"Perhaps you chose that moment to leave because he was tied up," he speculated. "We were moving so fast, my cane tip smoked as we walked down the sidewalk."

She stayed silent when Lyn put a gentle hand on her shoulder.

"You have feelings for Jack Carter, and it appears he feels the same. I'm happy for you, my dear."

Cheyenne pinched the bridge of her nose.

"It doesn't matter if we're attracted to each other, Lyn. We're too different and you know it as well as I do."

"Nonsense! I know nothing of the sort." He thumped his cane on the truck floor for emphasis. "Since your daddy's not here, I hope you'll permit me to offer advice in his place. You'll not do yourself or your daddy's memory any good by continuing to view the upper class here in Lexington as your enemy. It's a disservice to all those individuals among them who are worth knowing, such as Jack Carter. Why, I can even argue for myself in that regard."

"Uncle Lyn! I would never consider you one of *them.*"

"And why not?" he said. "The last time I looked I was accumulating wealth at the speed of light."

Her grip tightened on the steering wheel.

"It's different with you, Lyn. You came from poor beginnings just like we did. You worked hard to get where you are, and you've never forgotten where you came from. Carter had everything given to him and don't try to tell me otherwise."

She heard his "hmphh" as she turned into the drive which led to his house. Sharp regret followed her all the way down. She needed Lyn's approval almost as much as she'd needed her daddy's, and she hated even slight disagreements between them. When she pulled up to the front door, she was ready to apologize for her outburst, but he spoke first.

"Cheyenne, perhaps I'm meddling in something which is none of my business. I apologize." He turned to her. "I would like to ask one small favor, however. Can you at least promise you'll consider what I'm about to propose?"

She nodded, saddened by the possibility she had damaged their friendship.

"Try to give Jackson the benefit of the doubt. Allow for the possibility he might be different from the person you think he is." He put his hand on the door handle. "Please?"

She took a moment to answer and when she did, her words were far quieter than her discordant thoughts.

"I promise I'll consider it."

"He plays polo every Sunday afternoon at Jeb Daily's farm, out near Paris. If you stop by and watch, you'll gain some insight into his playing abilities, and get to know him better."

She gave the idea serious consideration because Lyn, and his advice, were too important to her. "Maybe."

He patted her shoulder and left the truck. As usual, when she drove away, he stood and waved until she was out of sight. Tonight, when she looked in the rearview mirror, she saw his reflection through a haze of tears.

****

Her truck came to a stop outside the clinic five minutes early.

"Chris, you can take off. Cheyenne's here." Jack stood at the front office window and watched her climb from her truck.

"Are you sure, Doc?" Chris said. "I don't mind staying until she gets settled."

Jack grinned and hitched a thumb over his shoulder. "Your butt. The door. Go."

Once outside, Chris paused at Cheyenne's truck where they shared a few words and parted after a minute. Jack didn't blame the kid. He liked to look at her, too.

"Hi," he said when she walked in.

She circled around him and placed her purse and small lunch bag on the reception desk.

He wasn't happy when she didn't meet his gaze or with the subdued tone of her "hey." Was she still angry from their earlier go-round? No, he'd sat across from her at dinner and she hadn't shown any animosity then. He was beginning to read all the nuances in her expressions, and this time he detected sadness.

"You slipped away before we had a chance to talk."

She rummaged through the bag like she was fascinated by the peanut butter sandwich and yogurt cup inside. Little fuzzy curls framed her face where her hair had dried and escaped her braid. He wanted to touch her hair but now was not the time.

"Did you and the other vets settle the issue of women's rights?" she asked. "I can recommend some reading material if you feel the need for enlightenment." She looked up from her bag. "You could start with the 19th amendment, then you might try a few oldies like *The Second Sex* or *The Feminine Mystique*, or maybe even a podcast."

"And these books and such will convince me women are as strong, physically, as men, and won't get hurt in a game like polo where there's direct bodily contact?"

"Polo is not a sport of much direct bodily contact unless you're talking about horse bodies. And it's not your decision to make. A woman has as much right as a man to play polo."

"I didn't say women shouldn't play polo," he said and matched her conversational tone. "I simply said I won't play against a woman. I think it's too dangerous, and that's *my* decision."

She tilted her head to one side with a quizzical smile on her face. "Okay. Fine."

Her attention strayed back to her bag. This was a new and different approach.

"That's it? You're going to let me win a point without arguing. Some activist you are."

"Just for the record, you didn't win. And I am an activist, or feminist, whatever that means these days. Tonight, however, I'm too tired to argue a second issue with you." She picked up her bag and started to walk away. "I need to put my food in the refrigerator."

She was through the door before he blinked. He went after her because she hid something, and he needed to find out what it was.

"What's wrong?"

She closed the refrigerator door. "Nothing. I'm just tired. The farrier came today. I cleaned my house. I got very little sleep—like I said, I'm tired."

A shutter came down and she closed him out as if she'd been about to reveal too much. He wanted to bring up what was happening between them, but just when he thought she might open up, she stepped back.

"Are you busy tomorrow night?"

For someone who radiated energy, he had never seen a person go as still as she did at that moment.

"Why?" she asked.

He moved closer. She edged toward the pop

machine.

"I'm not going to touch you."

He *really* wanted to touch her.

"I know," she said, more defiant than was necessary. She *wanted* him to touch her. There was a remnant in her eyes of the look she'd given him at the pool.

He shoved his hands in his pockets. "So, are you busy?" he asked again.

"Why?"

"I'd like to see you away from work."

"You saw me tonight away from work."

*Okay, so this isn't going to be as easy as I hoped.* But then, nothing with her had been easy since they met.

"I take it you're busy."

"Well, if you needed assistance on a call, I could help."

A light dawned. For whatever reason, she didn't want to accept a date. Therefore, he'd find an appointment and take her with him, even if he had to beg one from Mike or Win. And he'd keep doing it until he overcame her resistance, or his lust imploded, and he died of arousal poisoning. At this point, he wasn't willing to place a bet on what might happen. The only thing he knew for sure was she was worth every last ounce of his effort.

"As a matter of fact, I do need your help tomorrow evening. I forgot I have an appointment." He moved away, toward the door. "I'll pick you up at seven."

Chapter Twenty-Six

Cheyenne promised Lyn to give Jack Carter a chance. She wasn't ready to date him but maybe an assist on a few calls would increase her comfort with the idea.

She just hoped he didn't try to touch her. Or smile, especially the off-kilter grin where one side of his mouth curved up and his dimple appeared. Or look at her in his uniquely brooding way, with his eyebrows meshed and his pupils dilated until his eyes turned black instead of their usual warm brown.

All she needed to do was stay at least five feet away from him, not say anything remotely funny and not look into his eyes. *Crap.* Now she knew what it was like to meet a grizzly bear on the same hiking trail.

She made her rounds through the barns, marking notes on the clipboards. Mr. Tibbles' empty stall, now clean and ready for another inhabitant, made her pause. She might take another farm tour to see him again and to make sure they really didn't put him back in the barn on tour days.

The tight muscle in her neck spasmed as she sat down at the reception desk and checked the time. She wanted to call Lyn and he didn't stay up later than eleven most nights.

She rubbed the muscle as she dialed his number.

"Am I calling too late?" she asked, reassured by the sound of his voice.

"No, no. I'll sleep when I'm ninety," he joked. "What a pleasure it is to talk to you, especially after I rudely butted into your personal affairs earlier." He paused. "I apologize again, my dear. My only motivation is your happiness."

Cheyenne put her head in her hand. "I know, Lyn. I called to apologize to *you*. We never argue and I didn't like leaving tonight feeling there was an issue between us. Please forgive me."

He laughed. "By issue, I take it you mean Jack. From now on, you handle him however you choose. I'll stay out of it."

"Actually, you may want to handle him first," she said. "I'm worried about his ridiculous attitude toward playing against a woman in the match." She stopped to search for words. "I can step aside if you can find a man to play in my place."

"Do you want to step aside?"

"No, absolutely not. He needs his, uh, he needs an attitude adjustment." She almost said comeuppance, but Lyn didn't like the word. After all, he'd asked her to give Jack the benefit of the doubt. "I'm concerned about his refusal to play, though. How will you find another team at this late date if he carries through with his threat?"

"Don't you worry, Cheyenne. I have ways of convincing even hardheaded individuals like him to do what I want. As long as you're sure you still wish to participate, I'll make sure he's your competition.

"I want to play." She *was* sure, wasn't she?

"Good. Leave it to me, then. I can be very persuasive."

When they ended their call a few minutes later, she was surprised by the remaining unsettled feelings. Lyn might convince Jack to play, but it wasn't going to be easy. And when Jack found out she was the woman on the other team, he'd know he had been manipulated.

Somehow, manipulating Jack now wasn't as comforting as it had been. She drummed her fingers on the desk and looked for a job to do. If she was busy, her thoughts might not be as bothersome.

She got no relief from the monitors which made her enter the supply room behind the office. She hadn't spent much time in this room yet, mainly because there was nothing here of interest. Shelves filled with paper products, a large locked medical cabinet with medical instruments and drugs, a copier, and an old fax machine long past its prime were the most significant items in the space. A door on the far wall was locked. She assumed it was a maintenance closet.

After trailing a finger down one unit of shelving, she made a face at the lack of dust. She straightened a few stacks of paper before deciding to go in search of other areas less tidy. She noticed the lock on the drug cabinet door dangling and snapped it closed, getting way too much satisfaction when the latch clicked. She walked out and remembered the stacks of paperwork, now organized, Janie said, in Jack's office. Maybe she'd place them in cabinets, to further clean up the room.

It wouldn't hurt to look. If she didn't find something to do, she'd be left to contemplate what was happening between her and Jack. She shuddered at the thought as she headed down the hall.

****

A phone call at midnight wasn't rude when it was made on a Friday and if the person you called went in late on Saturdays.

"What?" Ben growled.

"Are you awake?"

"I am now, sadist. I can't wait until you have kids so I can interrupt your few precious hours of sleep."

"It's only midnight and you go in late tomorrow, right?"

"So? You couldn't call earlier? You left here at nine-thirty. Where have you been?"

"I told you I was going to the clinic."

"So, what happened? I assume that's why you're calling at such a heathenish hour."

Jack shook the ice in his glass.

"Sorry, I had to take care of the hole in the backyard, so Buck didn't escape again."

"Then you didn't go to the clinic?"

"Yeah, I went. I just wanted to explain my late call."

"And? What happened with Cheyenne?"

"I struck out. She doesn't want to go out with me."

"You don't sound unhappy therefore I won't issue any words of consolation. Wait, don't tell me. You have a plan."

"Uh, yes. How'd you know?"

"Well, remember when you were eighteen, and Dad wanted you to go to Harvard, get your law degree, then join him in private practice, but you had plans to join the Navy, and have them pay for vet school? Remember when Mom and Dad tried to fix you up with Abby Randall, the belle of the 2012 debutante ball but you married Sydney? Remember when Dad wanted to get you a position at Rush and Rosen Equine Center after you graduated and you decided instead to use your trust fund from Grandpa Van Allen to set up your own clinic with Win and Mike? Remember the night we…"

"Okay, okay. You made your point. Do you want to hear my plan for Cheyenne?"

"You have me on pins and needles."

"Wiseass." Jack got up to put more ice in his tea. "She's fighting the attraction for some reason. I think I might have some ideas why."

"Maybe it's your antediluvian thoughts on women playing polo?"

"Shit, not you, too. It was bad enough that Janie and Mike and Cheyenne ganged up on me but you can't possibly agree with them."

"They ganged up because you were—pardon me for saying this—wrong," Ben said, injecting the *duh* factor. "Wait a minute. I don't remember Cheyenne saying a word at dinner. Actually, her restraint was admirable considering how *wrong* you were."

It sounded as if Ben was warming to the topic.

"I'm beginning to think you're imagining her hair-trigger temper," he added. "Both times I've been around her, she's chill to a glacial degree. You, on the other hand, have been showing your reactionary butt a lot lately."

"I am not imagining her temper. Didn't you see her stalk into the house tonight?"

"Oh, you mean after you became the succubus from the black lagoon? I had to give Bryan another lesson on the facts of life all because of your pool display."

"Bryan sees you and Janie kiss. Don't lay that guilt trip on me."

"Janie and I don't exchange tongues when we kiss in front of the kids. It damages their psyches."

Ben's point caused Jack a moment of worry.

"Lea didn't see us, did she?"

Ben laughed.

"Lea's too young to notice. Bryan was the one with the confusion. He wanted to know if Uncle Jack and Cheyenne made a baby."

Jack choked on his drink. In between coughs, he managed to gasp "hang on" before he left the phone. It took him at least a minute to clear his throat. "I don't believe you," he said, once he came back on the line.

"I swear to God on a stack of bibles, his exact words were 'Sean Edwards said his sister knew a girl who got a baby in her stomach when she was in a pool. Were Uncle Jack and Cheyenne making a baby'?"

"Who's Sean Edwards?" Jack asked.

"He rides the bus with Bryan. He's a god-like sixth grader."

"I told you not to send those kids to public school. If they went to a private school, they wouldn't have to ride the bus."

Ben started laughing. "Jack, did you hear what you just said?"

"Christ, I sounded just like Dad."

They both laughed.

"Don't tell Dad," Jack said. "And, by the way, you and Janie are doing a good job with your kids." He stopped to clear his throat, again. "Cheyenne has a problem with our wealth—the way we were raised. She thinks because we were surrounded by money we're arrogant and condescending."

"Hmm, then I'd say you have a problem as well."

"What do you mean? I don't condescend." Jack insisted. "What am I supposed to do? Give away all my money, renounce my family, reinvent myself into a down-home guy so she'll accept me?"

"I notice you didn't deny your arrogance."

"I'm not arrogant. I'm confident. There's a difference."

"Perhaps," Ben said. "When I said you have a problem, I meant her perception of you. I'm not sure you'll be able to change her mind if her feelings are deep-seated and long-standing. The only way you have a chance is to get her to see you as an individual and not as just a member of the wealthy class."

"Yeah, that's pretty much my conclusion, too."

"So, what's the plan?"

"You mean beyond the usual Jack Carter charm?"

"That'll get you halfway to first base."

"Your optimism warms me."

Buck jumped into Jack's lap, and he bobbled the phone.

"Hold on. Buck needs human interaction." Jack adjusted his position so the dog was half on the couch with his furry legs stretched over Jack's legs.

"Why don't you introduce Cheyenne to your dogs? I haven't yet met a woman able to resist Buck."

"You think I should? I had a few other things in mind but I'll put it on the list. I'm going to take her on calls with me. Since Mary isn't able to work for a few weeks yet, I, uh, well, I asked Cheyenne if she could help out if we needed an assist."

"Devious. I assume you made it seem as if Mary rode along on calls in the past?"

"Yeah."

"Sounds like a plan. Anything else Janie and I can do?"

"No, I can handle it. The barbecue at your place tonight was a big help. Thanks."

"No worries."

Ben sounded like he was falling asleep so Jack shortened his next comment.

"One other thing. Although it kills me to say it, I changed my mind about the folder. I appreciate your effort."

Ben responded with a snore.

Chapter Twenty-Seven

Jack managed to scrounge two appointments from Win for Saturday evening. Luckily, they were almost twenty miles apart, which gave him and Cheyenne time to talk while they traveled. When he pulled into her drive at six-thirty, she must have been waiting. She walked out the door as he rolled to a stop.

He watched her stride down the sidewalk wearing the same thing she always wore—a white sleeveless cotton top, faded jeans, and boots. Except for the bathing suit and breeches—and the flannel nightgown but he didn't count that—he'd seen her in nothing else. Not that she didn't look amazing in just about everything, because she did, especially the white top with no bra. But he wanted to see her in a dress, or the black thing he discovered in her drawer. Then there were the silk stockings with the lacy, elastic tops. Where had those come from? They weren't current fashion, but he'd give just about anything to see them on her sleek, upper thighs.

"Hi," she said as she slipped into the passenger seat.

He braced himself for the scent. A second later it settled over him—fresh, flowery, her—just like he remembered.

Maybe this wasn't such a good plan. Earlier, he thought he had a grip on his urges, but it was possible he didn't. Otherwise, he might be able to breathe, talk, and look away, right?

"Hi." He swallowed and tried to shift into reverse. The truck lurched backward. "Sorry."

He turned to watch the driveway as he backed up. Thank God he wouldn't have to reverse all the way to the road. His driving skills had deserted him.

"I have the same problem," she said.

"You do?" He eased up on the accelerator.

"My truck idles fast in hot weather, too. It wants to drive itself at times."

"Oh, okay." His vision of them in her bed—naked—disappeared. Apparently, they didn't have the same *problem*.

"I've been meaning to take it in for a tune-up." She rolled down the window and waved.

"Who are you waving to?" He looked over her head.

"No one." She rolled up the window.

As they pulled out onto the highway, he studied the rearview mirror but didn't see anyone return her wave. Dinah and the foal grazed in the pasture, and her gray gelding pranced in the paddock next to the riding arena. Interesting. Had she waved to her animals?

"We may not get back before you need to be at the clinic. Do you leave your horses out at night?"

He was driving her to the clinic and picking her up tomorrow morning. It was all part of the plan.

"John Michael will see to the horses, but how will I get home tomorrow morning?" she asked.

"I'll pick you up in the morning. I have an early morning appointment." He pushed a package across the seat. "I packed a meal for you. Make sure it's okay."

Her jaw dropped when she looked at him and then at the large square bag she lifted onto her lap.

"Open it. If it's not something you like we'll stop somewhere."

She unzipped the bag and opened it slowly. Her hand snuck into the bag and came out with an apple.

"It's beautiful." She slanted a look at him. "I feel like a fairytale princess. Are you the evil queen or the bitchy stepmother?"

He frowned. "I'm definitely not the queen and the last time I looked I wasn't anyone's mother."

She laughed, and his body turned to mush.

"Okay, I'll admit I didn't see you as queenly, although you can be a bit imperious. So what character are you then?"

He mulled it over until she started naming them. "The prince who slays the dragon?"

He shook his head.

"The giant with the purple hair or the grinning goblin?" she added.

He scratched his jaw. "I don't remember any fairytale characters like that."

"I just made those up to see if you were paying attention."

*Standing at attention, maybe.* When she smiled like this, her eyes took on an exotic shape and turned up at the ends, enough to make the upper and lower lashes tangle. His hand drifted toward her. When he realized what he was doing, he grabbed her snack bag and pulled out the sandwich.

"Turkey bacon double-decker."

"With mayo?"

"Of course."

"I love turkey bacon double-deckers with mayo."

He wasn't sure how long they smiled at each other

or even what else they talked about the rest of the drive. His only cognizant thought was how irresistible she was in this playful mood. His control wouldn't last if she kept it up.

Yeah, he was playing with fire, and he knew it.

Jack didn't want the evening to end. When they pulled into the clinic lot one minute before her shift, he followed her into the front office and dismissed Chris with only a little trouble. Jack made an excuse about work in his office when she left to tour the barns, then he doubled back to watch her on the monitors. She stopped for several minutes at each stall and talked to all the animals while she conducted a careful check. Impatient with her delay, he was about to go get her when she started back to the office.

They shared Oreos and she gave him part of her apple. When he left, he finally knew what character *she* was.

The Thief of Hearts.

\*\*\*\*

Cheyenne pulled into the pasture made into a parking lot and found a spot between a classic low-slung coupe and an EV Model named Pricey. A small but engaged crowd surrounded the playing field, it was the middle of the second chukker, and she was feeling wild and reckless. Not even the money smell that hovered over the audience like a silver-lined cloud kept her from making her way to the sidelines.

His purple jersey had a three on the back. She should have known. Nothing less than a quarterback position for Jack Carter. The play was fast and just a hair short of rough. Good-natured shouts and vigorous grunts erupted from the players as they galloped their ponies up and back across the field.

She spared a second or two to identify Drs. Blake and Barrington, but it was Jack who held her attention. She convinced herself he was exhilarating to watch on the back of a horse, but the reasoning nagged at her until she had to admit the truth. She hadn't come today to check out the competition, not after last night, and their drive home this morning. She came to see *him*. For at least the next two weeks, at Lyndon's suggestion, she had agreed to suspend her doubts over their very different lifestyles.

Unfortunately, her guilt over participating in the charity match had increased hourly. Not enough to make her withdraw, but *maybe* enough to tell Jack beforehand.

The bell sounded at the end of the chukker. Twenty seconds later the ball went out of play and the players retreated to the sides. The third chukker resumed in three minutes. She watched Jack dismount and toss the reins to a handler who trotted away with the well-lathered horse, likely to bring over a replacement.

Jack whipped off his helmet and scraped sweat-heavy hair back with one hand. It embarrassed her when her breathing quickened. Even worse, she caught herself licking her lips when he lifted a bottle of soda to his mouth and exposed his equally wet throat as he swallowed. An overwhelming rush of heat vibrated through her.

She came to her senses when she noticed Dr. Blake hitch a thumb in her direction while he said something to Jack. Jack brought the bottle down and stared at her.

She had intended to come and watch without discovery. When Jack started walking toward her, however, she couldn't fight the kick of having him know she was there. Her spine tingled when the horn sounded, which signaled one minute before the start of the next chukker. He stopped, put his hands on his hips, and studied the grass before he pointed up to the stands, then pointed to her. When he looked back at her, he mouthed the word "stay" before he turned and jogged to his pony.

For a few seconds, she observed Jack's outstanding butt before someone spoke behind her.

"Cheyenne."

Ben Carter loped from the crowd and took her by the elbow.

"I have orders to remove you to the stands," Ben said.

She followed him without comment. She'd stay until the break and no longer. Another seven minutes would give her enough exposure without making her silly, googly-eyed, eager—to hear his voice and see him smile.

By the time she reached the small bleachers, her composure had returned. Besides Janie and Ben, Jack's mother was there.

"Mrs. Carter." Cheyenne shook hands with Rae Carter when Ben introduced them.

"Ben tells me you recently started working at the clinic."

"Yes, a few weeks ago."

Cheyenne's attention was torn between the match and curiosity about Jack's mother. There was something familiar about the woman and it had nothing to do with the physical characteristics she and Jack shared. She was tall and aristocratic-looking, with the same dark hair although hers was peppered with gray. Her eyes were deep-set and intelligent, and her expression conveyed dignity.

Yet Cheyenne experienced no unease in her presence. Mrs. Carter was wealthy but Cheyenne's typical reaction to someone of Rae Carter's station didn't surface.

A smatter of applause signaled a goal. It was Jack's team, but she wasn't sure which member had scored.

"Oh, why does he do that?" Mrs. Carter murmured, exasperated.

Jack rode off an opposing player, and his upper body invaded the other guy's space, both horses at top speed. It was allowed but it seemed his mother had a hard time watching her son do dangerous stunts on a horse at thirty miles per hour.

Rae Carter looked at Cheyenne. "He does that all the time, crowding the other player just short of fouling. It makes me nervous, to say the least."

Cheyenne smiled and filed the information away for future use.

"How do you feel about women playing polo, Mrs. Carter? Specifically, women playing with or against men?"

Ben turned to his mother when Cheyenne asked the question.

"Uh, oh, Ma, watch how you answer. Janie and Cheyenne both feel quite strongly on the subject."

"I think it's a woman's prerogative." She studied Cheyenne. "Do you feel differently?"

It was apparent Mrs. Carter and Jack shared more than just physical characteristics.

For the first time, Cheyenne questioned whether her perception of Jack's arrogance wasn't a little skewed. She had assumed it was a natural extension of his status and wealth. However, it was possible he came by it another way. Maybe he had a mother who was unafraid to speak her mind and that personality trait, which some might view as arrogance, had been passed down. Maybe it wasn't a result of his privileged upbringing after all.

"No, no, I feel the same," she answered, unable to shake the feeling Mrs. Carter knew what had just gone through her mind.

Janie leaned around Ben and put her thumb up. "Good answer, Cheyenne. Let's you and I try to bring Jack out of the dark ages."

"I take it Jack doesn't agree," Mrs. Carter said. Janie and Cheyenne shook their heads at the same time and laughed.

"I'm not surprised. Jack thinks women are physically incapable of competing fairly against men in certain arenas. He and his father share the same opinion." Mrs. Carter arched one slender eyebrow. "I like to look at the trait as charming and quaint. However, I imagine you younger women merely think he's biased."

She directed her remarks to Cheyenne.

"Polo isn't a game of brute strength." Cheyenne turned her gaze from the field. "In this instance, he's charming and quaint and wrong."

The older woman's mouth rose at one corner and a faint dimple appeared. "Do you play polo, dear?"

Cheyenne's guilt sparked. She wasn't able to lie to eyes so much like Jack's, not when they were leveled at her in steady assessment.

"I've played in the past," she hedged. She refused to provoke speculation over the charity match.

"Cheyenne owns a riding stable," Ben volunteered, as if unaware of the undercurrents between the three women.

When Janie sat back with a smile on her face, Cheyenne knew Janie had a hunch about the woman who played on the opposite team. As for Mrs. Carter's intuition, Cheyenne figured Jack's mother guessed everything else, including the way Cheyenne's private parts ached every time Jack came within touching distance.

Cheyenne fought the urge to fan herself. She didn't really care if Jack's mother deduced her interest in Jack as long as no one else discovered the *extent* of the interest. It was, after all, something she hadn't come to terms with and until she did, Cheyenne needed to retain whatever control she had for as long as possible.

"I, too, have past riding experience," Mrs. Carter said. "Not polo, but jumping, dressage, and the like. Would you ride with me sometime?"

Ben's mouth dropped in what could only be described as shock, then quickly closed. He focused on the playing field as if the game was suddenly of much more interest.

"I'd enjoy that." Cheyenne looked at Ben's profile, then at the field. The horn sounded and the halftime break began. As they stood, Cheyenne added, "You're welcome to come to my farm if you like. I have jumps and riding trails and well, just about anything horse."

It wasn't like her to beg. Not that she was, but the eagerness she heard in her voice was confusing.

Vaguely, she wondered if her attraction to Jack, chemical as she believed it to be, extended to the rest of his family. Lord. Was it possible to fall in love with a whole family?

"Ben!" Cheyenne heard Mrs. Carter's voice through

a fog as blood rushed from her brain and she plopped back down on the metal seat. Her heart pounded, her knees had grown weak, and the parched feel of her mouth made her bend over to keep from making a complete ass of herself.

"Cheyenne?" Ben said through the curtain of her hair. He had his hand wrapped around her upper arm as if any minute she might slide like a glutinous mass between the seats and splatter on the ground under the stands.

She broke out in a cold sweat. "I'm okay," she whispered and wished she might slide somewhere. She never fainted. It was too, well, humiliating, too shameful, too un-Modine-like.

"Take deep breaths," Janie said and held her other arm.

"Ma, get Jack," Ben ordered.

"Do you want to lie down on the seat?" Ben asked.

"Here he is, dear," Mrs. Carter said. Even in her distress, Cheyenne heard the concern in the woman's voice.

When Jack knelt next to her, she wanted to scream. She tried to sit up, but their faces were all blurry and back down she went.

"I know I'm an exciting polo player, but I've never had a woman faint because of it," Jack whispered.

She lifted her head and tried to warn him. The look on her face must have been enough. He stood, guided her head down through the metal seats, and held on to her while she barfed into the grass ten feet below.

Her daddy had told her there'd be days like this.

## Chapter Twenty-Eight

He couldn't stop laughing. It started while he held her up, to keep her from diving between the seats and onto the ground. It continued as he carried her down the stands to the back of Ben's SUV, which was parked in the shade.

She had her face pressed against his chest. She was either too weak or embarrassed to care, or she was crazy about him because he was covered with sweat and smelled like horse and a very manly man.

"Stop laughing," she croaked.

He laughed harder as Janie opened the back hatch, pushed the seats down, and spread a blanket. His sister-in-law gave him the evil eye as he placed Cheyenne in the car. He noticed his mother headed in their direction with a soda. Ben had rushed away, his face an alarming shade of green, to request a longer break from the umpire. Jack hoped the request was successful. Polo was impossible to play while slapping one's knee with boisterous glee.

"Jack, stop it," Janie scolded. When his mother handed him the soda and shook her head, he composed himself enough to pull the ring and hand the can to Cheyenne. She reached blindly with one arm thrown over her eyes.

He leaned into the car. "Drink."

She eased up on one elbow and brought the can to

her lips.

Ben came back to the car with Dale Demme, the fourth member of their team.

"Ump said five minutes." He looked at Jack. "I brought Dale along just in case. He's trolling for patients."

Jack started to laugh again, but his mother, brother, and sister-in-law simultaneously shushed him, so he quit. He helped Cheyenne up while Demme sat down next to her.

"I'm feeling better now," she said but kept her gaze on Jack when Demme asked questions.

"Ben said this came on suddenly." Demme lifted her wrist to take her pulse.

When she nodded, Demme pulled down her lower eyelid.

"Have you been out in the sun for a prolonged period today?"

"About three hours," she replied, taking another sip of soda.

"Did you stay hydrated while you were out?"

She hesitated and looked at Jack. "Yes."

Her expression turned mulish—the same one he'd noticed when she thought someone questioned her judgment.

"What did you do during those three hours?" Jack folded his arms across his chest.

She looked away. "Chores."

Demme told her to sit in the shade, drink, and stay away from chores for the rest of the day.

"Heat and dehydration, likely," he said. "Come and get me if you start feeling worse."

The horn sounded. Demme looked at Jack.

"Coming?"

"Yeah, in a minute."

Jack raised his eyebrows and looked at his family, who, sensitive to nuance, moved away with Demme.

He sat next to her. "I've got to go in a few seconds. You sure you're feeling okay?"

"Yes." She slanted him a look. "Physically. My self-respect is at an all-time low but otherwise, I'm fine."

He studied the field. Some of the players had mounted and now moved the ball around.

"Am I the only man you've puked on, twice?"

She covered her face with her hands. "I knew that's why you were laughing."

He smiled and pulled one of her hands away. He held it in his lap, before turning it over and running his fingers over the calluses.

"Yeah, that's why," he admitted. "Except when Demme came up, I laughed then because he's a podiatrist. A good podiatrist, but a podiatrist, nonetheless."

She managed a weak smile.

"What chores?" he asked.

She tried to remove her hand, but he held on. "What chores?" he repeated with more force.

"Hay," she mumbled.

He winced and she noticed. "My horses have to eat this winter," she said in defense.

"Hay bales weigh sixty to eighty pounds." He looked her over. "You weigh no more than one twenty. And the last time I checked, the temperature was ninety."

When he stood up to leave, he pulled her up with him, wrapped his hand around the back of her head, and kissed her forehead.

"No more haying."

"But…"

"No," he ordered. "And stay here until the match is over. You can drive me home."

He left her to simmer and sent Janie back to sit with her so she followed his orders.

As he trotted across the field, he thought he might be closer to figuring her out. She baled and put up her own hay to save money. She drank whiskey to treat the flu to save money. She rationed out her bite-size Oreos to make them last because she didn't have enough money to buy more. He didn't know why he hadn't thought of it before. Maybe, as she said, his life of privilege had made him too complacent.

She, Janie, and his mother sat talking in the back of the car, the hatch still raised. The three of them together made him happy. While he finished the game, he'd spend more time thinking about why he was so pleased and aroused by a woman who had hurled on him—twice.

\*\*\*\*

They watched the rest of the game from the car. Cheyenne drank iced tea from a pitcher Mrs. Carter brought over from her car. They talked again about riding together before Jack's mother left to pick up Mr. Carter from, of all things, a poker game.

The poker game was at a retirement center where Mr. Carter's best friend lived. It sounded a lot like what her daddy might do if he were alive.

"What is Mr. Carter like?" Cheyenne asked Janie after Mrs. Carter left.

"Nothing like Rae."

"Oh."

"He can be pompous." *Jack.*

"Ben and Jack call him toplofty." She chuckled. "I think it's an inside family joke. They've never shared it with me. He can also be charming, witty, bold, and as sweet as can be. His friends and family mean everything to him, even when he was drinking."

She lowered her voice and her features softened. "Has Jack said anything to you about his father?"

Cheyenne ran a finger over the seam in her jeans. "A little. He referred to a drinking problem."

Janie nodded. "Jack had the hardest time with his dad. They're very much alike in many ways."

"Toplofty?"

"Toplofty." Janie laughed, then became quiet. "I think he's just beginning to come to terms with his early life and his father's problem."

Cheyenne centered her gaze on the field and Jack. "It's interesting how we're all influenced by our family, even subconsciously. I'm just starting to realize how much my father shaped me."

They were silent for a minute.

"And Mrs. Carter?" Cheyenne asked.

"She's what you see. Reserved, solid as a rock, firm in her opinions, but not…"

"Toplofty," they said together.

"We should take our show on the road," Janie said with a warm smile. "Our timing is perfect."

"Uh, oh, did someone fall?" Janie stood up for a clearer view, then sat back down. "The other team. He's getting up."

"You know, Rae doesn't ride at all anymore. Ben and I were very surprised she suggested it to you."

Cheyenne wasn't sure how to respond. She sipped the remainder of her tea and waited for Janie to say more.

"In her early marriage, she tried out for the U.S. Olympic Equestrian Team and made it. Then she got pregnant with Jack, then two years later Ben came along."

Cheyenne made a conscious effort to relax. She now realized why the woman had seemed familiar. "What happened after that?"

Janie shrugged. "She tried again in the early nineties and qualified again. But, well, Jack, that is, Mr. Carter, my father-in-law…"

"It's okay. You don't need to go into details," Cheyenne said, and stood to stretch her legs and test her balance. A remnant of the chill she'd experienced earlier went through her but this time she was sure it had nothing to do with heat stress.

"Are you sure you're okay?" Janie asked.

Cheyenne waved her off. "I'm fine."

This appeared to be her day for discovery, and it was almost too much to digest. Was she falling in love with Jack Carter? If she was, would she end up like Rae Carter, who had delayed her dreams of riding competitively until she was too old to do anything about it? Hell, if she tried to answer either of those questions she'd go insane.

And why was she indulging in this introspective bullshit in the first place?

"Cheyenne, you're pacing. Why don't you sit down? The match is almost over."

Janie patted the place next to her.

"Janie, what is Jack doing for Mary's mother?" Cheyenne leaned against the back fender and hoped the change of subject might calm her agitation.

Janie bit her bottom lip. "You should ask Jack that

question."

"Will he tell me?"

"Probably not."

"I can keep a secret."

"I'm sure you can but he doesn't want anyone to know."

"Janie. Please. It's important."

The final horn sounded. They stood together to watch the players dismount and shake hands. Jack's team had won by a goal.

Janie didn't look at Cheyenne when she said, "You have to promise me you won't tell anyone."

"I promise."

"After consulting with Mary's family, the docs are paying for her mother to come to University Hospital for therapy. The hospital is known for its orthopedic care, and everyone concerned thought she might recuperate faster here."

Cheyenne took a deep breath and let it out slowly. "That's very generous of them."

"Yes," Janie agreed. "But you didn't hear it from me."

"Hear what?"

Chapter Twenty-Nine

The house was just as she imagined—large. The lawn was well-kept, weed-free, and beautifully landscaped. It was, in essence, a wealthy man's home in a wealthy neighborhood. Coming so soon after her conversation with Janie, the sight of it was even more of a shock than she'd expected. The man who owned this house could easily spend thousands of dollars to help an employee's mother get good medical care. What wasn't so easy to understand was the man's generosity of spirit.

When they walked through the front door, two chocolate Labs greeted them with typical Labrador joy, jumping on Jack and licking Cheyenne's outstretched hand. Their energy took her mind off the calculations scrolling through her brain.

"This is Buck and this is Annie," Jack said pointing first to the bigger dog. "Let me fix you a drink, just in case Demme asks if I kept you hydrated. Then you can look around while I shower. What'll you have?"

Cheyenne tore her gaze from the semi-circular stairway in the two-story foyer and knew what showed in her expression.

"Kind of pretentious, huh?" He gave her an awkward smile.

She nodded slowly, and he laughed. He seemed unfazed by her honest agreement.

"I intend to move soon. Actually, I've been thinking

about it for quite a while but never got around to it. My ex loved this house and had to have it. We lived here a year before our divorce," he explained.

Buck shoved his head under her hand to get her attention. When she petted him, he wagged his tail and trotted off.

The house was easily worth half a million. Of course, she was no authority on the price of real estate in Lexington. She wondered what her farm was worth—uh, no, she didn't.

"What?" Jack asked.

When she stared at him, he said, "You shook your head."

"Nothing."

"Okay." He didn't believe her. "What can I get you to drink?"

She smiled at his assumption she'd stay. The way he looked at her made her want to. "I should be going."

"I don't think so." His return smile had a mysterious tilt. "Demme said I needed to watch you for a while. I told him I planned to."

"Demme said that, did he?"

From the back of the house, a dog howled, and Jack flinched. "I'll get the drink and let the dogs out. How about apple juice on the rocks?"

"I love apple juice."

"How did I know that."

He headed down a hallway while she strolled into what she assumed was the dining room. It had no furniture which made the marble floor stand out. Her slow footsteps echoed off the walls.

"Some of the furniture left with my ex," Jack said behind her.

Cheyenne took the glass he held out.

"How long have you been divorced?"

"Six years," he said. "I, uh, eat in the kitchen."

"My divorce was eight years ago," she said. "We were only married a year. We were very young."

"Sounds like a valid excuse," Jack said. "I was definitely old enough to know better."

Cheyenne raised her eyebrows in question, but he didn't bite.

"Well, let me go take my shower." He sniffed the air. "I'm beginning to spoil. Make yourself at home and look around if you want. There's more pretension in the back."

Cheyenne laughed. This was crazy. What *was* she doing here?

She did look around because her nosiness got the better of her. The kitchen was large, of course, and very spartan. She speculated he probably didn't use the kitchen much. The breakfast room had a fireplace and the necessary furniture. She found the "pretension in the back" in the room off the kitchen, which she thought would be correctly called a "great room". The furniture was black leather, and the back wall was solid floor-to-ceiling windows. She walked through the great room into the center hall and noticed double doors to her left. She started to enter when she realized this was Jack's bedroom. He was singing in the shower.

She paused for a moment at the doors. With reluctance, she admitted his room wasn't bad. The carpet was thick and a deep blue. The bed was an unmade four-poster. Magazines lay on the floor by the bed and one entire wall was bookshelves. A huge skylight was positioned over the bed. It looked as if he spent a lot of time in this room, which made her nervous.

Back in the great room, she looked out the windows to see the dogs running around in some kind of crazy canine tag. She sipped her juice and tried to center her thoughts. Fear didn't sit well in the Modine makeup. She wanted to regain her balance. The best way to do so was to leave.

Instead, she turned and her attention caught on the painting above the fireplace. It was possible she had ignored it on purpose. Only the rich had their portraits painted. She recognized Jack and Ben and Mrs. Carter, although the painting was obviously done several years ago. The man who sat in the center was the focal point, however, since he was the only one seated.

Earlier she had believed Jack and his mother favored each other. His father's looks told her she'd been way off base. Father and oldest son so closely resembled each other they looked more like brothers than Ben and Jack.

Mr. Carter was a striking man. Jack even more so and Cheyenne realized it was useless to deny her attraction. A wave of sympathy for Mrs. Carter washed through her, unexplainable but real. Of course, if Cheyenne pitied Jack's mother, what did this say about her?

"Ah, the family Carter," Jack said from behind.

Distracted by the smell of his newly showered body, she said, "I've read there are those who can read family dynamics by looking at group family photos. Do you think the same is true of paintings?"

He frowned. "Hell, I hope not. Look at me."

She *was* looking at him, but it was clear he meant the painting. To be polite, her gaze went back to the wall. In the painting, Jack stood erect and stiff and at least a foot away from his father's right shoulder. The part in his short hair was noticeable and perfect, which even the painter's brush strokes had picked up. He wasn't smiling.

"If I remember right, I was fourteen and my voice was fluctuating all over the place. I was lusting after my freshman Biology teacher, not unlike how I feel now, although now it's a whole lot more complicated."

Just like that, the tension between them escalated to an uncomfortable level.

"You're strangling the glass."

She put the glass down on the nearest table and moved away.

His voice followed her. "Why did you come to the match today?"

She shrugged, as much to relieve the sudden knot in her neck as to show her fake unconcern. "I didn't have anything planned this afternoon. I needed a little diversion."

It was a flip answer. She didn't much care for it but he crowded and probed and she was a mass of wants and needs which made no sense. She really should leave.

"Well, yes, that sounds reasonable." He stood right behind her. "After two or three hours of the backbreaking work of stacking hay, I would opt for a restful diversion in the hot sun, sitting on hard, metal bleachers to watch a fast game of polo, in a crowd of strangers with whom I had little in common."

His words were far too perceptive. She turned on him, ready to do battle, only to be sideswiped by tears in her eyes. She gritted her teeth and watched him blur in front of her. He moved closer until his lips touched hers.

\*\*\*\*

Such a dichotomy, this woman. Jack tasted the

215

sweet apple on her tongue, the salt of tears on her cheeks. His fingertips traced her rigid spine while her hands touched his neck like butterflies. He wanted her strong and wild and uncontrolled on top of him, her shimmering hair falling around them as she searched for her own pleasure. He wanted her under him while he drove her beyond climax. With her, there wasn't anything he didn't want.

She clung to him, just like the other night, and he deepened the kiss until they were both undone with need. She sucked on his tongue, and in desperation, he nipped at her lips, their kisses taking on a frantic rhythm. He slipped his hand under her top, and fixed it to her now warm and pliant back, at the same time he reached for support behind her.

His knee touched the cool leather of the couch, and he moved her down. She slid her open lips over his jaw while he eased on top of her, their legs tangled together. He pulled her top up, and grasped the hair at the back of her head.

The heavy weight of her breast in his palm made them both moan. She stood it for a minute and writhed as he rubbed her nipple.

He licked her lips, their mingled taste fresh and arousing.

"I want you," he whispered as he eased off her top and threw it on the floor.

His mouth moved to her breast and he swirled his tongue around her nipple. When he drew the hard bead between his teeth and sucked harder, she whispered his name. He went to the other nipple, back and forth, until she vibrated beneath him. His hand slid down her smooth belly and inside her jeans.

She was pliant and ready where his fingers pressed and circled, and she locked her hand around the steely flexing of his wrist, guiding the depth and pace of his fingers.

"See what we have." His voice was rough as he brushed his face against her breasts. "And what we could have."

"Yes." Her tortured breaths pushed him further.

"Let me give you more." He unsnapped her jeans, pulled them off, and pitched them over her blouse.

"Open up."

When she did, his finger stroked faster, urgent now as she trembled and shuddered against him. He put his mouth to her ear and murmured raw, broken words that demanded her orgasm. Her tense body responded and began its ride to satisfaction. When she peaked, her cries filled the room, and he slipped his fingers inside her to feel the waves of sweet release.

They lay for a minute in silence as she recovered. He kept his hand tight against her, unmoving, while his lips touched her cheek. When her relaxation was total, he loosened his grip and rested his hand on her stomach. He was one big ache.

Apparently, she recognized his problem. When she moved to her side and started to unbutton his shirt, he placed his hand on hers.

"What...wait...maybe we should go to my bedroom," he said.

"Maybe?" Her sideways smile told him her intent was exactly what he wanted.

They made it to the bedroom, both of them naked when they fell onto the bed. She touched him in all the right ways as her lips grazed his face, neck, and chest while her hands roamed lower. She climbed on top of him as he grabbed a condom from the drawer of the nightstand.

Something in her eyes, a mix of honesty and desire and pure determination, made him realize that she, too, recognized this wasn't only about sex. She guided him inside her and her gaze never left his, until the tight sensation of her body forced her name from his lips.

When her hips began their rhythmic pumps, he lost all control. His hands, her body, his words, her struggle to breathe, all of it ended in devastating waves of release that drained every last ounce of his need. She collapsed upon his heaving chest and his arms surrounded her. A minute later, the last thing he remembered was her mesmerizing scent and the soft strands of her hair against his jaw.

Chapter Thirty

She left a note on the coffee table since he was still asleep.

It read "I have to go. I need time to think. Until I figure things out, no more sex or touching."

She got to the farm, checked on her animals, and purposely didn't answer her cell phone until she entered the house.

She read his text. —*I'm not going to leave you alone. I'll give you some time, but I want to be with you. I won't let you push me away and I won't pretend I don't have feelings for you. Just don't make me wait too long.*—

Cheyenne hadn't lied to him. She needed time to think, and sex confused everything. Or maybe her past life as a Berserker had returned to haunt her.

Bubba scratched at the closet door, but she didn't open it. She needed the dark, muffled silence to help her navigate through a maze of disbelief—caused by the amazing experience of climaxing all over him, and the possibility he was the wrong man who touched her in all the right ways. What kind of lunacy was this?

Apparently, the kind which made her replay the scene. The fullness lingered between her legs and she was unable to stop her thoughts. If she'd stayed one more minute, it would have taken hours to quench her thirst.

She was still mesmerized by his expression as he came. His avid eyes and the tight set of his jaw told her he was as lost in the moment as she was. And the words he'd whispered—Lord, if any other man had talked that dirty to her he would have earned a well-placed right hook.

She laid her head against the back closet wall and fought to calm herself. How in the hell had she made it home without causing a major tie-up on Route 25. Her truck was almost on the grass of the Henry Clay estate before she caught it. The next time they did anything like this at his house, she'd call Uber. Or they'd do it at the farm because driving after sex was, for her, too dangerous.

Good God. What was she thinking? No more sex with him until she got her head straight.

She *was* confused and she *really* needed time to think.

Would he abide by her no-touch rule? He said he wasn't going to leave her alone.

It didn't take a genius to figure this one out. She was in trouble—big trouble. She required serious advice—yesterday. Pammy? Billy? Lyn? A psychiatrist?

No, definitely not family. Lyn had encouraged her to give Jack a chance so he was out, too. She didn't have the money to hire a shrink. What she required was the opinion of someone who knew her well, someone she respected, who had some objectivity and detachment.

Only one person fit those requirements. All she had to do was swallow her Modine pride and get out of the closet.

\*\*\*\*

"Ben!" Jack yelled over the heads of the loud deli crowd. "Over here!"

He motioned his brother to the table he'd managed

to steal from a slow-moving older couple. He might have felt guilty if he hadn't arranged to anonymously pay for the couple's meal.

"How in the hell do you stand this?" Jack asked when they both sat down. "Do you eat here often?"

"No, not usually," Ben said. "I brown-bag most of the time."

Ben flipped his tie over his shoulder and slipped the menu from between the ketchup and napkin holder.

"I already ordered for you," Jack said.

Ben shoved the menu back in place. "How did you know what I wanted?"

"You're my brother."

Ben sat back and crossed his arms. "You look like hell."

"Gee, thanks."

"Rough night?"

"No. Yes."

Their sandwiches arrived with pickles and chips on the side. When the waitress left, Ben lifted his bun.

"Okay, you know me." He took a bite and chewed. "So, which is it? Yes or no?"

Jack had his mouth around his sandwich and mumbled incoherently.

"Have anything to do with Cheyenne?"

His answer was another mumble, even less intelligible, if possible.

"Yeah, that's a bitch, isn't it?" Ben said as if he understood. "Janie and I called her last night."

Jack swallowed. "Why?"

"Duh. We wanted to make sure she was okay."

Ben looked at him like he had lost it. "I know you found the whole vomiting episode hilarious, but she looked miserable." He wiped his mouth. "What was going on there?"

"It's a private joke."

"Joke? Jesus, Jack, how can you be so insensitive? You laughed so hard I thought I was going to have to administer oxygen."

"It's private," Jack repeated. "Just drop it, will you?"

Jack popped a chip in his mouth. "How was she when you called?"

"Cheyenne? I thought she took you home."

"She did."

"You were going to invite her to dinner. What happened?"

"She, uh, left, after, uh…how did she seem when you called?"

Ben eyed him with curiosity. Jack knew the look. "I'm going to hurt you if you don't tell me."

Ben gazed at Jack's plate. "I'll tell you if I can have your pickle."

Jack held out his plate. "Have at it. Now, tell me."

The crunch of the pickle was loud when Ben bit into it. "Fine."

Jack frowned. How did she get fine so fast?

"You're sure?"

"Mmmm." Ben's head bounced in the affirmative before he swallowed. "Why?"

"I'm switching to Plan B." Jack ignored the real question.

"Plan B? What happened to Plan A?"

"Plan B is an extension of Plan A."

"Drop back and punt?"

"Yeah, sort of."

Ben ate a chip. "Okay, you got me. What is it?"

"I'm going to be everywhere she is."

Ben frowned. "What?"

"You know, the old 'God and horse manure' philosophy."

Ben smirked but it was clear he didn't get it. "I think you're losing your grip on reality."

Jack swiped a hand through his hair. "Christ. I know."

Ben put down his sandwich.

"Janie said everyone at the clinic has noticed, especially after the pool episode."

Jack closed his eyes and tried not to imagine the circulating gossip.

"You're in love with her."

Jack stared at his brother's face and dropped his tasteless sandwich on his plate. "Shit, I know."

"Here," Ben said as he waved a pickle in Jack's face. "Have a pickle and tell me more about Plan B."

\*\*\*\*

If this was his idea of giving her time, he didn't know how to tell time. Now she knew what he meant when he said he wasn't going to leave her alone. It was as if he was everywhere she was.

First, there was the phone call this morning. The message had been brief and polite. Her knees had weakened at the sound of his drowsy voice.

"Cheyenne, it's Jack. Just checking to see if you're all right. I'll be in and out, but if you need anything, call me. You know the number."

Then his mother had called her and they'd made a date to ride on Thursday afternoon. Cheyenne was fairly sure he'd suggested his mother call.

And now this.

She scanned the invoice again. It was stamped "paid in full". She went after the man who'd given it to her. He stood next to a truck loaded with hay, now parked right below the door to her hay storage area. It looked like very good hay, alfalfa, or an alfalfa-timothy mix—clean, fragrant, and green.

The problem was, she hadn't ordered it.

*He* had.

"Mr., uh, Mr.," she called after the truck driver. "I didn't order this."

"Chuck." He smiled down at her. The guy was big and muscular with dark hair and a mustache. He wore a UK T-shirt and a sweaty ballcap on his head. When he pulled off his gloves, he poked a finger at the address on the invoice she waved under his nose. "This your address?"

"Yes."

"This your name?"

"Yes."

"And a real pretty name it is, ma'am, if you don't mind me saying so."

She didn't mind. There were more weighty matters to attend to at the moment.

"Chuck, I know you think you should deliver the hay to this address, but really…"

"Pardon me, ma'am, but if you could step aside, I need to get the elevator in position."

She swiped at the sweat trickling down the side of her face and tried again.

"Chuck, I can't accept this hay. You can't unload it."

Chuck looked at her with something close to pity.

"Ms. Modine, I'm begging you to take this hay. The man who ordered it said if we didn't deliver it he'd sue for breach of contract. Now, you wouldn't want that to happen, would you? Ma'am?"

Crap. He was whining.

She threw up her hands. "O-kay. Load it."

She stomped to the house with every intention of googling breach of contract. *He* wasn't going to get away with this "charitable" gift. She'd just have to figure out how to pay for it. She smiled when she pictured his reaction. He'd be pissed, for sure.

Later that afternoon, he called again, and her smile returned.

"Can you come on a call later?" he asked.

"What time?"

"Uh…" Papers rustled in the background. "Six thirty. I can pick you up at six. We can eat on our way back."

"I can't."

A brief yet heavy silence followed.

"Eat, or go on a call?"

"Both. I have plans." She did have plans—polo practice—but there was another heavy silence, so she knew he didn't believe her.

"Okay, no problem." He cleared his throat. "Did you get the hay?"

"Yes, thanks. I'll pay you as soon as I can."

His response was immediate. "That's not necessary."

"Please. I insist."

"All right," he said. "Why don't we take it out of your pay, a little each week?"

She brightened at his reasonable attitude. "That can

be done?"

"Sure."

"Well, that's great. I appreciate your acceptance of my decision."

"No problem. Oh, and Cheyenne, effective tomorrow, I'm giving you a raise."

He hung up before she could argue.

Chapter Thirty-One

It started all over again the next day. Her phone rang at six a.m. and startled her awake.

"Hullo."

"Hi," he said. His voice, once again, made her stomach flop.

"Why are you calling so early?"

"I have a surprise for you."

"God," she groaned. "Not more hay."

"No, even better. Can you be dressed and ready to go in half an hour? You don't have plans, do you?"

She rolled her eyes. "No, unless you call peeing and brushing my teeth *plans.*"

"Good. I'll see you soon."

"This had better be *damn* good." She hung up on him this time.

Damn good didn't even come close. It was the most thrilling thing she'd done since, well, Sunday. He picked her up, handed her a fresh cup of coffee as she got in the truck, smiled a wanton, sleepy smile, and drove her to Hunter Glen Farm to see Mr. Tibbles.

The morning air blew fresh and soft as they walked down the lane to the exercise track. While Mr. T pranced sideways and threw his head, the groom and Jack talked all the way.

"Let me take your coffee," Jack said when they stopped.

"Why?" She handed him the cup with a frown.

"Mr. Tibbles wouldn't like it if you spilled hot coffee on his neck."

She gaped at his grin.

"Dammit." She grabbed the front of Jack's shirt and pushed her face up to his. "This isn't a joke, is it?

"No, it's not a joke." His gaze searched her face like he wanted to kiss her but he didn't. "He's all yours for the next twenty minutes."

The groom laughed and handed her a riding helmet. Jack gave her a leg up and she took off, thinking about every overused cliché in the romance books she'd read as a teenager. The horse was so fast her eyes watered as they galloped against the clear breeze. When Mr. T finally worked off his edge, the beauty of his graceful lope made her eyes fill with real tears. When the time was up, she slowed the horse to a trot, turned, and headed back to the groom and Jack.

She dismounted, thanked the groom, and he led the horse to the barn.

"Well, tell me. How was it?" Jack finally asked when they got to the truck.

She stopped to stare at him. "Promise me you won't say anything when I tell you."

He nodded, his expression serious.

Assured of his silence, she closed her eyes and laid her hands over her heart. "I am so *touched* you did this for me." She stopped when her voice threatened to break and ruin a beautiful moment.

They drove back to her place in silence. His presence alone comforted her and he allowed her the freedom to savor the joy of the ride. He seemed to understand she had no words to express what was inside her.

When they pulled to a stop in her driveway, she placed a hand on his cheek.

"Thank you," she whispered and left before he tried to change her mind.

**\*\*\*\***

By the time Billy stopped by later that morning, she had almost come down from her high. Her brother adjusted her spine with his hug and they ate the lunch Pammy had prepared. Billy talked with his mouth full, pontificating on the Zen of hauling horses when Cheyenne realized the race was on for real.

"Hey, girl, that vet gave me a call yesterday."

She straightened on the bar stool, suddenly wary. "What?"

"You know, Jack Carter. The vet we met at the steakhouse a few weeks back. He wants me to haul some horses for him, from a horse rescue facility up east. Don't that beat all?"

"Why?"

Billy waved his apple around and squinted like he was deep in thought. "Didn't ask. We're meetin' at his clinic tomorrow to work out the details."

She bit her thumbnail.

"How's Pammy?" she asked, in an effort to detour her thoughts.

"Sexy as hell," Billy said. He took another loud bite of his tortilla chips. "Meaner than a snake. If that baby doesn't get here soon, I'm takin' the woman down to Red River Gorge and hiking her into labor."

"Have her call me."

The detour was a dead end. Why would he hire Billy to haul some horses now?

She spooned another bite of ice cream into her mouth. Billy was good at his work, of course, but why now? Was it yet another way to let her know he wasn't giving up?

"How are you and Carter getting along, by the way?"

"Okay," she hedged and tried to imagine what Billy might say to "I'm falling in love with him and it's the scarier than hell and why do I feel like I'm tarnishing Daddy's memory and turning my back on my heritage" but she didn't.

Of course, Billy being Billy didn't pick up on any of her vibrations.

"What's J.C. up to this week?" She injected as much nonchalance into the question as possible.

"Working his butt off, of course. We've got two drivers laid up. One of them did the tango with a little filly last week and broke his ankle. The other was playing softball over the weekend and ended up gettin' one of those pulls in his privates. I told J.C. we needed to lay down some rules about drivers doing the weekend warrior thing. Anyway, he's making a bunch of short hauls around town since we're low on staff."

His cell rang and he looked at the number.

"Speak of the devil." He smiled at her as he answered. "Bud. Shy and me were just talkin' about you. Oh. Hell. Now?"

"It's not Pammy?" she whispered, and he shook his head.

"Okay, I'll be right there," Billy said and hung up.

"Duty calls." He stood, and slid the phone into the back pocket of his jeans. "One of our trucks needs my tender loving care or we don't make a lot of money tomorrow."

She walked him to the door. "Don't forget to tell Pammy to call me."

"Sure thing." He hugged her again. "Want me to let you know what I find out about the vet's horses?"

She shook her head. The more she thought about it, the most logical explanation seemed the simplest. Jack just wanted her to know he hired her brother, not the what, when, where, or why.

Besides, he'd call later. She'd ask him then.

\*\*\*\*

When she answered the phone, Jack decided the gods were finally on his side. She had, after all, answered the phone in the middle of the day, at a time when she was usually busy with chores.

"Why did you hire Billy to haul some horses for you?" she asked.

"Why not? Is he unreliable?"

He heard what sounded like a boot tap against a metal appliance.

"No, but the timing's odd."

"Is it? Not if I want to get the animals here before Mom's birthday."

A metal lid squeaked open, and she said, "eat, Bubba."

"You're buying her horses for her birthday?"

"Yes. I heard you two are riding on Thursday. If she's going to start riding again, I think she'd like horses. I happen to be an expert on horses, by the way."

"She can ride here any time, at no charge."

"That's very nice of you. You're not just offering because she's my mother, are you?"

She frowned at his question. "No, why do you ask?"

231

"I'm not hiring your brother just because you're his sister, either."

Okay, he had her there.

"Actually," she said. "I feel honored to ride with your mom. With her experience, I'm sure she might teach me a few things."

Jack had heard something about Cheyenne's Olympic interest, maybe from Lyn, and he wondered if she still thought about it. His mother had valid experience, that is, if Cheyenne needed advice.

"Will you go out with me tonight?" he said.

"I have to work."

"Oh. That's right. Can I stop by and eat a late dinner with you then?"

"I don't know. If my boss catches us, I might get in trouble."

"I'll talk to him. We're good friends and I'm pretty persuasive."

Purring filtered through the line, and he suspected she held her demonic cat.

"If you think so, I guess we could eat together, as long as you don't touch me."

He waited to reply until he lost the argument in his head.

"Jack?"

"I won't touch you."

He wondered what they were doing to each other and when she'd end his torture.

"I'll see you later, then," she said.

****

He didn't touch her. They ate, talked, and laughed, but they didn't touch. After he left, she realized it didn't matter that there was no physical contact. His eyes made love to her, his voice moved over her like hot caramel, and his mere presence in the same room shot excitement straight through her.

And she was fairly sure she'd done the same to him.

Chapter Thirty-Two

For an early Wednesday evening, the steakhouse was packed. She and J.C. had arrived at the same time and found one vacant table in the middle of the room. Her restlessness increased when her chair was continually bumped by bodies as they passed back and forth. She didn't like it but there was no place else to sit.

As usual, J.C. was quiet. He had always been a man of few words—the strong, silent type her daddy used to say. Maybe this wasn't such a good idea. The activity around them and his non-communicative ways weren't conducive to helping her solve her problem.

She had completed her third napkin fan when his hand settled over hers.

"Since you called me, I was expectin' you to carry the conversation," he said.

She put the napkin down, took a swallow of tea, and said, "That was always one of our problems, J.C. Sometimes I wanted you to take the initiative."

"Well, it appears I have tonight," he responded without resentment. "But as I said, you called me. So, talk."

He sat back in his chair in his typical relaxed way and watched her. Except for a few squint lines around his eyes, he looked the same as always. J.C. was a tall, handsome, healthy Kentucky country boy with a slow charm and chill attitude that made her brother seem manic. When she looked closer, she amended her thoughts. He wasn't a boy anymore. His broad shoulders and toned thighs showed his maturity; maturity he carried with ease.

"See something you like?" He smiled, his blue eyes sparkling in a familiar tease, more like a brother than a former husband and lover.

She blushed. It wasn't fair to compare him to Jack. They were opposites in every way, which didn't make J.C. a bad person. He was just J.C.

Still, she hadn't come tonight to discuss Jack or their relationship with her ex-husband. J.C. was a busy man who looked pretty tired right now, so she'd better get down to it.

"Sorry," she said. "I'm taking up your time and I told you I wouldn't." She picked up the napkin again. "J.C., do you remember why I decided against trying out for the U.S. equestrian team?"

He shrugged. "I always thought it was the money. Your daddy didn't have any extra and you were always real touchy about asking him for some."

That was the accepted rationale, one she didn't find so acceptable anymore. "But why didn't I find the money somewhere? We married when I was nineteen. I started college. Why didn't I pursue it then, make my own money, or look for a sponsor or something? I mean, after our divorce I had only myself to think of. It would have been a good time to do it."

He leaned forward and put his arms on the table. "I remember Lyndon Tyree offered to help you. When you turned him down, I guess I thought you really didn't want it bad enough. Either that or your take-no-prisoners pride." He sipped at his drink and continued, "Tyree was

235

a second dad to you and Billy. Maybe you thought taking his money was the same as taking money from Walker."

She traced a finger through the wet glass ring on the table. He thought she hadn't wanted it bad enough. A wave of longing welled up inside her, so strong it almost choked her. She *had* wanted it, more than anything. When she realized she still did, the dismay left her speechless.

"Shy?" He waved a hand in front of her to get her attention. "Did you know Billy borrowed money from Lyndon to start his business?"

"You're kidding me," she said. "Are you kidding me?"

J.C. shook his head. "Don't let Billy know I told you though. He'd skin me alive."

"Then why did you tell me?"

"Well, we paid Lyn off last year." He looked around as if to make sure no one listened. "And I thought it might help you decide."

"Decide what?"

"Whatever it is that's botherin' you enough to seek my advice."

She stayed quiet, and he left her with her thoughts. At this point, she wished he'd take her attention away from them. She didn't want to think about the other reasons she hadn't pursued her dream, and how much of the choice had been within her control.

Again, he put his hand on hers.

"I don't know if this will help, but here's what I think. Don't worry about what you didn't do in the past, and why you didn't do it. You say it would have been the perfect time then. I say why not now? If you still want it, if it's as important as it seems to be, don't let anything stand in your way. What have you got to lose?"

She wanted to laugh and cry. What did she have to lose? The farm, Daddy's legacy, the respect of her family if she sold it to pursue a dream with no guarantee of success, maybe her damnable pride if she didn't succeed. She couldn't decide which was worse, or maybe they were all equally as hurtful.

There was, of course, something else. It was the most uncertain element of her life but it, *he*, felt as important as the others.

If she did this—sold the farm, found a coach, and started to compete in the required events with the required travel, she had Jack to lose.

And she was almost sure losing Jack might be the hardest loss of all.

\*\*\*\*

Cheyenne arrived home by eight. She fed and watered the horses, and walked into the house to hear the landline ringing. She'd had no Jack calls all day and after the constant communication of the past few days, her sense of deprivation intensified.

When she picked up the phone, her spirit rose with the sound of his voice. He asked to stop by. He'd had a late appointment, on a farm a few minutes away from hers on Winchester Pike. She started to say no but something in his tone made her hesitate. After her talk with J.C., she was more confused than ever about her problems. Tonight, with everything else on her mind, she wasn't sure she'd be able to fight the attraction. But Jack sounded odd, and she wasn't strong anymore where he was concerned.

He arrived ten minutes later. She handed him a soda when he walked in.

"Do you mind if I take off my shirt?" Her nerves skittered when she noticed a splattered arc of blood at the neckline.

Cheyenne swallowed the knot in her throat. She never used to cry. Why, now, was it suddenly an every-other-day occurrence?

"What happened?" She took his shirt, which left him in an undershirt and jeans.

"I almost lost a patient tonight." He sat at the kitchen table and rotated the soda can on the tabletop. This was the first time she'd noticed the tiredness in his posture, although he worked hard, all day, almost every day of the week. Of course, he worked like a man who loved what he did, but because he loved it, when things went wrong, he hurt more.

She put the shirt in the sink and turned on the faucet. Her reaction was off-kilter, probably unnecessary. He would throw away the shirt and buy a new one. But it gave her something to do with her hands. She now sincerely regretted her no-touch edict.

He took a long swallow from the can.

"Why didn't you call me?"

*Right, as if I could have made a difference.*

He searched her face. The shadow of beard along his jaw was blue-black.

"I called and texted. You didn't answer."

She'd turned off her cell during dinner with J.C. which must have been when he called.

"What happened?" she asked again.

"I was stitching up a minor head laceration on a filly when she freaked out. I'm still not sure what happened next. She reared up, and lost her footing on the stall floor, I think. Anyway, she fell over and fractured her back leg.

238

Win's doing surgery on her right now." He smiled without humor. "He's our best knife man, so to speak. I wouldn't have been any good anyway. Unsteady hands."

She wasn't sure what to say so she turned and swished the now dingy water. She tried to scrub away the stains, but it was obvious the shirt would always have a pink hue. Several seconds of silence passed and he came up behind her.

"I'm sorry," he said. "I can't keep our bargain tonight. I need you to hold me for a minute."

She turned without drying her hands and threw herself against him. They stood quietly for several seconds, wrapped around each other, and she wished he'd never let her go.

"Where were you, earlier?" he whispered into her hair.

"I met J.C. for a drink," she said. He stiffened, but she didn't release him.

"Do I need to have a talk with him?"

"No."

He tightened his arms.

"Christ, I'm getting hard."

She smiled. "I know."

He eased back and looked down at her. "I'd better go."

"No, not yet," Cheyenne said. "Let me throw the shirt in the dryer. Go into the living room. I'll be there in a minute."

He seemed about to say something. Instead, he turned and walked down the hall.

She went back to the sink, swamped by confusion. Why didn't she let him go? Her hands dipped again into the soapy water, and she rubbed harder at the stains, then squeezed the shirt and threw it into the dryer. When her thoughts of him quieted, she walked into the living room.

He was stretched out on the couch, asleep. His obvious exhaustion allowed her to slip off his shoes, and cover him with a throw—with a horse on it, of course. She slipped from the house to check on her animals one last time.

When she returned, he still slept. She took a long shower and climbed into bed. In the morning, he had already left by the time she awakened.

****

"You're looking energetic tonight, Jack," Win commented as he dismounted.

Jack mopped his face with a towel and gave Win a calculated look.

"Meaning?"

Win put his own towel around his neck. "Nothing, really. But if we'd been playing a match instead of practicing, we'd either be beating the shit out of our competition or suspended from playing in these here United States for the next decade."

"Yeah, well, with the charity match only a week and a half away, I was hoping to motivate you."

Win smirked. "You're worried about being beaten by a woman."

Jack made windmills with his arms. No matter how hard he tried, he couldn't work out the kinks. He didn't know which was worse—a perpetual erection or knots in his back that refused to relax. His attempt to give Cheyenne space this last week, with no touching, had made him a physical and mental wreck. Constant hard-on, muscle cramps, the concentration skills of a gnat, hair-trigger temper—he even wondered whether the episode with the filly was his fault or just a twist of fate.

"And you're not?" Jack asked, finally.

"I'm trying to keep it in perspective." Win sat back in his folding chair and propped his feet on a saddle. "It's a match for charity. Tyree has a right, hell, maybe an obligation to sell as many tickets as possible. You have to admit the man is a marketing genius. If playing a woman is going to sell more tickets, then more power to him."

Jack grunted. "I'm certain he's going to sell more tickets. Last time I talked to him, he said he's already at a hundred more than last year, and it's typical for at least twenty-five percent to wait until the week before to commit."

"Well, then, he had the right idea." Win glanced around. "Where the hell are Mike and Dale with the beer? I'm dry as a bone. Let's ask Tyree if he can move the date of the match next year to later in the fall. August is way too humid for a game as vigorous as polo." He motioned to the coming dusk. "If this inversion pattern doesn't clear up soon we'll be playing in fog."

A few patchy wisps hugged the low-lying areas down the hill.

Jack opened the small cooler at his feet and pulled a bottle of sparkling water out for Win, who waved it off.

"I'll wait for the malted stuff. Makes my belches more resonant."

Jack smiled without comment. He took a swig of the water and scanned the trees above them. The leaves were still as if he viewed a painting.

"How did ole' Tyree convince you to play, anyway?" Win asked.

"He told me I could pick the charities. What can I

say? The man is not only a marketing genius, he's a master manipulator. As long as it's for a good cause, one I get to choose, I guess I can be manipulated."

They both turned when a car came down the lane. Win got up to greet the liquid refreshment wagon. Jack stayed in his seat and tried to restrain his itchy palm from grabbing the cell phone on top of the cooler, to call her. If he heard her voice, he'd want to see her. If he saw her, he'd want to touch her. If he touched her, he wouldn't be able to stop. Besides, he'd gone back on his promise to her when he stopped after the filly injury. He didn't want to push until he knew she was ready.

Still, just one look was all he needed. When he saw it, whatever it took, they'd work it out if she'd let him into her heart. Once that happened, it was only a matter of time before he claimed her soul.

Chapter Thirty-Three

How had it come to this?

Cheyenne and Mrs. Carter neared the end of their ride and their horses ambled across the pasture after a pleasant trip on the trails. She had just spent a companionable hour with the mother of the man she had fallen in love with. A woman of the upper class who Cheyenne had started to think of as a friend. From a class of people she generally did not like. Just how did she explain this?

Equally as strange, how did she explain Jack? He was arrogant and wealthy, opinionated and hard-headed. He was the type of man she had never been attracted to. Yet here she was, with the hand of love waving in her face.

How had this happened?

She knew how. He was arrogant and hardheaded and charming and funny, a lover of animals, and a man who tried to help people in need. He also made her burn with a look. Reduced her to ash with one penetrating glance.

It was time to face the music. Cheyenne didn't know which end was up anymore and it was all his fault.

She could just kill him.

As they came in sight of the barn, Mrs. Carter said, "Jack told me you were an exceptional rider. I have to say I agree."

"You're no slouch in that department yourself. I can

see why you…" She stopped and wondered if a mention of the Olympics might upset Mrs. Carter.

"Why I what?"

There it was again—the Jack trait. Straightforward, no bullshit. Maybe it was the Rae Carter trait, too.

"I was going to bring up the Olympics, but I didn't want to if the subject is painful."

Mrs. Carter laughed. "It's not painful. On the contrary, I like to talk about those days. I feel special in spite of non-participation in the main event."

The woman didn't sound bitter, but Cheyenne didn't know her well enough to tell. It was possible she had no regrets, but Cheyenne didn't see how. Mrs. Carter may have made her choices with the knowledge it was right for her at the time. If that was the case and the decisions had been easy, Cheyenne envied her. At this point in her life, she didn't associate easy with any of her own decisions.

"Mrs. Carter, how did you decide, the first time? Was there something that allowed you to say this is a choice I can live with, no matter the outcome?"

"You're referring to my decision to choose my family over my riding, I presume?"

Cheyenne nodded.

"I remember a few sleepless nights. My husband knew riding was important to me and he was willing to wait a few years to start a family. However, Jack set his own schedule, even then. He was a lovely accident. And while I was busy enjoying him, Ben came along. They were both so wonderful, I didn't think much about my missed opportunity."

They entered the barn and dismounted. Mrs. Carter removed her own tack and brushed down Dudley. She seemed to enjoy the work of riding as well as the pleasure.

"When you tried later, didn't you feel, well, cheated? I mean, you must have had a strong desire to compete since you went back to it."

Mrs. Carter paused her brush. "Yes, at the time I was quite conflicted. As you probably already know, it's hard work to make the team. And I was much older by then, which made it even harder. But I regained my perspective. I might have won a place on the team four years later, but I chose to move on."

She studied Cheyenne. "I meant what I said before. Not many people have the distinction of qualifying twice for the U.S. team, with eight years in between."

Cheyenne's disappointment must have shown on her face. Her current dilemma hadn't lessened with Rae Carter's answers.

"Do you have an interest in competing at the Olympic level?" Mrs. Carter asked.

Cheyenne stalled. "Let me put the horses out." She released Dud and the mare she had ridden into the paddock and rejoined Mrs. Carter a minute later.

"I did," Cheyenne said.

"I think you still do."

Cheyenne took a deep breath and let it out slowly. "I still do," she admitted.

"Does Jack know?"

"I, uh, no, he doesn't."

Cheyenne picked up the saddles and bridles.

"Dear, may I offer a suggestion?" Mrs. Carter said as she lifted a saddle from the burden Cheyenne carried.

They studied each other.

"I know my son. I saw the way he watched you at

the match. You need to tell him."

Cheyenne winced. "I was afraid you'd say that."

That afternoon, after Mrs. Carter's departure, two new students arrived for their first lessons. One was a middle-aged housewife with a reawakened childhood desire to ride and the second student was a little boy whose parents wanted him to conquer his fear of horses. Both lessons ended successfully. The little boy even opened his eyes during the last five minutes as she led his horse around the barn.

By the time he left, she still hadn't heard from Jack. She went to take a shower before she left for the clinic when the phone rang.

"Cheyenne, it's Janie Carter."

For some reason, maybe because it was Janie calling and not Jack, Cheyenne's anxiety kicked in.

"Is everything okay?" she asked.

"Uh, yes, why do you ask?"

"No reason. Sorry, I've had a busy day. What can I do for you?"

Janie was slow to respond, which told Cheyenne something *was* wrong.

"Have you noticed anything unusual at the clinic lately, during your time here?"

"No," Cheyenne said. "I'm not sure I've been there long enough to know what is or isn't unusual, short of the dead body on the floor scenario. Why?"

Janie sighed. "I can't say. Something's going on that the docs don't want to broadcast yet. They've appointed me the preliminary detective. What that means is I'm stuck between a rock and a hard place. I know a little, but I can't tell anyone what I know."

"I understand," Cheyenne said, without really

understanding. "I'm just glad, well, everyone is okay." She'd almost said "Jack".

"Oh, yeah, everyone's okay except me, Win, and Jack."

"What's wrong with Win and Jack?"

"Win is worried about the situation here, the one I can't talk about, which means he hovers, you know, like a helicopter. He's loud and he blows wind everywhere, making staff duck for cover when he flies by." She made a frustrated noise. "Jack is, well, Jack. He's been working himself into the ground, as usual, but without his normal good humor. Of course, the accident with the filly really upset him, but I suspect other issues are making him hyper. You wouldn't know what those are, would you?"

"Uh, no," Cheyenne replied. She really liked Janie, but Cheyenne was a time bomb where Jack was concerned. Talking about it just made it worse. "What about the filly? Is she okay?"

"Yes," Janie said. "She's fine. The operation was successful. Her owners had no intention of running her anyway. She's too small. They'll be using her as a broodmare."

"That's good. Jack should be relieved."

They talked a few more minutes and were about to hang up when Cheyenne remembered the folders in Jack's office.

"Oh, Janie, I almost forgot. What about the folders on Jack's desk?"

Cheyenne thought she heard a gasp.

"Janie, are you okay?"

"Please, believe me, Cheyenne, I never approved of it. But Ben went ahead and put it together anyway."

"What are you talking about?" Cheyenne asked.

"What?"

"I'm not following you. What are you talking about?"

"The folder. What are *you* talking about?"

"I've been trying to organize Jack's office. Did you see my note? I wanted to make sure I followed proper procedure. I thought I'd work on it tonight, and get everything put away. The folders have been there since last week and I wondered if it's okay to work on them."

"Oh, folders, Jack's office, right," Janie babbled, and then gave a nervous laugh.

"Yes, I like to keep busy while I'm there."

"Please, that's a big help," Janie said. "I haven't been able to get to it yet, what with everything here in flux. Thanks."

When they finally ended the call, Cheyenne was still confused about Janie's misunderstanding over the folders, but the hush-hush office matter was even more of a concern. She'd noticed some of her Oreos missing but hardly thought that was any cause for concern. Maybe someone had stolen office supplies? Whatever it was, Cheyenne tried not to worry. She already had too much to think about.

Later, at the clinic, Cheyenne looked over her recently completed clean-up in Jack's office. In between her rounds, she'd filed everything in the cabinets behind his desk.

Ben Carter's name hadn't appeared on anything. Janie must have been preoccupied with the secretive matter in the office. Her words had made no sense.

Cheyenne flipped the light switch off and walked down the hushed hallway. Jack hadn't called or stopped by. She'd asked him to give her time, but it didn't help to not see him. She pictured a tennis match, with her as the ball. Call me, don't call me, touch me, no, no, no, don't, love me, don't love me—if the answers didn't come soon, she'd be on her way to the closet and never come out again.

Chapter Thirty-Four

Okay, he was weak and demented. But, hell, it was Friday, and he hadn't seen her in two days. He didn't want to wait anymore. She hadn't called, but he wondered why he expected her to. Oh, that's right, he was demented.

If he didn't already know it, it was obvious in her expression tonight. He really didn't need assistance on this call, but it was the only one he was able to finagle from Mike after he promised Mike his firstborn child. A yearling colt needed to be wormed. Fortunately, the process took only a few minutes, and the farm crew left them alone once they saw he'd brought his own assistant.

Since he picked her up, she'd been quiet and withdrawn. He couldn't even get a good fight started, not that he wanted to. Still, maybe a fight would be better than her current...aloofness.

While she took the horse from his ties and led him to his stall, Jack put his equipment away. She said nothing when she came back, and they walked from the barn in silence.

Five minutes later, they were back in the truck. He noted the time. It was only seven.

He'd ask but he already knew the answer.

"Are you hungry?"

*Are you as hungry for me as I am for you?*

"Yes," she said.

He was speechless. Somehow, his hands remembered how to insert keys into the ignition. "What would you like to eat?"

*Me?*

"I don't care. You choose."

All right. This was going reasonably well.

"There's a ribs place down…"

His cell phone blipped with excessive force. He wanted to throw the damn thing out the window when he saw it was the clinic number.

"Yes? You're kidding? Tonight?" *Shit.* "I know, I know. I'm on my way."

She looked at him when he signed off. "We need to postpone our meal for just a little longer," he said. "But I won't need your help with this one, so you can wait in the truck if you prefer."

"What is it?"

"One of my clients has a mare in heat and receptive. He wants to breed her tonight."

\*\*\*\*

Cheyenne closed her eyes and tried to block the scene below. Why had she insisted on coming into the barn? Was she possessed? Yes, the farm was famous, and the stallion was a multi-million dollar race winner. Even in this area of the world, a Derby-winning stallion was viewed as special. And she wasn't immune to the allure.

But this was a bad decision all the way around. Jack knew it, too. He'd stared at her when she said she'd wait inside. Once they got there, he'd pointed out the viewing room, up several steps from the floor action. His expression told her she was to come up here and wait or go back to the truck.

But how would that have looked? She didn't do retreat, especially not in front of all these men. She wasn't some hot-house flower and once again, Modine pride made her climb the stairs to the empty room.

The stallion's primal grunts drowned out the mare's squeals as the horses mated. She could hear it all, in spite of the heavy plate-glass window. A flush of heat traveled from her head to her feet.

It wasn't the frenzied animals caught in their copulatory dance that stole her breath. She'd seen horses breed hundreds of times. The ritual was odd under any condition, even odder in this sterile, businesslike environment. There was a handler for the mare, a handler for the stallion, and two other grooms who washed the genitals of each horse. Three more men stood on the sidelines with bored expressions, present only because, in the world of Thoroughbred racing, this was the safe way to conduct the procedure.

The lights in the room were off, thank God, but she stepped back from the large window. The stallion ejaculated, the flag motion of his tail an unmistakable sign of the act's end. In horseman's jargon, it was called the completion of the "cover".

Her attention strayed from the horses and centered on the man who stood apart from the whole scene. All her hard-won control threatened to shatter. Her nerves hummed from the strain of denial. She used the back of her hand to wipe beads of sweat from her top lip. Nothing was settled in her mind, she'd reached no conclusions on anything, but suddenly those issues faded into the background.

*Forget the man, concentrate on the animals.*

For a few seconds, it worked. The beauty of a fit,

sleek, Derby-winning stallion engaged in the beautiful act of procreation snared her attention. Then the stallion made his initial awkward attempt to separate from the mare and the handlers flew into action, which drew her gaze from the horses. She looked in his direction.

He stood still, his arms folded across his chest, his gaze trained on her.

****

Jack had never gotten an erection by watching horses copulate. Tonight, however, he'd walked in with one and the action in front of him didn't help. Talk about insane timing. When Win had phoned with the news of this breeding, Jack had nearly lost it. She'd finally consented to go out with him, an almost date, and this call had interrupted everything. If the client hadn't been one of their most important, he and Cheyenne would be somewhere vastly different right now, sitting across the table from one another.

He'd spent the last several minutes totally distracted. His gaze had strayed to the room above, with only a few glances at the horses. She was up there, somewhere, but she'd stepped back. At first, her white cotton top reflected from the lights on the ceiling. Now, he didn't see the white but that didn't stop him from looking.

He clamped down on his lust. It was fortunate he'd worn his work overalls. The boys here in the barn would taunt him no end if they guessed his problem, even if he *had* brought it with him. Busy now with cleanup, they passed a few comments back and forth. He'd have to get through that before he faced her.

He ran a tired hand along his jaw and tried to work up the energy to fight his need for her. Even after what had happened last Sunday, he was damn sure she'd object if he acted on it. Tonight, when he'd picked her up, he knew she still needed "time".

"Doc, we're through over here."

Jack moved to the mare. He checked for any injuries, going through the routine by rote. When he was satisfied with her soundness, he looked toward Brock Williams, the farm manager.

"She's good, Brock. What would it take for your handler to walk her around for a few minutes?"

"Ah, Doc, you know that's an old wives' tale. If the mare's not gonna catch, walkin' her ain't gonna do a damn thing to help."

Jack noticed Brock uttered the weak complaint with a grin.

"Humor me."

Jack peeled off his gloves, while Brock circled his finger as he looked at the handler. Jack threw the gloves in the trash and gathered his bag.

She was waiting for him to come up. It wasn't in her nature to come down to him. She was so proud. Normally, he viewed the trait as admirable, but tonight he wanted her to bend—a little—and give in to the inevitable. Because *they,* the two of them together, were inevitable. He'd waste no time in proving it to her if she only let him.

Brock met him in the center of the arena. Someone had turned off most of the lights. Except for the handler, the mare, and Brock, they were alone.

When Brock opened his mouth to make a comment, Jack made an abrupt turn to the stairway. One minute ago, he was dragging his heels. Now, he had to see her.

He took the steps two at a time.

\*\*\*\*

Cheyenne panicked as she watched him advance. She wasn't ready to pretend, again, that the bond between them didn't exist. If he waited one more minute, she might be able to gather herself. Unfortunately, one more minute wasn't enough. The vision of what they'd done on Sunday overwhelmed her and she was submerged in base desire.

She laughed out loud at the ridiculous situation. The echo of the laugh sounded like a moan. Telling him she'd eat with him, earlier, had been a big hurdle. Now, food was the last thing she wanted.

Cheyenne brushed back her hair with a shaking hand and knocked a forgotten hair band to the floor. She crouched down to grope for the band in the dark. The overhead lights flashed on, and she struggled to her feet.

"Are you ready?"

His tone was harsh—with tiredness? She wasn't sure but she hadn't heard the harshness for several days, not even when they argued.

She didn't look at his face. He waited with his hand on the door handle, and she sensed his stare.

"Cheyenne?"

Please, no, not that tone in his voice. Look at me, it said. I want you to look at me. Inch by agonizing inch, she lifted her gaze.

She saw the comprehension dawn in his expression. *Is that what he sees on my face? He knows now that I want him as much as he wants me.*

"Let's go." He turned and left.

She followed because she had no choice—no, that wasn't right. She'd made her choice, in one area of her life at least.

255

They walked the steps, across the now shadowed arena to the side door, with Jack ten feet ahead. Someone had placed a white blanket over the door window. Cheyenne paused until Jack opened the door and fog billowed in on the damp night air.

Their boots crunched on the gravel outside the barn. Otherwise, it was ghostly silent, the fog adding to the surreal atmosphere. Visibility was minimal and she slowed to a snail's pace.

A hard knock, followed by a curse, told her Jack had found the truck.

"Careful," he warned. She slowed even more while she moved in the direction of his voice. She bumped into him, and he reached out to steady her.

"Careful," he said again, a whisper this time. His thumb rubbed the inside of her forearm, before his grip tightened. He released her as if he'd touched fire.

"Get in. I'm going to get out of these overalls."

His voice had no give, nothing now to indicate he'd seen her vulnerability in the viewing room. Was it too late to stop this lust train in its tracks? If she couldn't control herself, he'd do the honorable thing and control himself, right?

While she listened to him take off his work clothes, the faint rasp of the zipper, and the muted thud of a dropping boot, she thought about giving him up to pursue her dream of riding with the Olympic team. A knot formed in her throat and she swallowed, glad the cab was totally black. He wouldn't be any happier than she would with a long-distance relationship. And he was too rooted here in Lexington with his clinic to come with her.

Is this how she was to make her decision? See which option hurt the least, and pick that one?

The slight creak in the driver's door jarred her from her pensive contemplation. She looked out the windshield at nothing. The door closed with a solid thud and the seat gave under his weight.

Seconds passed as she waited for him to start the engine. She gave a quick glance sideways and saw him stare straight ahead. Her nerves stretched to the breaking point as seconds turned into a minute.

"I know a place nearby."

She froze. He looked at her and she realized he wanted her to make the decision, the one decision that made all the others seem like child's play. This time, the option to leave wouldn't save her.

"Okay," she whispered.

## Chapter Thirty-Five

Jack didn't know what was on her mind. She looked out the windshield and hadn't changed position since he'd climbed in. He recognized what he'd seen on her face in the viewing room, though, and she'd given her consent, so he was holding her to it.

He bobbled the keys, caught them before they hit the floor, and inserted them into the ignition. Just before the motor turned over, the green dash lights cast a paltry glow and he looked again at her profile. Her chin was up, and her hair fell in loose ripples over her shoulders. He stifled a shaky curse and wondered if he'd make it as far as they needed to go before he lost it.

With the pea soup outside, he stopped his imaginings and what they'd be doing in a few minutes. He released the brake and eased down the lane. The service drive took them back to the main road but it was a hassle to hold the truck in the lane with only ten feet of visibility. He loosened his grip on the wheel and flexed his hands to ease the cramps in his fingers.

For a brief distance, as they climbed a hill, they rose above the vapor, which helped him locate the turn-off he sought. He found it at the last moment and slammed on the brakes before making a wide arc to enter the private lane.

He searched the gravel path for the familiar wide spot where he sometimes ate his lunch. It was a magical place in a far corner of Windemere Farms. Mature willow trees with gracefully drooping limbs surrounded a small pond full of ducks.

Under one of the trees was a wrought iron bench. The farm manager kept the area mowed and neat, but Jack had never seen anyone there.

The orange reflection disc caught his eye and he swung in to stop. Silence filled the cab when he killed the engine. The dark and fog hid the beauty of the place but it was close and he was desperate. He promised himself to bring her back in daylight.

*Christ, don't let her change her mind now.*

When she didn't speak or move, he had to say something. The first thing that came to mind wasn't exactly the best subject for the moment, but he said it anyway.

"This will be fast. I can't wait any longer."

"Okay," she said, finally.

He wasn't sure what he heard in her voice but he had no words to make her understand his need for her, a need that now required immediate action. He'd make it up to her afterward if he came out of this alive.

\*\*\*\*

Cheyenne sucked in a ragged breath, her hope for a little romantic foreplay flying out the window. Maybe last week had been an exception, and he wasn't a patient, unselfish lover. Big deal. They'd known each other for a month, she had instigated their Sunday encounter, and tonight might have been their first actual date if they hadn't been interrupted.

"Take off your top," he said.

Like a robot, she unbuttoned her blouse and unhooked her bra. It fell forward, but before she could pull it off, he moved over and placed his mouth on her breast, sucking her nipple between his teeth just like before. She arched her back, her arousal instant and devastating. All her thoughts focused on the play of his tongue.

He pressed one hand on her back to bring her closer. When he rubbed her other nipple, a mysterious mix of heady sensations intensified the familiar stirrings between her legs and the pulling aches signaled her body's readiness. Her hands gripped his hair when he lifted his mouth.

"Easy." He blew on her nipple which made it tighten even more.

"Let's go." He pushed her door open and urged her out as he scooted after her.

Her daze turned to confusion. "Wait. Where are we going?"

He took her hand.

"But the truck. I thought we were going to—in the truck…"

He shook his head before he moved in front of her and pulled her down a path he seemed to know.

"Watch the tree branches," he said over his shoulder.

They walked through a curtain of wet leaves that brushed against her naked upper body, creating an even more erotic sensation on her skin. Her nipples pebbled all over again, and gooseflesh rose on her arms.

"There's a seat here." He guided her hand to the seat before he moved behind her.

When he reached around to the front of her jeans, she shivered and realized he had come to the end of his wait. He unsnapped and lowered her zipper, his movements fast and firm.

"Kneel on the seat, put your hands on the back, and hold on," he said.

God help her, she was caught up in his excitement and climbed onto the bench. He pulled her jeans and panties down, which exposed her completely to the damp, swirling mist. The position was intense and carnal.

He unzipped his pants, and she heard the rip of a foil packet. His hands cupped her from behind, his fingertips pressed into the swollen flesh between her legs.

She gasped in pleasure as his fingers played around her opening.

"Jesus, God." He cursed low and rough. "Are you ready?"

"Yes," she whispered, and her fingers tightened on the back of the seat when he stretched her legs more, opening her as far as the jeans at her knees allowed.

"Push back toward me, just a little more. Hell, yes."

He slid inside her, and she realized carnal didn't even begin to describe the sensation.

\*\*\*\*

Jack lost part of himself with his first thrust, but she took every inch of him as he pounded into her. He wanted to touch her and allow her body to catch up, but the driving hunger didn't let him.

His thrusts sped up and he groaned with every pump, lifting her as his orgasm closed in. When he came, his hoarse shout carried into the night.

He fell forward and used her for support as he made a weak attempt to regain control. Groggy with a myriad of feelings, he tried to line up everything in proper sequence in his head. First, he'd tell her she was the best

261

thing that had ever, no, wait, he should give her three or four orgasms first, then he'd ask her to marry, uh, not yet, not before he told her he loved her.

She squirmed beneath him, and he forgot his list as he nuzzled against her neck. When she mumbled something, he finally found his voice.

"What, babe?" he whispered.

"Your cell phone is ringing. Answer it."

It was the emergency ringtone, or he wouldn't have answered, especially not now. He struggled to pull up his jeans and hoped the phone was still in his pants pocket. Five minutes ago, in the urgency of the moment, he'd wrenched open his zipper and practically ripped seams to get the material down his legs.

He found his cell at the same time she backed off the seat and pulled up her jeans. He watched her, and his inattention made the words on the other end of the line incomprehensible. In seconds, he recognized Chris Crockett's voice.

"Chris, slow down, kid. I can't understand you."

"Doc, someone's in the pharmacy! I don't know how he got in and I can't see his face on the video cam!"

Jack heard heavy breathing.

"Chris, don't go into the pharmacy," Jack ordered. "Stay in the office and call the cops. Do you hear me?"

"But, Doc, he's stealing drugs! He'll be gone by the time the cops arrive!"

"Kid, listen to me. Go back to the office, lock the door, and call the cops."

The line went dead. Jack looked at the phone and then at Cheyenne.

"What?" She moved toward him. "What's going on?"

He shook his head and redialed the clinic number at the same time he pulled her toward the truck. The hazy air was still thick, but they found their way in seconds. When they were both inside the cab, Jack gave up on the clinic and called the police.

He gave the information to the woman who answered the emergency line, hung up, and started the truck.

"Jack, what's happening? Did someone break into the pharmacy? Is Chris okay?"

"I'm not sure. The connection broke. Yes, someone was stealing drugs."

"Oh, God, no," she said. "I hope he followed your order."

Jack heard the worry in her voice.

"Yeah, well, Chris has a mind of his own, aka pig-headed. For some reason, I'm surrounded by that sort lately."

He didn't look at her but she shifted in her seat as she struggled with her top. Her silence made him think about what they'd just done. The whole night had been one of inconvenient distractions and he wished like hell there was a way to rewind the clock.

She tugged her blouse down and shifted position again.

"Are you moving around so much because you're turned on?"

"Maybe." She stopped her movement.

"Don't worry. If everything is okay at the clinic, I'll do you, tonight," he promised.

When she didn't respond, he took a chance and glanced over. Even in the darkness, he saw her bite her lip as she stared out the windshield.

"I'm worried about Chris, too," he said. "Let's not assume the worst. We'll be there in five minutes. Chris may be stubborn but he's not stupid."

The air grew heavy between them before she answered.

"That's not the only thing on my mind." She cleared her throat. "I have a confession."

Chapter Thirty-Six

*Not the only thing on my mind? How much more can my mind handle before it detonates?*

Jack, Chris, Jack, selling the farm, trying out for the national equestrian team, Jack. Cheyenne refused to lie to herself.

What was she going to do about Jack?

"A confession?" he said. Something in his tone sounded like hope.

"Yes, and cut me some slack, here." She pushed away her other cluttered thoughts. "I had no idea this was important at the time. A few weeks ago, I found one of the cabinets unlocked in the pharmacy."

"What?"

His tone affected her in a way she didn't need. It reminded her of their differences, differences she thought they had overcome.

"Why didn't you call me? Did you notice anything else that night, anything that looked different than normal?" he asked, and this time she detected concern, for her, in his questions. It was a pity her focus continued to be on the "what?." Combined with her anxiety and confusion over everything, especially her feelings for him, she flipped.

"Yes, little green men were running around in the paddock, throwing horse turds at each other. When their spaceship landed in the backfield, they all climbed on board and flew off."

"Cheyenne," he warned.

"No, I didn't see anything else," she countered. "Had I suspected someone had snuck in to steal drugs, I would have told you, no, make that Janie, since *you* were still clinging to my alcohol addiction at that point."

His curse was interrupted by the sudden glare of swirling lights that cut through the remaining wisps of fog. Three police cars sat in a haphazard fashion in the clinic lot, one with its driver's side door still open, as they pulled in. Jack turned off the truck but remained in his seat.

When Cheyenne opened her door, he grabbed her arm.

"Wait," he said. "We don't know what's happening, the fog doesn't help, and I don't like that open door on the cop car."

"But, but…Chris might need us!"

Jack's grip tightened and her protest died. He jabbed a finger at an indistinct shape as it darted from a side door of one of the barns. When the person ran across the paddock, Jack jumped from the truck and sprinted after him.

"What the hell!"

Cheyenne was on his heels in seconds. She needed Jack safe. He was too important to her, even if she didn't have the nerve to tell him yet.

****

The runner turned out to be the robber, a spooky figure wearing a hoodie, who became Sean Davis, the teenaged boy the clinic had fired three months before. At the last minute, Cheyenne won the race to catch Davis. She flew past Jack and lunged toward the kid, collapsing on top of him as they hit the ground.

Jack's hissy fit over her daring but unwise tackle was almost over when the police joined the melee seconds later. In between curses, Jack hooked his fingers over the back waistband of Cheyenne's jeans and dragged her off the kid's flattened body, which allowed the officers to cuff and walk Davis to one of the police cruisers. After a discussion with the cops, Jack ushered Cheyenne into the front office and ordered her to sit and stay before he went in search of Chris.

The pharmacy room door stood open, and Jack followed the voices that drifted out into the hall. Chris sat in a chair holding his head, while he talked to two cops who stood over him.

"What's going on?" Jack asked.

His concern for Chris lessened somewhat. The kid was coherent although he'd been roughed up, by the looks of the red bump on his forehead.

"Doc." Chris's face cleared with relief when he saw Jack. "I wasn't able to catch the guy, but he dropped the drugs before he ran out the door."

He pointed to the pile of boxes as Jack put a hand on Chris's shoulder.

"I thought I told you to stay in the office." Jack smiled, grateful for Chris's efforts, and looked at the cop. "Did you call an ambulance?"

"No, sir. The boy said he didn't need one."

Jack shook his head as he looked back at Chris. *Yeah, pig-headed.*

"I think it might be wise to have that bump examined, don't you?" Jack asked, but it wasn't really a question.

Chris rolled his eyes, which told Jack the kid really

did know an order when he heard one.

"Okay, maybe I should. Mom will worry if I don't," Chris said.

The cop ordered the ambulance, and Jack took the time to call Win, to tell him what had gone down that evening. Win promised to get a staffer to replace Chris for the rest of his shift. Afterward, Jack and the cops walked Chris out to the front drive to wait.

"Hey, that's the thief! How'd you catch him?" Chris pointed at Davis in the back seat of the police car.

Jack told the story but left out the part where Cheyenne did the take-down. When he watched her do it, he wanted to shake the crap out of her, after which he hoped he lost all memory of the incident, so he didn't develop fainting goat syndrome.

The ambulance arrived and the paramedics loaded Chris into the back before he asked any more questions. After a dialogue with the cops, they returned to headquarters, and Jack strode into the now quiet building, the after-effects of the incident coursing through his system. He entered the front office where he was greeted by silence.

Cheyenne had disappeared, of course.

\*\*\*\*

She watched the whole scene with Chris, Jack, and the cops on the office monitors before she left the front office. She needed to check on the animals in person.

All the offices looked fine. No open file drawers, no computers missing from desks, or any kind of damage to windows or furniture caught her eye. The cops had likely done the same, but they weren't as familiar with the clinic as she was. Besides, her need to get up and move had won out over Jack's hardcore order to sit and stay.

The last time she looked, she wasn't a dog.

Because Jack's door was wide open and a few files sat on his desk, she entered to put those files in a drawer, out of habit. Davis had come for the drugs, not to snoop at horse medical files.

She made a note to herself to tell Jack later where she placed the folders, to let him make fun of her for being OCD. Then, she'd remind him he'd be in deep doo-doo if his practice didn't protect the privacy of his wealthy clients. She might even harass him about his need to have paper copies of his records, instead of just storing everything on a computer or flash drive.

The desk drawer creaked as she pulled it out. It was almost full, so she flattened the folders already there to make room. As she did so, her gaze caught on one folder, a different color than all the rest. At the top, a paper with her name on it peeked out.

Without debating the right or wrong of her action, she picked up the folder and opened it. It took all of thirty seconds for her to realize what it was.

"What don't you understand about sit and stay?"

Cheyenne turned to look at Jack as he stood in the office doorway.

"What is this?" She held out the folder. "Is this the folder Ben gave you?"

He grimaced and looked away.

"How do you know it came from Ben?" he asked when his gaze returned to her.

"Janie said something about it last week, but I wasn't sure what she was talking about. Now I know."

"Are you going to let me explain?"

She wanted to leave, immediately, but he blocked the door. Apparently, he read the intention in her face.

"Okay, really, I can explain. The question is, will you listen?"

She dropped the folder on his desk and walked to the window. The fog had thinned, and the keys were probably still in Jack's truck since they'd left it at a run. She just needed to figure out the best method of escape.

"Will you listen?" he asked again. He'd moved closer. "I'd like to explain before you decide to use your tackling skills on me."

His agitation, reflected in the window, along with the concern in his voice pretty much spoiled his joke. While she was no longer immune to his feelings, his need to have her investigated, by *his brother*, humiliated her in more ways than one. Had Jack done this with all the applicants for the job? She doubted it. Only an arrogant member of the privileged class would think this was acceptable.

"You're going to explain whether I want you to or not." She wished she was capable of breathing fire. The thought of singeing every dark hair on his body gave her immense satisfaction at the moment.

His eyebrows rose but his expression was unreadable. Maybe he was surprised by how upset she was, or perhaps he thought she'd become his puppet after their blazing bench rendezvous.

Thinking of that, *now*, jarred her like nothing else. Less than an hour ago, she'd knelt on a bench, stripped almost naked, dripping with need—for him, only for him. Jesus, the New Madrid fault was causing tremors again and her feet were braced on opposite sides.

"Actually, you do have a choice. I can forego an explanation, and we can act like it never happened. After all, we both know where this is going, right?"

Chapter Thirty-Seven

"Explain." She had refused his gutless option. And she hadn't responded in any way to his "where this is going" remark.

He'd given it his best shot. He wished she didn't know about Ben's involvement. After all, Ben may have had her investigated, but Jack hadn't refused the information. Why didn't he destroy the evidence before she found it?

Her expression throughout his explanation remained indifferent, even when he told her it had been all about his alcoholic bias and rush to judgment. So he apologized. Again.

She accepted the apology with a silent nod, something he hadn't expected. Her look told him whatever brewed in her mind was serious. Every non-verbal cue, from her crossed arms to her roaming gaze, made him crazy, either with lust, or a far deeper sensation he'd never experienced, not even with his ex-wife.

When she requested he take her home, he wanted to bawl like a baby. Not that he didn't want to take her home. He did, but it was supposed to be his home, dammit.

They pulled into the lane that led to the farm, where the darkness and stray ribbons of fog obscured the barns beyond the house. He pulled up to the gate that opened to the sidewalk and turned off the engine. A heavy stillness filled the cab. To ease his mind, he got out and walked around to her door as she stepped out of the truck.

"It's not necessary for you to walk me to the house."

Her quiet voice told him he needed to confront the situation now.

"What's going on? Up here?" He pointed to his forehead and should have expected what came next.

"You tell me. It's your head," she said, her response more to his liking, even if she was perfecting her avoidance technique.

"Are you still thinking about the folder?" he asked.

"A little." Her gaze angled toward the house as if she wanted to get away, from him?

When she didn't say anything else, he asked, "And?"

She just shook her head.

"I'd like to know. Yeah, it's late, and the incident at the clinic was a hassle. But you're pulling back and that's not the way I want things to go from now on."

\*\*\*\*

If he only knew.

This whole night had been one jolt after another, like rolling down a back-country lane filled with potholes. They'd made earth-shattering love, dealt with the robbery at the clinic, and she'd found the folder. What else waited for them in the dark night?

Her escape strategy resurfaced. She wanted to dart into the house, grab some scissors and chop off her braid.

"What?" he said.

Nope, that definitely wasn't feasible. He was fast, even if she had managed to outrun him earlier when she'd tackled Davis.

"I'm thinking about cutting my hair," she said.

"No, you aren't."

He seized her upper arms and pulled her against him, close enough for her to see the unyielding purpose in his eyes.

The shock made her raise her hands to his neck, and she pressed a light thumb against his throat. All her negative thoughts disappeared when a naked need reappeared in his eyes.

"You know." She made an effort to expand upon her previous answer. "A Brazilian blowout is good at destroying frizzies. And it'd be easier to braid."

He mumbled something that sounded like "too many chemicals" before his mouth took hers. Her fingers slid up his throat to feel the movement of his jaw in rhythm with the stroke of his tongue as he ate away at her resolve to "pull back". His breathing quickened and his scent swept her under, as usual. He lifted her off the ground, their mutual lack of control telling her they were headed for another round of physical bliss.

She whispered his name, in between toe-curling kisses, and he reached behind her to open the truck door. He placed her onto the seat and eased her back, her desire sharpened by his sweet dirty words. He made short work of her jeans and panties and pulled everything down far enough to give him access to the swollen want between her legs.

When he buried his tongue inside her, she grasped his head and pulled him in. She begged him to hurry, and he used his teeth and lips to bring her home. Pleasure surged through her, tensing her hands and legs, and he angled her up while she bucked through her peak.

Her orgasm decimated her, but he didn't pull back.

Instead, his mouth found her again and he sucked her to a second orgasm that stiffened every muscle in her body. She cried out with her release and the aftershocks followed her as she slid back to earth. The night sounds returned while Jack placed light kisses on her thighs and stomach.

"I want to sleep with you tonight," he said. "Let me stay."

She didn't have the strength to refuse him. Not even the recent insult of the folder made a dent in the warm contentment that now spread through her. She answered without words and extended her arms toward him. He picked her up and carried her to the house. They didn't speak while they made their way through the dark.

Tomorrow, she'd think about life's thorny issues. Tonight, she just wanted to be with him, with nothing on her mind but the magic they made together.

****

The sweet scent of pancakes floated in the kitchen air when he backed through the side door. She had her arms around his neck, still half-naked as her jeans dangled beneath his arm. If he got his way, she'd be stripped bare in a matter of seconds.

Sadly, a rush through a dark room with furniture was a maneuver that begged for disaster. His knee hit a table leg, and he almost dropped his human package, in his hurry to get to the bedroom.

"Whoops," she snickered.

"Shit!" he said at the same time.

He eased her onto the fortunately bar-height table and bent to rub the bruise he knew would be there tomorrow.

"I can walk to the bedroom." Her voice carried a

tease. "It might be safer if I lead the way."

"No," he said when he stood up. "I know where it is, and I want to carry you. It's, well, romantic. Besides, I want you out of your clothes. You'd need to get back into them if you walk to the bedroom."

"Uh, not really. I could just take off everything right here. Actually, you could, too."

It took him two seconds to agree.

"Race ya," he said, his hands already on his shirt.

Clothing flew everywhere. A shoe landed in the sink and someone's buttons scattered over the tile floor.

Jack pulled the condom from his pocket as he tugged at his pants leg. The two-second delay gave her time to scoot off the table and race down the hall.

He almost fell as he ran after her, his pants still hooked to his foot.

"I won! I won!" She spun around like a ballet dancer.

He grabbed an outstretched arm and pulled her onto the bed. He used his teeth to tear open the packet and rolled the latex sheath up his erect penis.

"No, I won," he growled as he parted her legs and dove in. One thrust was all it took for her to arch up into him.

"Oh, my, I'm shook," she purred.

He plunged into her with warp speed and minutes later, reached the point of no return. Her soft body was his landing zone when he doubled over and melted into her.

When his breaths had settled back into their regular rhythm, she whispered, "I think we both won."

He grunted his agreement as he slid into sleep.

\*\*\*\*

A few hours later, she awakened to quiet words in her ear.

"What?" She turned to face him.

He smelled like a mixture of man, horse, and sex, her favorite scents, which made her want to reach under the covers and touch him.

"I'm sorry about the folder," he said in a voice deep from sleep.

"I know Ben put it together. I'll take out my irritation on him when I see him," she said, without any conviction, as she slid her finger down his cheek to his dimple.

He took her hand and kissed her open palm.

"Starting now, let's be honest with each other. I want to know you, way beyond what I read in the folder."

She feared the emotions his words triggered. For tonight, she didn't want to deal with those or any of the other issues that plagued her waking hours.

"I'd like to know you better, too. I have a bunch of questions, which I'll ask tomorrow, in daylight, so I can watch your facial expressions when you reply."

She scooted closer and tucked her head under his chin, in an effort to tell him without words that they needed to sleep.

He seemed to understand when his arm wrapped around her and he pressed his lips against her forehead.

A minute later, it appeared his understanding and hers were not quite in sync.

"What's one thing you wish you'd done differently in your life?" he asked.

*Crap.* Couldn't he have asked something easier, like her favorite dessert or if she kissed on a first da…

*Crap and damn!* They hadn't even had a real date.

Not that he hadn't tried but how had she gotten so easy? Duh. That answer was simple enough. She'd fallen in love with him.

"What's that look mean?" he asked when he pulled back. "I can see it even in the dark."

She shook her head, unsure how to voice the problems which once again demanded answers.

"So, we're only going to be honest with each other when it's convenient," he observed.

"Well, it is two in the morning. I'm not sure my answer would make much sense."

She wanted to be honest with him, in the intimacy of their first night together but she was too overwhelmed by the issues that battled in her brain.

"Hmm."

He knew what she was doing. Just that "hmm" told her he knew.

"I, well, when I was seven, I told Daddy I wanted to be a jockey, and win the Derby. He said I could be anything I wanted to be."

"So, what made you go to college and get a degree in speech therapy instead?"

"I had a friend in elementary school who had hearing problems. The other kids made fun of her, and I hated it. When she was finally diagnosed and got help, she told me about her therapist, and I guess it stuck with me."

She didn't tell him that the jockey idea became less appealing as she got older. Very few women made it as jockeys. In other words, success was possible but unlikely.

Until now, she'd never admitted to herself how much she feared failing.

"You're a great rider, though. Mom agreed. I knew it already, of course, after watching you at the dressage workshop and on Mr. T. Since you came back to Lexington, to start your riding business, it seems you still want to do something in the horse world."

In spite of her unsteady middle-of-the-night brain, she heard something in his words that made her pause. Was he just referring to her business, or had he heard about her reawakened Olympic aspirations? She hadn't talked to anyone except Pammy and J.C. about her on-again, off-again itch, and while Mrs. Carter had guessed, Cheyenne was certain the woman hadn't told Jack.

"Hey, whoa, babe, what's wrong?"

He held her hand and she realized she had one leg hanging over the edge of the bed. At his urging, she lay back down.

"I thought I needed a bathroom break, but maybe later," she said, finally, in an effort to explain her sudden movement.

"You sure?" he asked as his hand stroked her arm.

"Yeah. For some reason, my pregnant sister-in-law infiltrated my thoughts. She's always doing the potty thing."

"Uh-huh," he said, his confusion evident, something she found reasonable since her excuse only made sense to her. Had Pammy said something to Billy about the Olympic thing? Had Billy opened his big mouth when he and Jack discussed hauling horses for Jack's mother?

"I'm actually glad you sat up," Jack said, pulling her out of her introspection. "Seeing your body just now made me realize how sexually deprived I've been lately. Since you now appear totally awake, maybe we can address that problem?"

Without hesitation, she crawled on top of him. She'd deal with her suspicions tomorrow. Right now, the heady influence of his very sexy maleness made her body a tangle of cravings.

"Holy Jesus," he groaned as she straddled his hips. This woman on top thing had its benefits and within seconds she was certain they both knew she was the right person for the job.

Chapter Thirty-Eight

Early the next morning, they consummated their first night together with one of the most stimulating showers he'd taken in years, if not in his entire life. With the steam swirling around them, her mouth worked his penis until he had to grab the showerhead to remain standing. Whatever she was doing with her tongue paralyzed him. When he came he lost all sense of time and place, certain the water that pelted his face and chest was a tsunami that had skipped the California coast and surged inland.

"Gotcha." Her voice curled around him as he labored to return to lucid thought.

He looked down at her smug smile and became distracted by the wet hair that streamed down her sleek, naked body. The scene at the pool hadn't done her justice.

"You got me all right," he said. He reached behind her to turn off the water and pulled her to her feet. "I'm yours and it's not because of what you just did to me."

As she climbed his body to kiss his dimple, he rubbed his lips over her forehead, undone by a need far beyond the physical.

Yowling interrupted the tender moment, and they looked at each other.

She rolled her eyes and said, "Animals."

He opened the shower door with a smile. "Yeah. As

you know, I have the same problem."

The big white cat stared at them from the bath mat. Jack remembered the same sneer the morning after Dinah foaled when the cat found him in bed with Cheyenne. A hiss told Jack the cat hadn't forgiven him.

"Bubba, be nice," Cheyenne warned.

She wrapped a towel around her wet body and picked up the cat. "Let me get him fed. I'll fix us some coffee. Omelet okay for breakfast?"

His hunger flared at her suggestion, but he wasn't sure if it was the food, or simply eating with her that stirred his appetite.

"I love omelets, especially if someone else makes them."

\*\*\*\*

Cheyenne left him to dry off, and with her leaving, the world and all her current challenges *attempted* to invade the peace she'd experienced over the last several hours. At least she now recognized them as challenges, which was a step up from life-altering problems. Funny how a night of hot sex with a beautiful man altered a woman's thoughts.

She fixed the cat food, placed it on the floor, put the towel on her head, and started breakfast. With the Keurig set up and ready, she fixed her classic omelet recipe with cheese and salsa, singing along with her favorite country tune on her laptop while she cooked. Since she was naked and John-Michael was scheduled soon, she gazed out the window to make sure he hadn't already arrived. It was rare, but sometimes he came to the house with a question, and it might be awkward if he found her "nekkid".

"Smells good, but how in the hell am I supposed to

eat with, uh, well…"

Jack gestured in her direction while his eyes roamed her body and made her hot all over again.

"Let me finish cooking and I'll put something on."

"Okay, thanks, I think."

He strolled to the Keurig machine, punched a few buttons, and started the brew. She knew he still watched her, which made her smile. She placed the omelet on the plate, took it to the table, and turned to find him behind her, dragging the towel off her head.

"Wrap this around your body. I have no immunity where you're concerned."

She saluted, covered herself with the towel, and pushed him into a chair. Since he had about seventy pounds on her, all of it muscle, the task might have been hard had he not fallen into the chair without protest. He pulled her onto his lap and held her, which made them both laugh. His action dislodged the towel, however, and it fell to the floor.

She looped her arms around his neck. "I need to fix my omelet, but I can't if you don't let me get to the stove."

"How about if we share this one." He picked up the fork. "I'll feed you."

"But, but I'm still naked," she smirked.

"I know." He arched his eyebrows with a devilish look. "I'll work on my immunity, a little, while we're eating."

Seconds later, while she chewed her masterfully cooked egg-ceptional breakfast dish, his immunity attempt failed. The movement beneath her butt was far too familiar to ignore.

He took a bite and shrugged. "It's still early. I think

it's a leftover from my morning boner."

With the two of them eating, the omelet disappeared in a minute. He allowed her to retrieve the coffee, but only if she came back to his lap afterward. He'd picked up the towel, and draped it over her front when she sat back down.

They exchanged coffee-flavored kisses and talked about inconsequential things, which was fine with Cheyenne. It kept the heavy stuff away, floating in the stratosphere, her present peace and contentment undisturbed.

Their cups were half empty when he looked out the window and said, "Last night, when I asked what you wished you'd done differently in your life, I got the feeling you only half answered the question. You mentioned the late hour if I remember right. Maybe now you can expand on that answer."

She picked up her cup, but he took it away from her.

"You just had a sip," he said. "And I know your tactics."

She was definitely calling Modine after Jack left. There was too much coincidence here, and her brother's nature was set in stone. So was hers, apparently. She did the only thing she could think of to completely derail Jack's train of thought.

"You asked that we be honest with each other," she said and looked him in the eye. "I want that, too, which means I need to share something with you."

She didn't miss the slight frown on his face. "Please tell me this has nothing to do with the incident at the clinic last night?"

"No." Her next words came out in a rush. "It's about the polo match. I'm the woman playing on the other team."

He stood up and dragged her with him because she threw her arms around his neck as if she might stop his big blowup.

"See what just happened?" he shouted.

"What do you mean?"

"Look at us," he said. "You're clinging to me, naked, by the way, and I'm holding you because I didn't want you to fall when I stood up. It was automatic. How in the hell am I supposed to play against you in the match and not care about your well-being?"

"Are you saying I'm not capable of watching out for myself?" She squirmed in his arms, and he let her go when her feet met the floor.

"No, that's not my point," he asserted. "I can't believe this." He walked to the sink and stared out the window. Seconds passed before he turned to face her. She'd wrapped the towel around her again, and her stiff stance told him she wanted to rant. For some reason, though, her lips remained tight and unmoving.

"When was the last time you played polo?" he asked.

"Polo? I need to know how to play polo? I figure I can learn next week on the field," she said with a shrug.

He walked back to her. He had to get his thoughts in order and, if possible, calm down. To do both, he needed solitude.

"I have to go," he said. "Duty calls."

Her eyes rounded in surprise as they searched his face.

"No, I'm not going to rise to your challenge." He wrapped his hand around the back of her neck. She stiffened when he pulled her forward, but she didn't refuse his kiss. "I'll see you soon."

He had reached the door when she said, "Wait."

Hoping for something, an apology, her promise to withdraw from the match, any sign that she understood his reasoning, he looked back. Her gaze was on the floor, and she said nothing else. He walked out without a word.

****

John-Michael's arrival a few minutes after Jack left alerted Cheyenne to her unclothed state and she marched to her bedroom, where she found a clean pair of jeans and a random top. Her over-sensitized woman parts yelped when the seam of her jeans rubbed against them, but she was too disheartened to care about something as unimportant as underwear.

Once back in the kitchen, she turned off the Keurig, dumped the rest of her coffee down the sink, and retook the chair to stare at nothing. Minutes later, Bubba decided she needed feline therapy, and jumped into her lap. After massaging her thighs with his claws, he circled twice, and settled into his typical front paws inward, head down position, and sent a loud purr through her dead quiet kitchen.

The polo match was a concern, and it pricked at her self-control. Oddly, she almost understood his logic. Aside from the whiskey/flu episode, stupidity wasn't something she embraced, and it was definitely stupid to deny the superior strength of men over most women. That didn't mean she totally agreed with his viewpoint. She really did believe polo was a sport of agility, speed, and accuracy of shots, which usually counteracted strength. She'd make sure to bring it up, again, the next time she saw him.

Bubba started to knead again, which added more

holes to the already-worn denim of her jeans.

"Owww, cat. Your therapy isn't welcome right now." She picked him up and placed him on the floor, ignoring the plea in his eyes.

For a brief second, she thought again about withdrawing from the match. Lyn had already sold several tickets based upon the lure of a woman playing. The match was next weekend, and finding another woman to replace her was, likely, impossible. Cheyenne didn't think Jack would allow the issue to ruin what was happening between them, although she knew he wasn't happy. They needed to talk it out, as soon as possible. And once they resolved their differences on that issue, she had to bring up the other one. Her head started to throb, which made her massage her temples.

The Pammy-Billy tune began to play on her cell phone, and she wondered if she had ESP. *Had* Pammy said something to Billy about the revival of Cheyenne's Olympic aspiration? Did Billy's big mouth relay that information to Jack, when they'd met to discuss transporting Rae Carter's horses? She finally located the phone in her jeans, the ones she'd ripped off last night that still lay in the corner of the kitchen.

"Shy? That you?" Billy said, in his usual happy-as-shit mood.

"Yes, Modine. Bubba hasn't figured out cell phones yet," she replied.

"Bad Bubba. I guess he's not as smart as I thought he was."

When she didn't say anything, Billy, for once, seemed to pick up on her state of mind.

"Shy? What's up? You don't sound so good."

"Well, it's early, and I didn't get much sleep," she

said. If she was going to skewer her brother, she needed to talk to Pammy first. Then, she'd deal with him in the easiest way possible—an entire roll of duct tape over his mouth. "Is Pammy up yet?"

"No, I'm lettin' her sleep for a few more minutes. She's not gettin' much shut-eye these days, either," he said. "Actually, she's the reason why I'm callin'."

"Oh?"

"Yeah, I'm headin' up north to pick up those horses the vet bought for his mom. Will you check in on Pammy for me? Maybe call or text her each day?"

"Yes, I can do that. How long will you be gone?"

"Until the day before the match. J.C. told me he'll keep an eye on her, too."

"Good idea," she said. "Maybe I'll take the kids one day next week, to give her a little relaxation while you're away."

"I'd like that, sis. Thanks. I'll probably leave this afternoon. If I can, I'll check in with you while I'm gone. Pammy doesn't like me breathin' down her neck, well, except when we—"

"Billy, please." She shook her head. "Don't go there, for Christ's sake."

"Uh, okay," he said. "Anyway, thanks again. I appreciate it."

"Sure. And Billy?"

"Yeah?"

"Tell Pammy to call me later today. I need to talk to her about something. It's important."

## Chapter Thirty-Nine

Jack called the clinic to let them know he was running late, to avoid the same freakout that happened the morning after Dinah foaled. It had only taken ten minutes to return to Windemere Farms and the grove of willow trees where he and Cheyenne had made love.

In the morning light, as the sun climbed over the hills, the view of the pond and the distant pastures brought him some much-needed composure. He still wasn't okay with playing against Cheyenne in the match, but as he sat on the bench and watched faint ripples glide over the water, the knowledge was easier to handle.

At this late date, they had to play against each other. Lyn's efforts deserved their participation, but damn, he wished the circumstances were different. How could he live with himself if she got hurt? What if, for example, the ball hit her in the eye, or she fell off the horse and in the furious action she was trampled, or she got hit with a mallet, his mallet...

Two ducks floated from the clump of horsetails on the other side of the pond, followed by six ducklings in a row. Babies. Just like that, his thoughts were overrun with baby Cheyennes as they ran around the house, the house where he and Cheyenne lived as husband and wife. The images appeared easily, which told him the match was likely going to be one of the harder things he'd ever done.

God, he had to stop this mind-blowing speculation. She was an excellent rider, so he doubted she'd fall off a horse. He'd played polo long enough to know how to swing a mallet, likewise with his team members. As for the ball-in-the-eye possibility, he flinched and pulled out his phone.

"Lyn," he said when the old guy answered. "I'm a little shocked you're home."

"Well, Jackson, it is only eight twenty in the morning. I plan my days to start after nine, due to my advanced age. To what do I owe the honor of this *early* call?"

"I'd like to request both teams wear face guards with our helmets at the match next week. Do you think the other team will have a problem with that?" he asked.

There was a delay in Tyree's response.

"I believe the other team will be amenable to the small change," Lyn said a few seconds later. "I'll contact them today with the information. May I ask why you feel this is necessary?"

It was Jack's turn to pause.

"Cheyenne told me about playing for the other team," Jack said. "For some reason, I thought the guards might make it safer for all concerned."

"Ah, I see. I am pleased she told you. However, I know you have some difficulty with the idea of playing against a woman. Does this mean you've changed your viewpoint?"

"Not entirely, but I'm trying."

Lyn chuckled. "I hear the disinclination in your tone. If it's of any help, she started playing polo in high school, and if I remember right, she played with a team in South Dakota, most of the time she was there."

Well, at least now he knew she wouldn't learn the game at next week's match.

"I know she's a great rider," Jack agreed. "But she's only five-three and weighs nothing. I don't think my concern is unwarranted."

"No, your concern is valid, even more so if you have feelings for the girl," Lyn said.

The old man was fishing. Jack wasn't in the mood to bite.

"Lyn, what do you know about Cheyenne's Olympic ambitions?"

"Why, er, well, she once expressed a desire to try out for the team."

"Once? You mean she no longer has that desire?"

"No, I didn't mean it that way. Perhaps it's better if you ask her."

"I tried. I didn't exactly get an answer."

Jack's earlier question hadn't been specific to the Olympics. He had purposely made it vague to allow her to bring it up. Her mention of becoming a jockey had been a definite detour.

"Ah, the Modine avoidance technique. Let me guess. Did she bring up her participation in the polo match when you asked her?"

"Yeah. You got it. The second time I asked. Why won't she talk about it? Any ideas?"

"Knowing Cheyenne, it's likely something to do with money, but you didn't hear that from me."

****

Cheyenne stumbled into the house around two, after several hours of work in the barn. John-Michael had finally ordered her away when he found her stuck in the manure pile. He gave his order in a respectful way, of course. If she remembered right, he'd used words like "hell's bells" and "Shy, move your ass", but she was too exhausted to recall the rest.

Her second shower of the day produced some clarity of thought. She needed to contact a realtor to find out the value of the farm, and maybe talk to Lyn about his connections with any sponsors. The idea of selling the farm still made her stomach flip. The only consolation was the look she imagined on her daddy's face when she told him she wanted to do this—badly. He would say "you do it, darlin', and don't let anything stop you".

Then, of course, there was Jack. She'd decided to give herself a year to make the team. After paying off the loans, the leftover money should last that long. A year was enough time to tell her if she had a chance. But what about Jack?

The towel she'd worn this morning hung on the back of the door. She wrapped it around her and remembered how she and Jack had played with it just hours before. The images in her head were bittersweet. She wanted back the time they'd spent together.

She'd tell him tonight, at the clinic, and start with his idea to sell his house. Then, she'd mention the possibility of selling her farm. If she approached it in a casual way she thought it was doable. Once the farm topic was out and if his reaction was positive, she'd proceed to the Olympic idea and the wait. *Please God, make him understand why I need to do this.*

She wobbled to the bed, more tired from her mental exercises than the farm chores. Since her shift at the clinic was an all-nighter, she needed a nap. As soon as she lay down, someone knocked on the front door. She scrambled into a T-shirt and jeans before she hurried through the living room to see Pammy staring through the window.

"Why are you still driving in your condition?" Cheyenne asked as she opened the door.

Pammy waddled into the room with a foil-wrapped something in her hands.

"I don't care anymore," she answered. "When you get this fat, nothing matters except baby movement, and I know mine's headed in the right direction."

She held out the foil object, a pie plate by the looks of it.

"What's this?" Cheyenne asked.

"It's a peace offering." Pammy grabbed the sleeve of Cheyenne's T-shirt and pulled her toward the kitchen. When they got there, Pammy made Cheyenne sit down, before she ambled to the silverware drawer. She returned to the table with a spatula, fork, and plate.

"I made you a pie," Pammy said. "Actually, I made it for Billy and the kids, but he's gone, and the kids went over to the neighbors for the afternoon. When I found myself eyeing it, I decided I owed you an apology and what better way to apologize than with a peanut butter pie?"

"Why do you owe me an apology?" Cheyenne asked and took the plate Pammy handed her. She wasn't about to turn down peanut butter pie, even if peanut butter *was* a staple of her diet.

"The last time I was here, I butted into your business, and I'm thinkin' I really had no right to do that. Before Modine left today, he told me you had to talk to me about something important. I assumed my butting-in was what you wanted to discuss."

Cheyenne chewed her first bite of pie and shook her

head.

"What? Wasn't that it?" Pammy asked.

"Okay, this pie is really good, and I'll take it, but not as an apology." Cheyenne swallowed the peanut buttery goodness and cut another piece. "I wasn't mad at you and you didn't butt in. I needed to hear your opinion. After thinking about it, you were right. I'm not the type to be in business for myself, at least not right now."

"You aren't?" Pammy said, clearly surprised. "What, uh, what are you going to do? I mean, the farm, the new riding arena, and the barn, your loan? Did Billy forget to tell me about this?"

"No, I haven't shared this with him yet. Old 'loose lips' Modine is dangerous with too much information." She took a last bite of pie and swallowed. "That's actually why I wanted to talk to you."

Cheyenne took her plate to the sink, rinsed it off, and placed it in the dishwasher.

"You wanted to talk to me about Billy?"

Cheyenne leaned back and felt the warm breeze from the window flow over her shoulders.

"Did you by any chance tell Billy about our discussion on the Olympics?" Cheyenne asked and hoped her mild approach didn't sound critical.

"Uh, I might have. Why?"

"I think Billy told Jack, er, Dr. Carter."

"Oh, it's Jack now, huh?" Any other time, Pammy's knowing smile would have aroused Cheyenne's tenacious tendencies. Today, not so much. "Billy thought there might be something going on with you two, even that night at the steakhouse. Of course, then, he suspected a possible murder plot."

"Yes, well, things have changed, between Jack and

me. And I've also come to the conclusion I need to rethink the Olympic possibility. I don't want to look back and regret not trying."

Pammy struggled to her feet and walked toward Cheyenne with her arms out. When Cheyenne met her halfway, not even the baby bump kept her from stepping into her sister-in-law's kind hug.

"I'm proud of you, girlfriend. Billy and I always thought you should do this, but it had to be your decision."

Cheyenne clung to Pammy like a lifeline.

"But you see my problem, right?" she said as she laid her head on Pammy's shoulder. "Trying out for the team takes time and travel and lots of effort, not to mention a bunch of money."

"So, you either get some sponsors or..."

"I'm thinking about selling the farm."

"Well, then, you've solved your problem, haven't you?"

Cheyenne sighed again. "Not really. I'm in love with Jack Carter, and I think he feels the same. How in the hell do I tell him I love him, and then say "bye-bye, Jack, see ya in a year or so. Don't wait up'."

"Oh, yeah." Pammy patted Cheyenne's back and tightened her hug. "I see your point. Life's a bummer, isn't it."

## Chapter Forty

Jack tried not to accost her at the door when she arrived at the clinic, even though every nerve in his body twitched with tension. He'd spent the day purposely not contacting her, but that hadn't stopped his hand from dialing her number like a programmed Cyborg.

He was in his office chair when the front door squeaked. Thankfully, he'd applied Gorilla Glue to the leather seat to keep him in place. Otherwise, he'd be the white on her rice.

It took her forever to walk down the hall to his office door. When she got there, she stared him into speaking first.

"What happened this morning isn't going to happen again. I take responsibility for my overreaction."

She bit her bottom lip and looked a little less loaded for bear when she stepped into the room. Her gaze didn't leave his.

"And I apologize for not telling you sooner about playing for the other team," she said. "When I asked Lyn if I could play, you and I were butting heads over, well, you know, and I wanted to get even. Still, that was a few weeks back and I should have told you before this morning."

He nodded, his relief tangible. It seemed she had gotten beyond their earlier disagreement.

"I'd like…"

"You asked…"

They both spoke at once and he motioned for her to proceed.

"No, you go first," she said. She stepped toward him, and he caught her scent.

"Did you wear your hair down just to tempt me?" he asked.

One corner of her mouth crept up and the soft look he wasn't able to resist entered her eyes.

"Is that what you were about to say?"

He met her at the front of his desk.

"I forget. Come here."

\*\*\*\*

The locked door that Cheyenne assumed was an entrance to a maintenance closet turned out to be a room with a bed, a small kitchen, and a bathroom. Once Jack pulled her into the room, they headed to horizontal.

The mattress gave under them, and Jack found her zipper at the same time her fingers crawled up under his shirt. She managed to get his shirt off as she lifted her hips off the mattress. He yanked off her jeans and dropped them over the side of the bed.

Next, he removed her shirt then slipped his hands under her back and rolled so she was on top. His gaze centered on her response when his thumbs grazed her nipples.

Just when she thought she couldn't get any more turned on, he flipped her beneath him and kissed her like he was going under.

Or maybe she was the one going under. She was pretty certain her need for him, for all of him, couldn't get any deeper, and the thought made her pull back. Their lips separated with a loud smack which echoed through the room.

He looked down at her, the surprise on his face clear in the muted light.

"What's wrong?"

She shook her head. "I...I know this isn't the right time or place to say this, but I need to tell you, now."

She inhaled and closed her eyes.

"I love you." She didn't imagine the heavy quiet that followed her words.

"Okay," he said, finally. "Does that mean you'll actually go on a date with me?"

Her eyes flew open, and she struggled against his hold. How could he be so flip over the hardest confession she had ever made?

"Let...me...go!" Her vigorous movements against his heavy body had no impact but she kept on.

"Stop." His tone didn't calm her. She almost fell apart when he pulled her arms above her head and locked a hand on both her wrists.

"I said stop. You're going to pull a muscle or throw out your back. If that happens, how in the hell will you ride in the match?"

For a brief second, his challenge made her ease up. The leftover shudders and her chaotic emotions made it impossible to focus on his next words.

"Did you hear what I just said?" he asked.

"No." She tried not to look at him and feared what she might see on his face. It did no good, though. She couldn't erase him, as close as he was.

"I haven't been able to think of anything else but you since the night Dinah foaled," he whispered. "I know we've only known each other for a month, but that's no longer important to me. You make me crazy, and I mean that in the best way possible. I love you, Cheyenne, so, no, I'm never letting you go."

\*\*\*\*

He saw the calm return before fat tears slid down her cheeks.

"Thank God. Saltwater. Just what I needed," he murmured, as he licked the moisture from her jaw and neck.

When his mouth worked its way up and back to hers, he kissed her slowly, to make her understand that she had his heart. He slid inside her with as much patience as possible and hoped she knew he meant what he said. He would never let her go.

His thrusts were deep and measured, until her moans and the movement of her hips told him she neared her climax. When she came, she cried out his name, and he almost lost control.

He didn't stop until he brought her to a second climax, their bodies in perfect sync. She lay limp and sated beneath him when he shattered, and the moment became etched in his brain. It didn't get any better than this, and he couldn't believe how lucky he was to have found her.

"Damn," he said.

They lay side by side as his fingers combed through her hair. He smiled down at her sleepy face and her happiness touched his soul.

"Look what you've done," she mumbled. "I have to work for the rest of the night. How am I supposed to do that in a post-orgasmic daze?"

"I hear ya. That's why I made some plans before you arrived." He brushed the hair back from her face and shoulders. "Since Chris didn't work his whole shift yesterday, I asked him to come in around midnight. He heard you needed the night off since you have polo practice early tomorrow morning."

"I do? That's news to me."

"Yeah, well, you won't be riding a horse, if you catch my meaning."

"I think I do," she said, her response even more drowsy than before. She managed to return his smile, though, so things were trending in the right direction, even if she couldn't keep her eyes open. "What time is it now?"

He shifted to look at the clock on the wall.

"Maybe eleven thirty," he said. "Clock's a little hard to read in the dark. And, of course, our phones are somewhere in that pile of clothes on the floor. We seem to do that a lot lately."

She started to sit up.

"Not yet." He put his hand on her hip. "We have a few more minutes. I'll help you check on the horses before he gets here."

He kissed her eyes and the tip of her nose.

"I love you," he said. "And because I love you, I'm feeling a little hyper about playing against *you* in the charity match."

She started to speak but he laid a gentle finger against her mouth.

"Promise me you won't do anything extreme on the field."

"Hey, don't forget I've seen you play," she said. "I won't do anything extreme if you don't."

He gave an exaggerated sigh. "I guess I can dial it back, a little. The problem is, what one person thinks is extreme may be what another person calls energetic. I think we need to talk about this in more detail just so we know we're both on the same page."

Hearing him say "I love you" again made her want to stay right where they were for the rest of the night.

"When Chris arrives, let's go to the farm," he said.

That was a better idea, so she agreed, and they left the bed together.

They gathered their clothes and helped each other dress. Since he'd offered, they both checked on the horses and returned to the office, to find Chris had already arrived and was settled in front of the monitors.

His forehead sported a small bandage, but other than that, he looked eager to work.

He stood when Cheyenne followed Jack into the room.

"Cheyenne?" Chris said. "How are you?"

She smiled at the kid's obvious interest. "I think I should be asking you that question."

He touched the bandage. "I'm good. No problem. I hear you're playing polo tomorrow. Is there anything you can't do on a horse?"

The question was innocent and straightforward, but she noticed Jack's grin from the corner of her eye. She kept her smile brief but friendly.

"Well, I haven't won the Derby yet," she said.

Even though she and Jack hadn't yet talked about the *other* subject, they had expressed their love, a major victory in her mind. It gave her extraordinary hope, hope she couldn't have imagined earlier that day.

Jack's expression told her he felt the same.

Chris cleared his throat and Cheyenne realized the kid suspected something.

"Bud, I'll leave the clinic in your capable hands,"

Jack said. "Don't hesitate to call if you have any questions, or need help. Let's just hope tonight is much quieter than last night."

"Yeah, Doc, you got that right. I'm planning on it."

He waved them off and sat down as they walked out the front door together.

In the still, quiet darkness, Jack chuckled. Before she got in the truck, he turned her around and backed her up against the door.

"I think Chris knows something," he whispered and gave her a light kiss.

"Ya think." She grinned and kissed him back. "Why?"

"Well, could be my shit-eating grin when I look at you. Or, possibly, the haphazard way your shirt is buttoned."

"What?" She looked down and noticed the hem of her top hung lopsided against her jeans.

"Sorry. My bad. I didn't notice until we came back to the office," he said.

She rolled her eyes but wasn't the least bit concerned.

"Or it could be the pheromones we emit whenever we get within ten feet of each other," she offered as she nipped at his chin.

"You'd better stop that," he said, his lips a mere inch from hers. "Chris is probably watching from the window and my resistance is zero where you're concerned."

"It's your late-night beard. I love the scratchiness."

She nipped again, then licked him.

"Okay, I'm done. Get in the truck. I'll follow you."

He turned her around and smacked her butt, but waited until she was behind the wheel before he walked away.

For the first few minutes of the drive, her mind swam with happy thoughts. Halfway there, reality intruded, and she gazed in the rearview mirror. Leaving him for weeks and months at a time made her question fate. The idea of a long-distance relationship reappeared and like before, she dreaded the idea. Still, she had a few days to think things over. Maybe there was another solution, and she just hadn't discovered it yet.

Chapter Forty-One

When his phone blipped, he thought about not answering. After all, it was past midnight and they'd just gotten to the farm. He'd spent the last ten minutes of the drive with thoughts of hot sex and maybe a marriage proposal if it was a good fit. He looked at the number and immediately wished he hadn't.

It was Lyndon Tyree. Jack had to answer.

"Lyn? What's going on?" he said, while he watched his woman climb from her truck.

"Jackson, sorry to bother you at this late hour. I need a favor and it's something I couldn't put off until tomorrow."

"Everything okay?" Jack rolled down his window and waved her into the house. She understood and walked to the front door.

"Yes, all is well, maybe more than well. I found the stallion and mare for my perfect polo pony. Remember, we talked about it a while back, and you said you'd check them out for me."

"Uh, okay, I can still do that. Are you saying it has to be tonight?"

"No, no, no. But I just got off the phone with the owner, and they've had two other offers. That's why I wanted to tell you as soon as possible. We need to see them. Tomorrow."

Jack saw the light come on in the kitchen.

"All right. Is it the farm over in Versailles, like last time?"

"Um, no. It's in Santa Cruz."

"Santa Cruz? As in California?" Jack's grip tightened. Finding the perfect pair of horses to produce the world's best pony had been Tyree's main objective for the last century. And Jack *had* promised to examine any horses Lyn found suitable, and the old guy had only needed him twice in five years.

"Yes, in California. The mare is an Argentine-Thoroughbred cross, and played in the U.S. Open Polo Championship twice. The stallion has won several Best Playing Pony awards and—"

"They sound impressive, Lyn," Jack broke in and tried not to sound impatient. "What's the plan?"

The light in the kitchen flicked on and off several times.

"If your partners can take over your cases for a few days, I reserved two seats on United, from Louisville to San Jose. It leaves tomorrow at noon. I promise we'll be back Thursday, at the latest."

Jack swiped a hand down his face. He'd intended to spend the next several days with Cheyenne, every hour he wasn't at work. Now, he'd have to wait for their first real date on Thursday night, *if* they got back early enough, and *if* the time change didn't screw with his biorhythms. He needed decent sleep to play in the match on Friday, so he wouldn't be the player who hit the ball that hurt Cheyenne.

"Jackson? What do you say?" The man's voice was filled with hope.

"Okay, Lyn, I'll go. We need to get that pony born and playing before you reach ninety."

Lyn laughed and thanked Jack before he ended the call.

As Jack walked to the house, he tried to figure out how to break the news to Cheyenne. Fortunately, the light was still on in the kitchen. Unfortunately, she leaned against the counter, waiting for him. He'd hoped to use the extra thirty seconds as he walked down the hall to refine his approach when he told her the news.

"Who were you talking to? It's twelve thirty in the morning. Please don't tell me it was an emergency call?"

"No, not exactly an emergency." He guided her down the hall. "We have tonight, at least."

"Tonight?"

"Let's go to bed. I'd rather tell you when we're naked."

They walked through the bedroom door. She didn't know it yet but this was going to be a night to remember if he had anything to say about it.

****

Cheyenne spent the next two days plotting payback against Lyndon Tyree. When she recognized how ridiculous and selfish her thoughts were, she acknowledged the one positive about Jack's sudden departure. This was how it might be for the next year, with her travels, seeing Jack mostly on Facetime, and only occasionally in person.

She still hated the idea, and because she did, her decision to travel the Olympic path stayed a thorny mess. Yes, she knew a long-distance relationship wasn't her thing, and she believed Jack might feel the same. There was no way she'd be able to do her best riding if their separation put her in continual emotional turmoil. Why did she even think it was possible to balance the two?

It was time to talk to Rae Carter again. Cheyenne's guilt over a discussion with Jack's mother before she and Jack had discussed the issue caused a measure of unease, but she needed to resolve this problem. If she was able to do it before Jack came home, all the better.

****

"You'll never guess who I talked to earlier today."

"Who?" Jack asked. He and Lyn were finally back at the hotel, after a long day at the farm that owned the two horses. Jack was about to call Cheyenne, but when his mother's number popped up, he had to answer.

"You have to guess," she said. "I'll give you a hint. We went for a ride."

Jack smiled, for two reasons. His mother was riding again, and the horses he'd purchased for her birthday were an appropriate gift. As well, he wanted his family to get to know Cheyenne since she'd be part of the family soon.

"Okay, I'm thinking you went riding with Cheyenne," he said.

"You're such a smart boy." She laughed. "Just like your father."

"So, how was the ride?" he asked. Cheyenne hadn't told him of her plans to ride with his mother, which made him assume it was a last-minute decision, by someone.

"It was great! I can't believe how long it's been since I rode on a regular basis. Maybe I thought I was too old to get back into it, but it makes me feel young again, so I'm making some changes in my life beginning, well, three weeks ago."

"Good for you, Mom," he said. "Where did you ride today?"

"At Red Fox Farm, of course. It's a great little farm,

and the trails are quite lovely, in the woods in the back, with the creek running through it. I can't believe Cheyenne wants to sell it."

Jack snapped to attention.

"Sell what?" he asked.

"The farm," she said. "She's thinking about, oh, maybe I shouldn't, I just wanted you to know we had a good ride. She seems like a fine young woman. I really like her. Maybe you can bring her over for dinner, soon, so your dad can meet her."

For a moment, he didn't know what to say. Cheyenne intended to sell the farm? Why hadn't she told him? And what didn't his mother want to say? Did they discuss Cheyenne's Olympic ambitions and did selling the farm have anything to do with that?

Jack thought about Cheyenne's reaction when she found out who had finally given Jack all the details. Grilling Lyn hadn't worked. He said he was uncomfortable talking about it and had repeated his suggestion that Jack ask her. Lyn's reaction indicated Cheyenne now dealt with something significant, which had motivated Jack to pursue the information from another source. Combined with his mother's slip, it was apparent the Olympic pursuit was about to happen sooner rather than later.

"Jackson, are you there?"

"Yeah, Mom, I'm still here. I'm glad you two got together. In case you didn't already know it, Cheyenne and I are, uh, seriously involved."

"Yes, dear, I noticed. After all, I'm your mother and you've always been fairly easy to read."

"Damn, I think I'm embarrassed. Remind me never to play poker with you."

She laughed again and he heard what he imagined was the sound of her younger voice. The introduction of Cheyenne into his mother's life was an additional bonus, one that made him almost as happy as having Cheyenne in his life—almost.

The sinking feeling in his gut, though, told him he needed to talk to Cheyenne soon, or else he'd be crying to his mommy. The problem was, he didn't want to discuss the serious stuff on the phone or via Facetime. He wanted to put his hands on her and bury his nose in her hair and that required they do it in person.

He told his mom he loved her, signed off, and wished not for the first time that he and Lyn had completed their mission. Instead, he dialed Cheyenne's number, just to hear her voice.

Chapter Forty-Two

Jack's call came while she chased her nieces around the house. They'd made up a game called Pony Express, but Cheyenne thought they put a little hide and seek into it, just to rev things up. Not that they needed revving. No wonder Pammy happily surrendered the girls for the day when Cheyenne suggested they come over. They were two bundles of boundless energy.

"Hello, my man," she said, and ducked into the quiet bathroom.

"And good afternoon to you, sweetheart," Jack said. "Why are you breathing so hard? Did I interrupt something?"

"By something, are you speculating that my breathing hints at heavy-duty, no-holds-barred, hands everywhere, out-of-this-world, sex? That's a no, Super Doc."

"Okay. Just wanted to be sure. You're only allowed to breathe like that when it's my hands, or other body parts, doing the duty."

"Sounds good. I can live with that."

"So, what's going on? You're not out in the barn lifting hay bales at this time of day, are you?"

He sounded a little miffed, which made her feel good, in spite of his absent-without-leave status.

"No, but it's only seven. Trust me, I've lifted hay bales later than this. And in case you don't remember, the second floor of the barn is now packed with hay. I believe I have enough to last until 2025. As for my heavy breathing, my nieces are here. If I can get them tired before I take them home, my sister-in-law might be able to relax tonight. Since you sent Billy up east, it's my job to help her out."

She stuck her head through the door and heard the bed squeak, followed by giggles, followed by Bubba scrambling down the hall in terror. The girls were mattress-jumping in her bedroom. That meant she had a few more minutes to talk before she needed to check on them again.

"Tell me about the nieces," he said. "Will I get to meet them at the after-match dinner?"

"Doobie, er, Debbie is five and Jess is almost four. Yes, I believe they'll be at the match unless Pammy pops. She's due any day now."

"The Doobie name. Where'd that come from?"

"The Doobie Brothers. You know, *What A Fool Believes, Minute by Minute, Listen to the Music*. They were on Daddy's playlist when he was out working in the barn. Doobie is my nickname for her. She's a mini-me."

"O-kay. Maybe I'll ask my folks about that music, although I don't remember them listening to it," he said. Apparently, his parents weren't hip like her Daddy. Everyone over fifty should know about the Doobie Brothers, for God's sake.

"If she's a mini-you, I'm sure I'll like her," he added.

The kids started to scream which brought Cheyenne to the door again. She held the phone against her chest, so she didn't yell in Jack's ear.

"Girls, quiet please." Bubba ran back up the hall in the opposite direction. His hair stood on end and the look on his face was even more petrified than before. She shook her head. It was probably time to take the girls home.

Otherwise, she'd have a cat with PTSD.

"I miss you," he said, out of the blue.

Of course, she teared up because his words made her think of leaving him. Since her ride with Mrs. Carter, she'd been all over the emotional map. The woman's answers had been helpful, but Cheyenne still wasn't comfortable with her choice.

She sniffed and swiped at her nose.

"You're not crying, are you?"

"No."

"Don't cry, babe. I'll be home in a few days. Everything will be fine."

The knot in her throat tightened and she almost told him then. When she swallowed, her inner fortitude reasserted itself and she pushed away the fears.

"I know," she said. "I just wish you were here."

He stayed with her until she stepped back from the edge. When she heard the kids bare feet slap on the hall floor, she told him she had to get the girls home before dark. He said he'd call her later to say goodnight.

When his second call came, she promised herself she'd be back in the saddle, on solid ground, even if the ground *was* littered with horse apples. In the meantime, she needed to think about some new horse cliches. The old ones were seriously tired.

****

The British team arrived on Thursday morning and were adjusting to the time change, according to Lyn's

311

message. Cheyenne took this to mean the Brits were ensconced in their opulent suites at *21C* while they snored away their jet lag for most of the day. Her irritation with Lyn had disappeared when she heard his upbeat tone, even though he *had* taken Jack away from her for most of the week.

What Lyndon hadn't mentioned was the call she received from "Crush" McVey as she sat down for dinner. It was her first restful moment of the day after classes and barn work. When she included the phone and email discussions from two financial advisers and three realtors, her day had been both mentally and physically draining. Therefore, her talk with Crush hadn't been all that positive.

"Ms. Modine," he said, in a typical upper-crust, royal family accent. "My name is James McVey, and I understand you are our fourth for the charity match this Friday."

"Yes, Mr. McVey, you are correct. I am your fourth." British speak intensified her long-standing dislike for the moneyed class, but she realized that feeling was no longer as intense as it had been, likely due to the Jack influence. And she and the Brits were on the same team so it was probably good her dislike had slipped a few notches. Her realization of the fact told her this was yet another matter she and Jack needed to examine, if he ever returned, that is. Right now, it seemed like he'd been gone forever.

"We plan on practicing tonight at seven. We will need you there, if at all possible."

The "if at all possible" was an afterthought to soften his request. Otherwise, he'd issued it as an order, rather than a congenial offer from a team member who wanted to meet a player he'd never played with before.

"One moment, please, Mr. McVey," She rose from her chair. "I must check my calendar to make sure I am available."

She put down the phone before he replied, and almost laughed when she realized her diction now matched his. The notebook she retrieved from her desk in the dining room was blank, but she needed it to make the flipping pages noise. If she didn't do something to reroute her irritation, mild though it was, she might have to grab his balls upon first meeting, a gesture that wasn't at all conducive to sportsmanlike conduct.

"Mr. McVey, are you still there?" She flipped the pages and made sure the sound carried over the line. "It appears I can make it tonight. However, it will need to be seven thirty instead of seven. Is that doable for you and the other members?"

A heavy silence preceded his reply.

"Yes, Ms. Modine. We will see you at the Tyree farm at seven thirty."

They disconnected after mutual goodbyes, and Cheyenne decided a ball grab wasn't enough. The phone call was definitely frosty. If their in-person meeting wasn't any better, she'd switch to a ball-squeeze with fingernails. Either that or play his ass into the ground at the match and send him home with a bag over his head.

\*\*\*\*

Two of the Brits leaned against the side of the barn, helmets in hand, as they watched her approach. The other guy, the one she thought was Crush McVey, churned up dirt as he paced in a circle near the open barn door. The ponies were saddled and in their stalls. When Grant Dawson, Lyn's barn manager, walked out the door and waved, she returned his wave, grateful for at least one friendly face. Grant was the younger brother of Joe Dawson, her farrier. The Dawson family had lived in the Lexington area for decades and Daddy had used Grant and Joe's father for his more complicated shoeing needs. She smiled at the memory but lost the smile when her gaze returned to the Brits.

They now stood and stared at her like the Palace Guard at Windsor Castle.

"Hello, gents," she said, with a salute and click of her boot heels. "I'm Cheyenne Modine, your sub for the match tomorrow. Shall we get started?"

"Cheyenne, which horse are you riding tonight?" Grant asked, ready to head back into the barn.

McVey cut in before she replied.

"I'll take the bay," he said. He still stared but his expression had relaxed. "I imagine Ms. Modine would fit nicely on the buckskin."

The buckskin was a good pony, if small. No doubt McVey had looked them over beforehand, perhaps the way he looked her over now. Too bad he hadn't picked up on Culligan's tendency to shake. The bay, AKA Crazy Culligan, had been a polo pony for years but it took several minutes of play to work out his nerves.

"Are you sure you want Culligan?" Cheyenne took the reins from Grant, adjusted the stirrups in preparation to mount Beau, the buckskin, and waited to see if McVey picked up on her warning.

"Absolutely," McVey asserted, making an effort to mount Crazy, while the horse danced sideways in anticipation.

"Right, then let's get to it." She sprang onto Beau's back in one fluid motion. One of the other riders, a young man with blond hair and dark blue eyes, raised his eyebrows, his attention split between her and McVey. However, McVey was too busy to notice. He had managed to mount Crazy, but the horse didn't want McVey's other foot in the stirrup. It flopped several times while Crazy did his half-prance/half-buck move.

"Nice to meet you," Cheyenne said, holding out a hand to the blond guy, who now sat astride his horse. "You must be Ian?"

"Yes, yes, I am," Ian said and shook her hand. "And this is Rod Guinness."

Rod held out his hand with an equally friendly expression and said, "No relation to the beer folks."

"Too bad," she said. "I guess that means we won't be hitting the bar for some free drinks after we play."

McVey interrupted his laughter.

"We'll play two against two for this practice," he said. "Mr. Dawson, might you bring us our mallets?"

Once the mallets were in hand, they headed out to the field. Cheyenne had one objective in mind. Relieve McVey of his holier-than-thou attitude, and wipe the smug smile from his face. To do that, she needed to play her best, hopefully without breaking the horses' legs or giving Rod or Ian a groin pull.

## Chapter Forty-Three

Jack and Lyn arrived in Lexington at eight p.m. While he was happy to at least get back the day before the match, Jack was exhausted and he suspected Lyn felt even worse. The last several minutes of their drive had been in silence, and when Jack looked at his passenger, the old man's chin had fallen to his chest.

As Jack drove down the winding driveway, the activity in the left pasture caught his eye and he slowed to watch what looked like a polo practice. Only four players were on the field, but the action was fast, vigorous and competitive.

His foot hit the brake when he recognized Cheyenne on the buckskin. She had just cut off a player on Crazy Culligan to steal the ball, after which she directed an accurate strike to another player. The guy who took the ball hit it through the goal, a certain score if it had been a real match.

Jack was beyond happy to see her, even though he tried not to notice the skill he'd witnessed with her play. If he thought too much about the upcoming match, he'd have to fight the visual of her pinned beneath a thousand-pound horse. His brain was far too tired to deal with that at the moment.

"Why, it's the British boys and Cheyenne," Lyndon said, now fully awake, which made Jack laugh.

"That was a very fine move on her part," Lyn said.

"And she stole the ball from McVey, which is not an easy thing to do, as we both know."

Jack silently agreed and put the truck in park.

"Want to get out and watch?" he said, his mind already made up since his woman played with three men from the opposing team, and he was jealous.

"Of course." Lyndon was halfway out the door with his reply. They met up at the front of the truck and walked together to the pasture fence.

Across the field, the players and horses had gathered in a group. When one of the players pointed to Jack and Lyn, Jack saw Cheyenne's head twist in their direction. In a flash, she spurred her horse toward them at a dead run. The horse stopped five feet from the fence, the stop so abrupt the animal's back hooves kicked up dirt. She sprang off his back, threw her helmet to the ground, and launched herself into Jack's open arms, in spite of the fence posts that separated them.

As they kissed, Jack heard the Brits laugh and Lyn's chuckle. It didn't put an immediate stop to their locked lips, but when his calm returned, he pulled back and grinned at her.

"I thought you'd never get here," she said, breathless, her arms tight around his neck.

He gave her a quick kiss, eased her back to the ground, and slid through the fence. Once through, he picked her up again and buried his lips in the fuzzy, damp hair on her neck.

"Lyn took pity on me," he mumbled. "He got tired of my sad puppy whine. Am I right, Lyn?" Jack looked back at the old man, who had settled his arms on top of the fence, his expression one of pure pleasure.

"Yes, Jackson, you read me right. Fortunately, I now

own the perfect sire and dam for my future ideal polo pony. They should be here next week, by the way."

He directed his last remark to Cheyenne before he nodded and looked behind them. Jack put Cheyenne down and they turned to greet the other team as they rode up and dismounted.

McVey was the first to speak. Jack didn't miss the curious glance on the man's face, a glance that shifted between Jack and Cheyenne.

"Hello, Doc," he said as he shook Jack's hand. "Good to see you again. Are you ready to take a beating in our match?"

Jack smiled, familiar with the guy's psychological games.

"I'm ready if you are, McVey, although I'm pretty sure any beating is heading in your direction, not mine."

McVey's cheeky expression didn't flinch.

"Yes, well, we shall see, my friend. Whatever the outcome, I'm sure you and Ms. Modine won't allow your feelings for each other to affect the play. In other words, there'll be no conflict of interest since she'll be playing against your team, right, mate?"

\*\*\*\*

Cheyenne waited for a "mine is bigger than yours" confrontation between Jack and McVey. Before they unzipped, Lyndon's calm voice interrupted with perfect timing.

"Now, gentlemen—and Cheyenne—let us remove to the house for the best bourbon in existence, and some light refreshments. I'm sure your practice has left you in need of hydration since the temperature is hovering in the eighties."

McVey backed up and looked at Lyn.

"We appreciate your offer, Mr. Tyree, and shall join you as soon as we see to our horses. Ms. Modine, Dr. Carter?"

"Thanks, but Cheyenne and I need to go." Jack looked at Cheyenne and saw her agreement. "It appears we've both had a long day."

Jack's gaze returned to the Brits.

"After all, if my team is going to win this match, I need to overcome my jet lag."

The men walked toward the barn, amid talk and laughter. McVey led Cheyenne's horse along with his own. She didn't miss his wink before he left, and apparently, Jack didn't either, since he cursed under his breath all the way back to the truck.

They dropped Lyn at the front door, Cheyenne got into her truck and followed Jack, who suggested they go to her place first. Due to the delay in their return, she knew Jack needed his rest, which meant they wouldn't be together tonight. It wasn't what either of them preferred, but Jack had mentioned, once again, his need to be alert when he played. Cheyenne heard the worry in his voice and knew he referred to her.

As she drove into the dusky sun, the evening breeze wafted through the open window, bringing in the scents of freshly mown grass and wildflowers. She breathed in and replayed her talk with the realtors. For once, selling the farm didn't jar her as it had. With Jack's return, as well as his presence in her life, the anxiety had quieted. She'd achieved a balance between her regret, and her anticipation over what might happen in the future.

When they arrived at her house, she met him at his truck. He climbed out and she jumped on him again because it was impossible not to.

Halle Kenton

Their kisses were slow and sweet but when she caught herself eyeing the bed of the truck, she drew back.

"I know you're tired but I really wish you could stay," she said. She gave him her pouty look and he shook his head.

"I do, too, especially when your lower lip does that come-on thing." He bent down and kissed her again. "But I can't, and we both know why. I really need sleep and I won't get any with you in the same bed."

She laid her head against his chest and mumbled "okay" as his hand played with her braid. For a few minutes, they stood in the quiet night before he spoke again.

"When I talked to Mom earlier today, she told me she wants your family to sit with ours at the match."

Cheyenne lifted her head in surprise.

"Really?"

"Yeah, Mom and Dad rented a tent, with chairs, by the way, so your sister-in-law has somewhere comfortable to sit. I talked with Billy when he got home last night and told him."

"What did he say?" As usual, her thoughts danced around the subject of the haves and have-nots. The chirping of the crickets grew louder as she tried to picture the Modine and Carter families all under one tent.

"He said he appreciated the offer," Jack said. "And I know what you're thinking."

She looked up at his attentive gaze.

"What am I thinking?"

"You're wondering if they'll get along. Why don't we wait and see, instead of jumping to conclusions," he suggested.

The crickets quieted at the same time as Cheyenne's

heartbeat. She didn't think it was a coincidence.

"Okay. Sounds good," she said and smirked when his eyebrows rose in disbelief.

Chapter Forty-Four

The clinic was in chaos on Friday, due largely to Jack's unplanned trip west and the delayed return. Win and Mike had some much-deserved rest in the early morning but all of them were overrun with appointments until late afternoon. Jack glared at his desk, once again covered with files and papers.

He picked up the Gainesway Farm folder to check on the stallion he'd examined last week, but his thoughts drifted to his Cheyenne deprivation. She wasn't any happier than he about their separation over the past week, but at least he'd implemented Plan F in the few free moments of his busy day. Plan F, of course, had nothing to do with the f-word and everything to do with forever. It would go into effect on Sunday, after tonight's polo game, and tomorrow night's dinner with his family. He picked up the ring between calls that morning and couldn't wait to see her face when he opened the box.

As well, on Sunday, they'd get all the heavy stuff out in the open, before he proposed, that is.

"Jack?" Janie's voice filtered down the hall.

When she came to the door, he closed the folder and looked up.

"Yes?"

She stood framed in the doorway.

"Just wanted you to know I've got Chris and Mary all lined up for staffing the clinic tonight, and Gray, will, with great reluctance, be the vet on call."

"That's good. Gray's still coming to the match, right?"

"Of course. Has phone, will travel," she said with a smile. "Said he wouldn't miss it for the world. He wants to see Cheyenne and the British boys beat your pants off."

"Huh. Ain't gonna happen," Jack said. "Not if I have anything to say about it."

He was more concerned about playing against Cheyenne than winning the game, but he realized that concern would always be there, no matter what she was doing. Bailing hay, driving down the road, making omelets in the kitchen...

"What's that look mean?" Janie studied him. She seemed about to ask more but he cut her off.

"Nothing," he said. "Have a lot on my mind. You know, the match, dinner with the folks, selling my house..."

"You're selling your house?"

*Damn.* That wasn't something he'd planned on telling anyone, at least not yet. He blamed the slip on his half brain, the other half still somewhere in the Rockies.

"Uh, maybe."

Janie walked in and sat down on the other side of the desk. She looked at him with an expectant smile.

"I'm sure I've mentioned it before now." He started to rearrange folders in an effort to convey he had no time to talk. Janie didn't move.

Instead, she leaned forward and put her arms on the edge of his desk.

"Yes, but why now?"

He shrugged but didn't look at her.

"It's time I did something about it."

From the corner of his eye, he saw her discerning look. She rose without another word and walked from the room.

*Shit.* Jack wanted the information to stay secret for a few more days. If it spread through the family, someone was bound to say something, possibly tonight. That meant he needed to implement Plan F before Sunday. A thought popped into his brain and he looked at the clock. McVey was the perfect choice to help Jack achieve his goal. Jack knew the Brit would agree it was a brilliant idea.

****

Lyn had outdone himself in his preparation for the game. Cheyenne even speculated he manipulated the temperature. A soft, dry breeze blew in from the southwest, the thermometer read seventy and no clouds ruined the bright blue sky.

Billy, Pammy, and the girls, along with J.C. had arrived and blended easily with the Carter families. For once, Cheyenne experienced no shock when she arrived and saw how well everyone got along. Even now, as she and the other players readied for the match, she watched the Modines and the Carters together with something that felt like hope.

J.C., in a flannel shirt, jeans, and work boots—clean, thank God—sat and talked to Ben Carter, who held a glass of champagne with his Ray-Ban sunglasses pushed up in his hair. Rae Carter had just said something funny which made Pammy, her hand on her bump, cackle with laughter. Mr. Carter played with the kids in the children's area that Lyn had equipped with slides, trampolines, swings, and a merry-go-round. In the background, behind the tents, Billy pitched horseshoes with Janie and the UK Director of Athletics.

Maybe Billy wouldn't need that Maalox after all. If he did, Cheyenne knew Demme was in the crowd. As for her, the rapid thud of her heart no longer had anything to do with whatever lines existed between the upper and lower classes, and everything to do with Jack.

The two teams met in the center of the field a minute later, shook hands, and wished each other a good game. Jack whispered "be careful" in her ear, and moved away to mount his pony. As Cheyenne watched him walk away, she noticed a look between Jack and McVey that confused her, but Lyn announced the start of the game and there was no time left to think about it. After that, the field blurred, and Cheyenne welcomed the active play. Her mind forgot, for the next hour, the Olympics and choices and her likely separation from the quarterback on the other team.

The first chukker ended with no goals. Both teams had played serious defense, and so far, no fouls had been committed. Cheyenne questioned whether the absence of Jack's rougher habits was due to his concern for her or just leftover tiredness from his trip. Whatever it was, she hadn't missed the look of pure love in his eyes when he glanced her way. That look allowed her to keep all her concentration on him, and the moment.

"Ms. Modine, did you hear my instructions?"

Crush gave her his inquisition look and Cheyenne shook her head, unashamed by her drifting thoughts.

"Sorry, Crush, I had a few other things on my mind. Unless your instructions were for me to remove myself from the team, I say we just get back on our ponies and do our best. Oh, and by the way, I noticed the change in the wind direction, and I still intend to score the winning goal."

The slight crimp in his smile told her he held no grudge against her pronouncement.

Both teams mounted up and played their asses off in the next chukker. The crowd roared when Mike Blake scored the first goal, followed by Crush's goal soon after. During halftime, with two chukkers finished and two to go, all of them stood on the sidelines while they inhaled liquids, wiped their faces and necks, and tried to catch their breath as the ponies were changed once again.

She and Jack now played eye sex, and Cheyenne knew all the players noticed. Apparently, Ben Carter did, too. While some of the spectators stomped field divots during the half, Ben said something to his brother that made Jack shake his head. Ben barked a laugh, flashed a grin at Cheyenne, and walked back to their mid-field tent. When he joined the rest of the family, he whispered in Janie's ear and earned a smack on the arm.

With only a few minutes left in the game, Cheyenne found her best move. Since she and Crush had changed positions, she now had the responsibility of scoring the last goal at the same time she played defense against Jack, of course. Her attention narrowed to the span between the posts, and her man's athletic moves. The ponies flew down the field and it seemed like they were the only two in play.

The ball whizzed toward her. Cheyenne groaned, slid sideways on the saddle with only one foot in the stirrup, swung her mallet in a crazy arc, and sent the ball straight through the posts.

When she righted herself, cheers and claps saturated the air. The audience stood and chanted her name as she trotted across the field. It didn't seem to matter that the home team had lost. She took a moment to acknowledge their salute by removing her helmet and waving it in the air, which caused them to cheer even louder.

She joined Jack and the other players mid-field, where everyone shook hands and ended the game with smiles and laughter. Jack edged his pony close to hers and Cheyenne read his expression.

"What exactly was that last stunt? Did you not hear me say be careful?" he muttered and dropped his mallet to the ground.

"Uh, that was my U.S. Grant imitation," she said. "See, I was Ulysses in a past life—"

He shook his head and dismounted, handed the reins to McVey, and pulled her from her pony. When her feet met the ground, Jack wrapped a hand around her upper arm, gave McVey a nod, and in a mysteriously synchronized movement, the other players led their horses from the field. Her anxiety flared when Jack's hand tightened and held her in place. What exactly was going on?

He released her arm and answered her unspoken questions.

"We'll talk about your past life in a minute. Right now, though, we need to talk about our life, here, together."

With that, he dropped his helmet and went down on his knees.

****

"Jack! No, God, not here. What the hell!"

Her gaze darted to the now silent crowd and he saw the panic on her face.

"Please, Jack, we have to get off the field," she

begged. Her eyes filled with tears and, just like that, she was close to a meltdown. "We need to talk. You, you can't…"

She stopped and made an obvious effort to control herself.

He used the moment to pull the ring box from his back pocket.

"I agree we need to talk, later," he said. "First, though, listen to me. I know you want to sell your farm. I'm buying it for Mom. She wants to start a horse rescue, and your place is perfect. I also know you want to try out for the Olympic Equestrian Team, and I have no doubt you'll make it. In fact, I have some sponsors in mind, if you need them."

Her eyes widened in shock, and her shoulders shook as she cried harder.

"But Jack, what about…" she said.

"Us?" he asked.

She gave him a weak nod.

"When you make the team, I plan to offer them my services. I happen to have some skills with horses, you know."

She tried to speak, and he put up his hand to stop her.

"We'll work it out, whatever you need." He opened the box and held it up. "First, though, you have to marry me. Will you marry me?"

She fell into his arms, and they collapsed onto the grass. Jack hugged her and laughed his ass off. Somehow, as they rolled on the field, he found her hand and managed to slip the ring onto her finger.

A microphone squawked and interrupted the moment.

"Jackson," blared Lyn Tyree. "I assume that's a yes?"

Jack gave a thumbs up, and the crowd erupted—again.

Epilogue

Jack saw her look at the ring in the moonlight. The contentment on her face made him delay sleep for a few more minutes.

"Do you like it?" he asked again.

She turned toward him and slipped her folded hands between her cheek and the pillow.

"I love it," she whispered. "It's beautiful and you're beautiful and life is beautiful."

He blinked and managed a slow smile. "I think that's my line, or maybe we both have the same line now."

He moved closer and snuggled against her. She fitted her head under his chin and sighed.

Seconds passed, and his eyelids drifted shut. He was almost asleep when he heard her murmur, "Who told you?"

He yawned and tried to give her a coherent answer.

"Mom let it slip. I guess when you and she rode together, you two talked about it."

"Your mom told you I planned to try out for the Olympic equestrian team?"

"Uh, no, not that. She mentioned you were going to sell your farm and, well, I figured that meant you were ready to pursue your goal."

"Ah, so it *was* Billy," she said. "I suspected as much." Her tone indicated only mild irritation which made his response easy. Besides, they were engaged now, and they had promised each other honesty from now on.

"No, not Billy." Jack yawned again and settled in for a good sleep with the woman he loved. "It was J.C."

## A word about the author...

Halle Kenton spent her Ohio childhood reading when she wasn't begging her daddy to buy her a horse. She wrote her first poem in the second grade and has since graduated to historical and contemporary romance, always with a dash of humor. She graduated from Otterbein College with a B.S. in Equine Science, and the University of Kentucky with a Master's Degree in Library Science. Halle left her day job as a Reference Librarian and Branch Supervisor to (happily) write full-time. She has written articles for a travel magazine, and a regional history publication, and was awarded the Molly for historical fiction, by the Denver RWA chapter. hallekenton.com